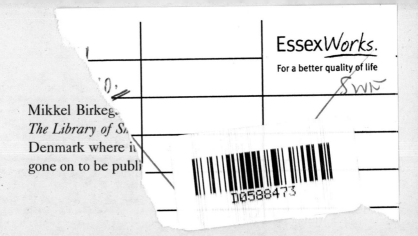

Mikkel Birkeg

The Library of S

Denmark where i

gone on to be publi

D0588473

Also by Mikkel Birkegaard

THE LIBRARY OF SHADOWS

and published by Black Swan

Death Sentence

MIKKEL BIRKEGAARD

Translated from the Danish by
Charlotte Barslund

BLACK SWAN

TRANSWORLD PUBLISHERS
61–63 Uxbridge Road, London W5 5SA
A Random House Group Company
www.transworldbooks.co.uk

DEATH SENTENCE
A BLACK SWAN BOOK: 9780552776806

Originally published in Denmark in 2009 as
Over mit lig by C&K Forlag ApS

First publication in Great Britain
Black Swan edition published 2011

Addresses for Random House Group Ltd companies outside the UK
can be found at: www.randomhouse.co.uk
The Random House Group Ltd Reg. No. 954009

The Random House Group Limited supports The Forest Stewardship
Council® (FSC®), the leading international forest certification organisation.
All our titles that are printed on Greenpeace approved FSC® certified
paper carry the FSC® logo. Our paper procurement policy can be
found at www.randomhouse.co.uk/environment

Typeset in 11/14pt Caslon 540 by
Kestrel Data, Exeter, Devon.
Printed in the UK by
CPI Group (UK) Ltd, Croydon, CR0 4YY

2 4 6 8 10 9 7 5 3 1

Death Sentence

Prologue

Until recently I had only killed people on paper.

As it happened, I was good at it. Good enough to make a living from it and so experienced that I could refer to it as my job. Being able to write full-time in a country the size of Denmark is something of a privilege, but there are those who will argue that I'm not a 'proper writer' or what I write aren't 'proper books'.

I have had to put up with criticism, ridicule even, my whole career, and at times I have secretly agreed with my detractors. It's not easy to admit, but when critics accuse me of laziness and cynicism, of resorting to shock tactics to make up for weaknesses in a plot, they are not altogether wrong.

But the story you're about to read is something else entirely.

I know it will be unlike anything I have ever written. Normally I'm invisible, the anonymous narrator who reveals the story without drawing attention to himself. But this time I can't hide. I have to reveal myself. And this introduction is primarily for my own benefit, a reminder of my project, a wagging finger, telling me what to do and on what terms. That's what motivates me.

Because I must go on and I must do so alone.

I'm cut off from the world. There are no distractions. At night, the darkness and the silence are as dense as though I were in a bunker. No sounds or impressions can reach me.

But then again, I don't need outside inspiration.

What follows here has already happened to me and merely needs communicating through my fingers and a keyboard to the computer. The events of the past week have forced me to train the spotlight on myself and document what's happened while it's still fresh in my mind and I have sufficient time left. There is no filter. No possible interpretation or perspective can show me or my role in the story in a better light. A shame, really, but no matter how tempted I might be to embellish the distressing and dreadful incidents I have taken part in recently, this time I can't make it up.

In a way, it's liberating.

I don't need to lie.

The technique is different, too. I won't have to resort to a range of literary devices to serve the plot or build the tension. I can write it as it is, without beating about the bush. The protagonist won't need to look in the mirror to give the reader an idea of his appearance because the protagonist in this story is me, Frank Føns, a 46-year-old writer, of medium build and height, slim, with dark hair, a closely trimmed beard and a pair of steel-grey eyes which I have been told don't blink very often.

There, that's that out of the way.

Had it not been for the gravity of the situation, I would probably have relished my newfound creative freedom. I have some regrets I didn't try this experiment earlier. Not that I haven't launched into literary experimentation before, but I discovered early, too early perhaps, a formula that worked and I've stuck to it ever since.

But not now.

The rules of the game have changed.

I have been freed from my own and others' expectations and conventions. I don't need to worry about conforming to rules determining what a writer can or cannot do. Just as well, really, as I'm forced to start with one of the biggest clichés in the genre, the event that set everything in motion, a telephone call . . .

Tuesday

1

No one dares to ring me in the morning.

People who think they know me expect me to be hungover. Those who really know me know that I write in the morning and hate being disturbed. I was in 'the Tower', as my older daughter had once nicknamed our holiday cottage, and when the telephone rang, I wasn't actually writing. True, I was at my desk, the computer was on and a mug of steaming hot coffee was next to the screen, but my thoughts were elsewhere. From my study on the first floor I had a view of the garden below. I was wondering if it was worth raking up the leaves today or whether I should wait until the autumn gales had shaken the last of them loose.

My gut reaction was to ignore the telephone. Calls at this time were never good news, or they would be unimportant, cold-callers or wrong numbers. I let the telephone ring five times before I grunted my name into the handset.

'Your body has turned up,' I heard down the other end.

It was Verner. He never introduces himself. Verner is

one of the people who think they know me and yet hasn't grasped that he can't ring whenever he feels like it.

I was in no mood for games.

'What do you mean?'

'Someone has committed your murder.'

'Which one?' I asked, failing to suppress a yawn.

Verner worked for Copenhagen Police and he checked police procedures for me. He didn't regard being a writer as a proper job, but he was still proud to contribute to the process. Sadly, pride had gone to his head and given him the impression he had the right to ring me at any time with ideas or suggestions.

'The murder in the marina,' he exclaimed. 'They've found the body of a woman in Gilleleje Marina, mutilated and bound in chains.'

I closed my eyes and pressed two fingers against my temple. My mind was still drifting between thoughts of raking up leaves and guilt at not having produced that day's quota of words. Verner's news sank in only slowly.

'Is this a joke?' I asked, mostly to say something.

'I'm telling you, this is your murder.'

'What possible connection—'

'The woman was alive and equipped with an oxygen tank when she went in,' Verner interrupted me. 'She has the same physique. Everything matches. Even the weight used to hold her down.'

'A marble bust?'

'Precisely.'

'And you're sure it happened in Gilleleje?'

'Yes.'

My head started to ache. The murder Verner described

did sound exactly like one of the killings in my new novel, *In the Red Zone.* It was the story of a psychopathic psychologist who subjected his patients to their greatest phobia, not in order to cure them, but to kill them in a way that realized their worst nightmare. Hence the murder in the marina involved a woman who had a fear of drowning. The psychologist dived down with her and studied the woman's panic as she ran out of oxygen and suffocated. He got off on her terror in the cold dark water, her pupils widening and her screams muffled through her mouthpiece and the mass of water. I had murdered other characters via their fear of needles, tight spaces and spiders. Not one of my best efforts.

'Frank?' Verner's tone was harsh.

'Yes, I'm still here,' I said.

'What should we do?'

I shook my head. 'It's impossible. It must be a coincidence.'

'She's dead, Frank. *That's* no coincidence.'

'But the book has only just been printed,' I protested. 'It hasn't even been published yet.'

Verner had to get back to work. He was on the beat in Copenhagen and dealt mostly with prostitution and petty crime. Murder wasn't within his remit, so he had nothing more to tell me the first time he called. Thanks to an extensive network within the police force he was normally able to sniff out the information I needed for my books, be it arrest procedures, traffic regulations or ways to kill people. He assured me he would follow the investigation during the day and keep me posted.

It seems to me now that not telling anyone about the possible connection to my book was an unfortunate decision. However, Verner had supplied me with confidential information for years and was probably panicking at the thought of the consequences if he was found out. I was probably too shocked to think straight, though for a moment I fantasized about how the publicity could boost sales. I quickly dismissed that idea, though. It was just as likely the police would stop publication out of respect for relatives or concern for the investigation, and I needed the money. In the last ten to twelve years, I had written a book every eighteen months, and I relied on the income. Not that I lived a life of luxury. Since the divorce, the cottage had become my permanent home – contrary to the terms of the lease – and although it was in reasonable nick, it wasn't exactly a palace.

'The Tower' was one of the older holiday cottages in Rågeleje, third row from the beach, on the north coast of Sjælland, with a spacious garden consisting mainly of lawn surrounded by tall birches and spruces. It was only ten kilometres from Gilleleje Marina, where I regularly bought fish from stalls on the quay.

It was local knowledge that made me pick the marina as the crime scene in *In the Red Zone*, but now it felt like a mistake. I couldn't imagine ever shopping at the marina again. In fact, I couldn't even begin to understand why anyone would commit a murder in the sleepy little fishing village.

So I decided to potter around the cottage doing odd jobs in an attempt to forget that a woman had been killed. It wasn't easy. I work with death every day. Not an hour goes by without me thinking about new ways to kill people or inflict pain and injury. I turn ordinary household articles and utensils into murder weapons or instruments of torture all the time, but only in my imagination.

Now someone had tried it out for real.

I never got round to raking up the leaves or writing the 2,500 words that constituted my daily target. An hour later, having given up on keeping thoughts about the murder at bay, I comforted myself with a whisky, even though it was only just gone eleven. I sat on the terrace and watched the autumn sun battle large drifting clouds. Piles of fallen leaves were spread around the garden. The wind took hold of the tall trees and shook them, and sometimes a cloud of birch seeds would scatter across the terrace. Several of the tiny three-leaved flakes landed in my drink. They floated around on the surface like pieces of a puzzle, and I studied how they sank to the bottom of the glass as they absorbed the liquid.

I have never quite understood the English phrase 'copycat murder'. I assume it has nothing to do with cats. In Danish you say that a murderer 'aped' another, which makes more sense to me. I can imagine that apes, like children, enjoy mimicking someone else's movements. The more I thought about 'copycat', the more absurd it seemed.

I had drunk my whisky and so I went to fetch another one, along with one of the advance copies of *In the Red Zone* I'd received a couple of weeks ago. Back on the terrace, I flicked through the book and found the place where the murder occurred. It was roughly two-thirds in and

17

lasted seven pages. The murder was the book's emotional climax, the scene I tended to plan most carefully.

Kit Hansen, the name of the fictional victim, is a beautiful 28-year-old redhead, slim and fit with large breasts. Her fear of water and of drowning stems from a tragedy in Sharm el Sheikh, where she and her boyfriend go diving by themselves only a few days after completing their training course. They get caught in a fishing net on the seabed. Kit manages to free herself and tries desperately to save her boyfriend, but he is helplessly entangled and she is forced to watch him drown. Bereaved, and laden with guilt, she has to return to Denmark and tell his family how he died, after which she suffers a breakdown. She loses her job with an advertising agency, withdraws from the world and becomes increasingly dependent on prescription drugs. Some time later her neighbour falls in love with her. He is the only person to look after the reclusive woman and slowly his love is noticed and reciprocated. With his help, she quits taking the pills. He also encourages her to see the psychologist, Venstrøm, who ultimately murders her. The story ends with the neighbour killing Venstrøm, but not before he has been subjected to a torture based on his fear of needles.

I flicked back in the book to the description of Kit Hansen and wondered to what extent she resembled the murdered woman – or, rather, vice versa. If it really was a copycat killing, did the real victim have red hair? Did she have a scar on her shin where the fishing net had cut right through to the bone when she struggled to free herself at the bottom of the sea in the Egyptian diving paradise?

How far would the killer go to find a victim who matched the fictional character?

The alcohol was starting to take effect. My body felt heavier and it was getting harder to think clearly. I reread the chapter where Kit Hansen was murdered. Things seemed more and more unreal and I started to doubt if Verner had even called me. Perhaps it had all been just a daydream, a subconscious displacement activity to avoid doing any work.

I decided to go to Gilleleje to see for myself. I needed to find out if a murder really had been committed and, if so, try to establish how far the circumstances surrounding this murder matched mine – or if Verner was simply being paranoid.

2

The Toyota hadn't been exercised for several months and it protested loudly when I turned the key in the ignition. Finally, it surrendered and I drove along the coast to Gilleleje. Most of the road was flanked by holiday cottages and spruces, but in a few places there was a clear view of the sea. The waves had white crests and in several places the beach was reduced to three to four metres of shingle by the salty foam. It was high tide.

There were few people out and about. November is well outside the tourist season and the cafés and pubs had put away their outdoor furniture, leaving me room to park the Corolla on the marina, close to the quay.

The book didn't state precisely where in the marina the murder was committed so I stayed in the car, peering out through the windscreen. The strong wind formed sharp crests on the waves in the basin. Many of the boats had already been put into dry dock for the winter. Those that remained ground restlessly into one another, producing the unpleasant squeal of rubber against rubber, drowned out only by the noise of steel wires lashing aluminium masts.

Five cars were parked on the far side of the basin; one revealed itself to be a police car. I suddenly felt dizzy and grabbed the steering wheel, closed my eyes and inhaled sharply. I sat like this for a while, breathing as regularly as I could. Relax, I told myself. There could be hundreds of reasons for the police to be in the marina; it didn't have to mean that Verner was right.

After a few minutes I summoned up the courage to open my eyes. Some people were standing around the cars, but more had gone out on to the breakwater and were looking out to sea. There was no police tape as far as I could see.

I left my car and strolled to the far side of the basin as calmly as I could. As I approached I could hear voices and the crackle of police radios. A couple of divers in wetsuits were sitting at the back of an open van drinking coffee in silence. A uniformed officer followed me with his eyes as I passed them. I didn't look at him, but carried on walking towards the breakwater. Out there twenty or thirty people had gathered, adults as well as children, all peering out to sea. Some had brought binoculars and cameras. I joined a group and followed their gaze.

A hundred metres out were two boats, a large yellow and red rescue boat and a black rubber dinghy. Four buoys with red flags marked out a square of twenty metres by twenty metres.

'They fished out a woman this morning,' a voice chirped up. 'She didn't have any clothes on.'

A red-haired boy of about ten, wearing a yellow rain-coat and blue wellies, was standing on a bench next to me.

Around his neck he had a pair of binoculars almost as long as his upper arms.

'She was completely white,' he carried on. 'And red.'

'You saw that?' I asked. My voice was trembling slightly. He nodded eagerly.

'I've been standing here all day.' The boy planted his hands on his hips and turned his gaze towards the boats. 'They came this morning. Loads of divers and police officers. At first, they told me to go away, but I kept slipping past them. They've given up trying to get rid of me now.' He smiled and stuck out his chest.

'And . . . the woman?'

'She was completely white,' he repeated. 'There were chains around her and a stone.'

'Did she have red hair?'

Wide-eyed, he turned to look at me. 'How did you know that?'

I shrugged. 'You just told me she was red as well.'

He nodded. 'She had red hair. But she was also red here and here.' He made a cutting movement with his hand across his chest and then his throat. 'And on her arms and legs.'

I didn't know what to say, or if I could even speak at all, so I turned to look at the boats. We stood like this for a couple of minutes until I cleared my throat and pointed to his binoculars.

'That's a very smart pair of binoculars you have there. Could I borrow them, please?'

The boy nodded and lifted the binoculars over his head. 'But I want them back if anything happens.'

I put the binoculars to my eyes and zoomed in on the

boats. In the rubber dinghy a man in a wetsuit was sitting down and holding a rope that trailed over the side and into the water. The dinghy was rocking precariously and every now and again he was forced to take one hand off the rope and grab hold of the gunwale for balance.

Obviously I knew there wouldn't be an outline of the body on the surface on the water, but I think I had expected something. At any rate, I felt disappointed. There should have been some evidence that a violent act had happened there, but the water revealed nothing, and only the boats and the buoys suggested the area was special.

'What's happening?' the boy asked.

'Nothing,' I said and gave him back his binoculars.

He lifted them to his eyes immediately to make sure he hadn't missed anything.

'Do you think there's another one?' His voice sounded hopeful.

'There won't be,' I said and turned around to walk back to my car.

'Are you a policeman or something?' the boy called out, but I ignored him and carried on walking.

As I passed the officers on the quay, they threw me a look filled with contempt.

'Get a good eyeful, did you?' one of them sneered as I passed them.

I sympathized. Rubbernecking is tasteless, but I hadn't come out of curiosity. At least, not the kind of curiosity that drives some people. I wasn't here to get a rush of adrenaline at the sight of blood, bones, intestines and brain matter. Though they were my props when I depicted murder and mutilation in my books, my inspiration didn't come from real-life accidents. Simply closing my eyes sufficed. The images my own brain could conjure up were more than enough.

But, yes, I saw what I came to see in Gilleleje Marina.

3

While I drove back to the cottage, I tried to work out how many people had read *In the Red Zone*. My editor was the first person to read the script and I guessed that probably three or four other people at the publishing company, as well as a couple of bookclub editors, must have seen it. The book would be published in a few days; it had been printed, so the printers must have had access to it for a month or two. I had received thirty complimentary copies in the post and it was likely that several copies had been sent to reviewers and to bookshops as pre-orders. Of my thirty copies, I had sent one to Verner, given one to my neighbour, and sent one to my ex-wife and one to my parents.

In total I estimated that somewhere between one and two hundred people had had access to the printed text of *In the Red Zone*, but both my publishers and the printers had the electronic version and that tends to appear in the strangest of places. I once received a printout of my sixth book, *Nuclear Families*, where the names of the victims had been replaced with mine and my family's. I didn't take threats like that seriously. I had grown used to letters that attacked my work or me personally, but on that occasion someone on the inside had leaked the electronic version of the script. My publishers couldn't explain it, but took the opportunity to enhance their security procedures. However, this was now some years ago and such precautions quickly become ineffective if they aren't reviewed at regular intervals.

The bottom line was I had no way of knowing who or how many people had access to *In the Red Zone*, so I was none the wiser when I pulled into the drive of the Tower.

'Hello, FF,' my neighbour, Bent, called out as I got out of my car.

He was standing in his own drive wearing baggy army trousers, a far too tight black T-shirt and resting an axe on one shoulder. During the summer he had chopped down seven or eight trees on his own property and three on mine, and most of his garden was littered with timber in all lengths and widths. He had an artificial leg, but he was remarkably active and insisted on splitting all the wood into logs by hand.

'Hello, neighbour,' I replied and tried to produce a smile.

'We're running a bit late today,' he said, grinning.

He was referring to our afternoon ritual of meeting up for a drink or two around three o'clock. Bent drank beer and I had a whisky, usually a single malt, Laphroaig or Oban. For me, it often marked the end of my working day. I rarely wrote for more than five or six hours and I had started to value human company after thinking about my book all day. My discussions with Bent were seldom very sophisticated and at times I got irritated by his prejudiced views about immigrants, women or politics, but he was always friendly and willing to lend a hand whenever I needed it.

'I think I'll have to make my excuses today, Bent.' I pointed to my temples. 'I've got a splitting headache.'

'Oh, all right,' he said, sounding disappointed. 'I guess it must be hard work committing all those murders.'

'What?'

'Coming up with them, I mean.'

'Oh, right, I see. No, I think it's something else,' I lied. 'Might be flu.'

Bent nodded. 'OK, I hope you feel better soon.' He swung the axe from his shoulder and was about to carry on chopping, but stopped when I called out to him.

'By the way, have you started the new book?'

Bent shook his head. 'Not yet,' he replied. 'I haven't finished your last one yet. I'm not a fast reader and when I've been outside most of the day, I fall asleep once my head hits the pillow.' He grinned. 'I'm not saying your books are boring, it's just all that fresh air wears me out.'

'That's quite all right, Bent. I was just checking.'

'See you later, FF.'

FF was the nickname he had given me shortly after we met. It was not only the initials of my name, but also of his favourite beer, Fine Festival, which for him was the perfect trade-off between price and strength.

Bent was only ever known as Bent. He came from a working-class family. His father was a blacksmith and his mother a housewife until Bent and his brother, Ole, were old enough to look after themselves, when she got a job as a cashier in the local supermarket. Even though Bent did well at school, he started an apprenticeship at fifteen and became a smith like his father. But the trade bored him, so he was delighted when his name came up for National Service and he was sent to the barracks in Næstved. He showed considerable promise and jumped at the chance to pursue a career in the army, a career that saw him posted to Iraq. He loved being stationed abroad and extended his posting several times – until he saw one of his mates ripped to pieces by an IED and was himself hit in the leg by shrapnel. The doctors couldn't save his leg and after three years' service abroad he was invalided out with miserly compensation.

Back home in Denmark, he realized he had no chance of getting a job and took early retirement at the age of twenty-six. He was in the habit of saying that his experiences in Iraq had aged him forty years, so technically he had reached retirement age.

He kept his army haircut and usually wore camouflage clothes and army boots, possibly out of habit, but more I suspect because it was important to him to remind himself and those around him of his past.

The mental calculations I had done on the way home were still buzzing around my head. I checked the stack of *In the Red Zone* that was on my desk. My publishers appeared to have short-changed me by one book on this occasion. At any rate, I'd given away four, but only twenty-five copies remained, including the one I had taken out on to the terrace earlier.

These days I'm rather wary of handing out copies of a

new novel until it has been reviewed, so it was unlikely I'd given one away and forgotten about it. In the past I had given away books when drunk, sometimes with preposterous dedications to entice the recipient into bed, but it was several years since I had last done that.

I poured myself a whisky, which I knocked back before calling Verner. He wasn't back from work yet, his wife said, so I asked her to get him to call me. For the first time since moving to the cottage, I was actually waiting for the telephone to ring.

Which it did after another two whiskies.

Verner had worked late to find out more about the Gilleleje murder. He got a bit annoyed when I told him I had been to the marina. He couldn't see why I would want to do that; on the contrary, he said, I ought to stay away to avoid suspicion. But I had nothing to hide, and I reckon the real reason for his anger was that he thought I didn't trust him. It was a poor start to the conversation, but after I made a couple of placatory remarks, he got to the point.

'I've got some bad news for you,' he began. 'Turns out the dead woman wasn't a redhead after all.'

'And you call that bad news?' I burst out. 'That's brilliant!'

'Not really. She has short black hair, but when they found her, she was wearing a red wig.' He waited a couple of seconds for the penny to drop. 'The killer put her in that wig to make her look like the woman in your book.'

I didn't interrupt him again.

Verner told me someone had reported seeing light in the water last night. A couple of divers were sent to

29

investigate this morning and had discovered the body. The light originated from a powerful diving lamp aimed straight up at the surface and it had clearly been placed there to make sure she was found. No one appeared to have noticed any boats anchored in the area.

The police believed the woman had been dead for thirty-six hours when they found her, and they established that she had been alive when she was immersed and would probably have been conscious for at least fifteen minutes before she suffocated to death. The cuts to the body were caused by a sharp knife or scalpel and inflicted underwater.

In my book I had given the victim those cuts to attract small fish so she would feel them nibbling little chunks off her, but Verner told me there were very few bites to the body and they definitely hadn't been inflicted while she was alive. Somehow I couldn't help feeling annoyed about this difference.

'Do you know who she was?' I asked.

'A local girl,' Verner replied. 'She worked in a bookshop in Gilleleje High Street. Mona something; I don't remember her surname.'

My heart skipped a beat.

'Mona Weis?' I said.

Silence down the other end of the telephone.

Then, 'Yes . . . do you know her?'

'You just told me she worked in a bookshop in Gilleleje. I've signed books there a couple of times and I've met her, that's all.'

'Hmm,' Verner grunted. 'And yet you can remember her surname?'

To my ears his question was tinged with a certain amount of suspicion, but then again he is a copper.

'It's an interesting name,' I replied. 'Authors collect interesting names.'

In truth there was a completely different reason why I remembered Mona's surname. I had indeed signed autographs in the bookshop in Gilleleje High Street and that was where I had met her, but it had turned into more than just an incidental meeting.

I can't deny that Mona was the inspiration behind Kit Hansen in the book – apart from the hair. Mona Weis had short black hair, as Verner had said, but came across as incredibly feminine. Her face was narrow and she had luminous blue eyes, a fine pointed nose and a small round mouth that made her look as if she was constantly blowing kisses. She was tall and slim without being gangly. Later, when I addressed her as Cleopatra, she rolled her eyes and said she had heard that one before. It failed as a compliment, but I couldn't help it, she really did look like her.

I was due to spend two hours in the bookshop and I signed a grand total of four copies, of which one was a borderline sleazy dedication to Mona. The shop wasn't very big, but they had found room for me in a corner where they had displayed a selection of my books and put up a till to serve the hordes of fans expected to queue up to buy a copy and get it signed by the author. It was Mona's job to operate the till, so we had ample time to talk, and flirt, in two hours while we waited for customers. She offered to add a little something to my coffee to help both of us stay awake and to my delight the next cup she brought me had an overpowering taste of whisky. We drank a lot of coffee and became increasingly animated, something the other staff members couldn't help noticing.

Afterwards we went to the Kanal Café or the 'Carnal Café' as the locals call it, where we carried on drinking whisky. It was there that I called her Cleopatra and she told me she couldn't stand my books. I must have looked taken back because she quickly added that she liked me very much. She said she was fed up with dating fishermen and country bumpkins who drank beer and only ever talked about cars. At this point we both agreed there was no reason to stay in the café, and we returned to her flat, two rooms above the town's photo shop, where we tore each other's clothes off as soon as the door had slammed shut. We fucked like rabbits, changed positions and places constantly, but my most vivid memory was being ridden by Cleopatra, whose blue eyes practically glowed down on me.

She tired of me after six weeks. I wasn't surprised; she was twelve years younger than me and I was just grateful for the time we had together. She told me little about herself and I didn't encourage her to tell me more. We were lovers at a time when we both needed someone, that was all.

Yet her death hit me like a blow to the chest. I hadn't seen her for over two years, but the thought of *anyone* dying in this way, let alone her, made me feel nauseous.

Down the other end of the telephone, Verner cleared his throat.

'Listen, Frank. I have to ask you a question.'

'Of course.'

'Can you account for your whereabouts these last three days?'

4

Of course, I couldn't prove what I had been doing or where I had been on the days Verner was asking about. Most of my evenings ended with a glass of red wine in front of the fire or the television and the three days he wanted me to account for had been no different. I didn't have a solid alibi, and I knew what that would mean if it had been a crime novel: I would have been the prime suspect. Not only had I described the murder, I also knew the victim, and it wouldn't take much imagination to come up with a motive of jealousy.

I didn't tell Verner how close Mona Weis and I had been. Our fling was probably known to most people in Gilleleje and I knew it was only a question of time before rumours about it reached the police, but I needed time to think. I was upset at Mona's death, but I had the sense to finish the conversation as quickly as I could. This involved me promising to come to Copenhagen to speak face to face with Verner.

I was going to Copenhagen two days later anyway for the launch of *In the Red Zone* at the Forum Book Fair, and we agreed that I would arrive a day early so we could meet. I wasn't happy about it.

Life in the small seaside village of Rågeleje had taken root in me and with every trip to the capital I felt more like a stranger. The noises had grown louder, the tempo faster and the people more distant. They were unaware of each other's presence and pushed their way through the streets in their own bubble as defined by their car, music device or mobile telephone, or sometimes all three at once. If I had stayed in the city – as I had always sworn I would – I would most certainly have turned into one of them, but now I was a tourist. It was no longer my home territory and, with every visit, it took me longer to rediscover the old rituals and familiar ease. Simply navigating my way down Strøget was a major effort and necessitated an endless string of apologies because I could no longer read the pedestrian traffic in the street.

All the same, I needed to get away from the cottage. I wandered restlessly between the kitchen, living room and study, thinking about Mona. I convinced myself that if I physically distanced myself from the murder, I would once more be the master of my own thoughts. If nothing else, the impact of the city would at least be a distraction.

My annual trip to the book fair was carefully planned to ensure I spent as little time in the capital as possible. This year I had meetings with my publishers, a couple of interviews, three signing sessions at the book fair and one reading. In addition, I had squeezed in a visit to my parents, an evening with my best and only friend, Bjarne, and now a meeting with Verner.

This meant I had to change my hotel reservation. I

always stay in the same place, Marieborg Hotel, in Vesterbro near the city centre, a tradition maintained since the first year I no longer had a fixed address in Copenhagen. Had I wanted to, I could probably have stayed with my parents or with Bjarne, but I liked being able to retire to my own space, and the hotel lay in a side street where I would get peace and quiet. The staff knew me, always gave me the same room and were politely interested without being intrusive. Part of their deference was due to the fact that I had used the hotel in my book *As You Sow*, where a corrupt police superintendent is murdered by a prostitute he has double-crossed. The murder takes place in room 102, where I usually stay, and the hotel manager had even put up a small plaque on the back of the door mentioning the murder and my name. In the bedside table drawer there was a copy of the book in addition to the Bible.

When I called the hotel it turned out I would be unable to stay in room 102 on this occasion. The room had been booked for a week and prepaid for a couple of additional nights by another guest. This information angered me and I raised my voice to the poor girl at the other end of the telephone. I tried to explain that I always stayed in that room and that I had made my booking a fortnight ago. She apologized profusely, but no special requirements regarding room 102 had been registered in their booking system. As compensation, she offered me the extra night I needed for free. It failed to improve my mood.

My meeting with Verner would take place on Wednesday in the hotel restaurant. I knew I had to tell him the truth about my relationship with Mona Weis, if he hadn't already sussed it out, but I wanted to supplement it with my own theory as to what was going on. The only problem was I had no theory.

As I couldn't get to sleep anyway, I turned my thoughts to solving the mystery. I approached the situation as if it was one of my own novels. My books are usually constructed around a central murder, a crime so vile it remains in the reader's mind long after the book has been read. Once I have devised that particular scene, I get to work on the plot and the list of characters. In this case, the murder was already in place, but the cast and the plot were completely different to my book. I had to create a new storyline from the same starting point.

I soon realized that I was top billing. The question was: which role was I playing? Would I be the mentor, the scapegoat, or was my challenge to take on the part of the quick-witted detective who solves the case and saves the day?

The thought that someone might be inspired by my murders wasn't novel. In the countless interviews I have given, the question is nearly always asked: 'Aren't you scared that someone might commit your murders in real life?'

I'm not boasting when I say that my murders are so complex in execution and so well integrated into the storyline that any reconstruction would be both difficult and pointless. I always spice the crimes up with exotic and horrifying details; they are meant to be unforgettable, they bear my trademark and they leave the reader in no doubt they're reading a Føns thriller. Secondly, there were several practical obstacles. In order to commit the murder in Gilleleje Marina, the killer would need access to a boat. The diving equipment had to be untraceable and the murder itself take place unnoticed in an area with plenty of boat traffic, even this late in the year. The victim would have to be selected, kidnapped, transported and murdered before anyone reported her missing. Such things take time and preparation, and nothing can go wrong.

In fiction, this is straightforward. The reader has been drawn so effectively into the story that different rules apply and events need only make sense within the framework of the novel. It must seem plausible not only that the villain is so cunning he might actually get away with the most outrageous scheme, but also that he has the motive to carry out the extensive fieldwork and the crime itself.

However, that's not the answer I give to journalists. When asked if I'm scared that someone might try to copy my murders, I inevitably launch into a lengthy speech about how art has always been accused of implanting something in people, as if that something wasn't already there. Cartoons were once regarded as dangerous and morally corrupting, then it was the turn of cinema films, video films, role-play and, most recently, computer games. My point being that if someone commits a murder, it isn't prompted by a book, it's because that person is bad. Book or no book, the murder would be committed.

This argument not only shut up the journalists, it also made sense to me.

The murder of Mona Weis, however, made no sense. Mona wasn't scared of water or diving. The act of killing her made sense only because it was done with considerable adherence to the script, a script I just happened to have written.

So perhaps Mona wasn't the only victim?

No matter how revolting the murder was, I couldn't ignore that I had a level of involvement. Someone wanted to get rid of Mona and had used my method, possibly in order to point the finger at me. It could be a boyfriend with a temper; she might have told one of her boorish fishermen about our relationship, bragged about it, possibly. Through her work, she might have got hold of a copy of *In the Red Zone* and waved it in front of the killer like a red rag.

This was my theory after a whole night of speculation, piles of notes and ever bigger glasses of whisky. I was convinced this was how everything connected. There were no other options. The more I thought about it, the clearer I could visualize the scene, and I had an overwhelming feeling that I could have found the killer by looking in the telephone directory or walking down Gilleleje High Street. A huge wave of relief washed over me and I looked forward to meeting Verner and telling him how it had all happened – I would be Sherlock Holmes to his Inspector Lestrade.

I was positively looking forward to going to Copenhagen.

5

Becoming a writer was never a conscious decision. It's as if I was given no choice; all I can remember is writing, even before I actually knew how to. As a boy, I never drew cars or houses like the other children, but copied letters from newspapers and books. And I'd be convinced I had written a story, even if I had only copied a shopping list. Afterwards I would 'read' the story aloud to my parents, who listened willingly and were always encouraging.

Once I learned to write, it became my favourite occupation. Again, I would write when everyone else was drawing. I would imagine the drawing I could have made, but draw it with words. 'The Red Indian on his horse sets fire to the fort with a burning arrow' was one of my earliest works. I had a clear picture of the scene and could visualize it down to the last detail when I read my text. It frustrated my teachers and worried my parents so from time to time I would draw the occasional picture, mainly to reassure them. However, the alphabet always crept in: the elephant was an 'a', the house was an 'H' and birds 'm's against the blue-shaded sky.

After the first few years at school we stopped drawing pictures and my parents could heave a sigh of relief and start delighting in the top marks their son got in Danish. I wrote articles for the school newsletter and published my own stories, which I painstakingly transferred to blueprint paper, printed and handed out in the lunch break. It attracted a fair amount of attention, mainly because I did it all by myself.

At high school, I continued with my writing. I became the editor of the school's weekly newsletter, *Posten*, in my first year and my sarcastic reporting style and acerbic editorials quickly made me one of the popular students. My appearance changed. I dyed my hair black, dressed in black and listened to The Cure. On special occasions I would wear black nail polish and eyeliner. I took up smoking, favouring obscure east European brands without filter, and my choice of alcohol was cheap whisky, usually J&B or King George.

To my great surprise I discovered that an inspired pen was extremely effective when it came to the opposite sex and I proved, on several occasions, that you could write the pants off a girl. Afterwards I would write up the conquest rather successfully as pornography and sell it. I always made sure that I obscured my 'victim's' identity, but most of them worked it out anyway and some even felt honoured to be included in my library. It all enhanced my popularity and I attracted a small group of disciples. In best Cyrano de Bergerac style, we helped bashful students out of their painful state of virginity by writing love letters for them, or we forged letters from parents, in return for payment, obviously. There was nothing we couldn't achieve with a great script or a poem, and this gave us the idea of forming a writers' commune – a creative utopia where we would do nothing but read and write. We would devote ourselves to the written word with an earnestness and reverence worthy of monks. Our combination of pomposity and naivety makes me smile when I think about it now.

My parents assumed I would become a journalist. I had the talent and the grades for it and since I had shown an interest in the profession by writing school newsletters, their ambitions on my behalf were understandable. But it held no attraction for me. Journalism was too restrictive. I didn't want to end up writing for *Ekstra Bladet* or some other tabloid. Control of the story and the word was crucial to us, and our view of literature as the finest medium of all left little room for compromise.

To my parents' dismay, I and two of my writing buddies realized our dream of setting up our commune, the Scriptorium, as we named it, in a six-room luxury flat on Nørrebro near the Lakes in Copenhagen. This was before the area was renovated so the rent was still manageable even though the size and the location were at the top end.

My mother especially worried a great deal, but I think my father was so confident I would regret my decision and find my way into journalism eventually that he talked my mother into indulging my 'fad'. The compromise we reached was that I would start a degree in literature, primarily to become eligible for a modest state-funded student grant. However, it didn't quite cover our expenses, so my flatmates and I had to take whatever casual jobs we could get in order to pay the rent. In this respect we weren't picky at all and we delivered letters, worked in shops and washed bottles at Carlsberg Brewery.

Much of our income was spent on cigarettes and whisky, which we believed fuelled our creativity. We often drank ourselves senseless during writing sessions lasting well into the early hours of the morning.

My two partners in crime were Bjarne and Morten. Bjarne was a huge, even-tempered bear of a man who wrote poems about nature and more spiritual subjects. He was impossible to provoke and often acted as a lightning conductor for the other two of us, whose tempers were more volatile. Bjarne and I had plenty of nicknames, but Morten was only ever known as Mortis because he was tall and pale and the subject of his writing was inevitably death in some form or other. His writing style was uncompromising and he was very sensitive to criticism. If we said anything negative about his work, he might not speak to us for days.

For my part, I experimented with different types of writing, but most of my output had strong sexual under-tones. In this way we had, in our own opinion, covered the three most important subjects: life, sex and death.

When we weren't writing, working or pretending to be studying, we partied.

Our parties were always popular and five or ten new faces would show up every time. This was quite all right with us, as long as they behaved themselves and brought a crate of beer, a bottle of spirits or something stronger. I don't think our neighbours liked us all that much, but they never complained.

The most memorable party, for many reasons, was the

Angle party, which we held three years after moving in. We had all tried to get our work published, but apart from Bjarne, who had managed to get a selection of his poetry published in an underground literature magazine – for no payment, of course – our efforts had been in vain. I had had 'pretentious and lacking in structure' thrown in my face after my first attempt at a novel, and Mortis was told that his texts were banal, naive and riddled with linguistic errors and clichés. It didn't worry us or, more accurately, we refused to show our disappointment, and we reassured one another that we would never compromise our integrity.

The turning point for me came with *In the Dead Angle*, a genre study of a crime novel, in which I describe a murder from every possible angle, hence the title. Even though it was fairly flimsy and experimental, the publishing house, ZeitSign, liked it and offered to publish it. To this day I can't imagine what the editor, Finn Gelf, saw in it, and I gather he was rather isolated in his view that it was any good, but at the time I was bursting with pride and delirious with success. I had cut a notch in the pistol handle of art, knocked my dent in the bonnet of literature and I felt close to immortal.

The critics slated *In the Dead Angle* and it barely sold two hundred copies, but when we held the Angle party, the publication date was still months away. I was thus blissfully ignorant of the reception the book would later get and simply wanted to throw the greatest party ever. There would be more guests, more alcohol and more drugs than ever before; plenty of girls and live music. Everyone was invited. And everyone came. The flat was swarming with people, of whom I knew only half.

That morning I had been to Nyhavn and had the book's ISBN number tattooed round my upper arm, a ritual we had pledged to undergo with the publication of our first book. I had to take off my shirt again and again to show I had kept my promise, and most guests were duly impressed with the armband tattoo.

It happened in this sea of people, as it sometimes does when crowds gather, that suddenly a corridor opened up and I could see from the far side of the living room all the way to the front door.

Line was standing in the doorway.

She was wearing a short dress and high-heeled shoes, an outfit somewhat out of sync with the rest of the guests, who were dressed more casually, but she appeared oblivious to it. Her mousy brown hair reached just below her jawline and her face was rather ordinary with strong eyebrows, high cheekbones and a narrow nose. She looked nothing like a model and seemed out of place both as far as her dress and the party were concerned.

What knocked me out was her smile.

I know it's a cliché and I would never have the audacity to write it in a novel, not even a romantic one, but that was what happened. She had a small wry smile that revealed a little of a row of perfect teeth and she exuded warmth and spontaneity. It took my breath away. Her gaze swept around the room and our eyes met for a brief moment before the crowd closed the gap between us.

During the time the commune had been in existence, we had all had our fair share of girls. We often scored at our own parties; it was a bad night if none of us got lucky. I wouldn't go as far as to say there was competition between us, but it was a source of huge satisfaction to turn up for breakfast the following morning and introduce a girl with rumpled hair wearing only a man's shirt.

When I saw Line that evening, I made a vow. She wouldn't be another party trophy. This time my aim wasn't a few days or a couple of weeks of casual sex. This was the real thing and it meant I had to be careful. I mustn't sabotage my mission with crass remarks uttered under the influence of alcohol and drugs. On the contrary, I would try to avoid her. I might exchange a few words with her, so she would at least remember me, but my main aim would be to try to find out who she was and how I could see her again. I would woo her with a persistence and a chastity worthy of a Shakespeare play, but not until I was sober.

After about an hour I began to worry that she might have left. Perhaps she had even come to the wrong address – her clothes suggested it – and now she might be at her real destination, a couples' dinner party at my neighbour's with a five-course menu and matching wines. It was almost unbearable. I kept moving to keep my nerves under control, constantly checking if she was still around. It became increasingly difficult to maintain my cool exterior as host and harder still to focus on the conversations I got caught up in. If she had gone, all was lost.

I was more or less resigned to drinking myself senseless when I heard a woman's voice behind me.

'You're not easy to find!' The music was loud so she had to shout.

I turned around and came face to face with her smile. She laughed when she saw my reaction.

'It's OK, I have been invited.'

'No, it's just . . . I thought you had left,' I stuttered and regretted it immediately.

'Congratulations on the book,' she said, holding out her hand. She had a drink in her other hand.

I took her hand. It was warm and dry and she gave my hand a quick squeeze.

'Thank you!' I shouted over the music. 'Who are you?' I asked before I could stop myself.

'My name is Line and I'm a dancer!' she shouted back, but thanks to the music I didn't catch all of it.

'A chancer?'

She started to laugh and it was impossible not to laugh with her. Then she placed a hand on my shoulder, pulled me closer and leaned into me at the same time.

'My name is Line and I'm a dancer,' she repeated, with her mouth very close to my ear.

I was aware of my face burning and I could feel beads of sweat on my forehead. She took a small step away from me without removing her hand from my shoulder and looked expectantly at me.

'So . . . what are you waiting for?' She looked me up and down.

I realized we were on the dance floor and she started to move, very slowly. I followed, encouraged by yet another one of her smiles, and we danced for fifteen minutes without speaking. Her blue eyes studied me. Every time I made to say something, she raised her eyebrows and leaned into me as if she wouldn't want to miss a single sound I uttered. As a result, I couldn't produce one word and she would move back with a grin. At last I had to surrender and laugh with her. I laughed from relief, so heartily that it brought tears to my eyes and everyone around started to laugh with us without knowing why.

When I had regained control of my voice and my body, I pulled her into me and hugged her.

'I'm already crazy about you,' I whispered into her ear.

Then it was her turn to blush and look away.

We were inseparable for the rest of the evening; we danced and laughed and talked. I had rediscovered my eloquence and told her of dreams and hopes I had never revealed to anyone, and she rewarded me with an intimacy and openness I had never experienced in another human being. In her company, personal space was reduced to zero and it felt like the most natural thing in the world to put my arm around her or hold her hand even though we had only known each other for a few hours.

Suddenly it was six o'clock in the morning and Bjarne started to clear up. Line and I sat alone on a sofa. The pauses between the words grew longer. I remember I genuinely didn't want her to stay, something that surprised me a little, but I wanted the first time we slept together to be special. She may have been thinking the same thing because she leaned towards me and gave me a long kiss. She was sorry, she had to get to work, she said, but she would like to come back again if that was all right. I traced her fantastic mouth with my index finger and said she would most certainly have to.

But Line didn't come back. Not the following day or the day after that. It was dreadful. I drove Bjarne and Mortis insane with my speculations about why she hadn't contacted me. Perhaps she had only been toying with me, or worse: she had been in an accident. There was no end to my disaster theories. Mortis grew very irritated with me and it wasn't until later that I realized why he was so touchy about Line.

For Mortis, it wasn't only the word that was important, but the medium itself, the physical book that contained the written word. He placed great emphasis on paper quality and binding and could be elevated to a state of ecstasy when holding a particularly well-produced example in his long slender fingers. He thought little of new publications; the paper quality was poor, the pages too thin and the glue in the spine inadequate. His passion drove him to visit antiquarian bookshops in Copenhagen in a constant search for the perfect volume.

I think the hunt itself mattered to Mortis. There wasn't a single second-hand bookshop in Copenhagen he hadn't explored, and he had set routes he patrolled at regular intervals in order not to miss out on anything. He never wanted us to come with him on his trips. Nor do I think we would have appreciated them in the same way he did and we would probably have ruined the experience by joking or making fun of him. Nevertheless, we benefited enormously from his obsession. If we were looking for a book, he could usually tell us where we would be most likely to find it and we rarely made a wasted journey.

It was on one of his patrols that he ran into Line, around the time I was getting my tattoo in Nyhavn. The Angle party was happening that night and Mortis had to shorten his usual route to get back to help with the preparations. In a second-hand bookshop in Vesterbro he noticed a girl browsing. She moved between the bookcases with great care and there was something about her posture that caught his attention. Some people just seem more relaxed and at home in their body than others and this was the case with Line. 'She was at ease with herself,' Mortis later said to Bjarne, without being able to explain what that looked like. I knew exactly what he meant. Line possessed an acute physical awareness that made her graceful in everything she did.

Mortis summoned up the courage to invite her first for a coffee and later to the party that same evening. I think he exaggerated my talent and importance as far as the reason for the party was concerned, and I'm fairly certain he hinted strongly that his contribution to my forthcoming book was considerable. Anyway, he managed to talk her into going.

I had no idea that Line was there at his invitation, but nor do I think it would have made a difference. Mortis wasn't her type and she wasn't his, although he would never admit it. I don't know what he had expected would happen between the two of them, but the upshot was he felt I had stabbed him in the back.

Four days after the party, I could bear it no longer. Line had told me she worked in a health food shop near Nør-report station and I decided to go there. I braced myself for every kind of rejection and entered the shop with a feeling of just wanting to get it over with. The shop concept was American. Jars, pots and bags of health remedies filled shelves that lined aisles so close together you could barely squeeze past the other customers. The staff wore green uniforms with a white cap, to make them resemble nurses, I suppose. The shelves were no taller than I could peer over and I quickly established that Line wasn't there.

The assistant behind the till was a blonde woman in her thirties. A badge gave her name as Alice. She smiled warmly as I approached her, but when I stuttered my question, her expression changed to one of concern. My heart started pounding. All the terrifying scenarios I had imagined in the last few days came back to me in one mad clamour.

Alice told me that Line's mother had died.

I'm embarrassed to admit it, but I felt an incredible sense of relief and I believe my lips curved into an inappropriate smile. The shop assistant sent me a baffled look until I got my emotions back under control. This might explain why she was somewhat reluctant to tell me where I could find Line, but eventually I coaxed the surname, Damgaard, out of her and left the shop.

The telephone directory took care of the rest. I knew she lived somewhere in Islands Brygge and luckily there was only one Line Damgaard listed in the area. Now that I knew the reason for her disappearance I was happy and apprehensive at the same time. I debated long and hard with myself about the wisdom of contacting her and I experienced a growing sense of concern that was entirely new to me. It was this feeling that decided the matter. When I cycled to Islands Brygge later the same afternoon, I was motivated more by compassion than infatuation.

Islands Brygge wasn't as upmarket in those days as it is now. The streets seemed narrow and dingy. It was a part of the city where the weather was always grey and the residents scuttled along the pavements or into their cars to disappear down potholed roads without looking back.

There was an entryphone outside Line's block, but the door was wide open and I went straight inside the stairwell. Even though it was a sunny day, few rays could penetrate the grimy windows. I switched on the light and saw worn steps and pale green walls that were in dire need of a lick of paint.

Outside Line's front door I had second thoughts. Should I intrude on her grief? I was about to leave when I heard music coming from her flat. I leaned closer. It was Billie Holiday. I had discovered Blues myself during that period and it was probably the music that decided the matter. I took a deep breath, straightened up and knocked on the door.

A moment passed before I heard the lock click and the door gradually open. There she was, barefoot and wearing a long black dress. Her hair was slightly rumpled and her gaze focused on the floor, but when she raised it, she found mine and I saw that her eyes were red. If she was surprised, she didn't show it. A small smile formed on her lips and without saying a word, she held out her hand to me. I took it and squeezed it. She held on to my hand and pulled me inside, closed the door and led me into the flat to the sound of Billie Holiday's hypnotic voice. In the living room was an unmade sofa bed with crumpled sheets; clothing was scattered around it. The record player sat on an upside-down beer crate and LPs filled another crate next to it. Slowly, Line guided me to the bed, still without letting go of my hand, and lay down. I stepped out of my shoes and lay down close to her. Even through my clothes, I could feel the warmth from her body. I put my arms around her, and she pulled the duvet over us both.

I don't know how long we lay like this. The music soon stopped. Every now and then we slept. Sometimes she cried very quietly; I could feel her body tremble against mine. We didn't speak. Our communication consisted of small squeezes or light touches. There was nothing sexual about it – we were fully dressed – but I had never experienced anything this intimate before.

'My mum has died,' she said after a long time.

'I know,' I whispered and stroked her hair.

She turned to me and looked into my eyes. 'I've missed you so much,' she said. She snuggled up to me and started to sob.

I said nothing, but I held her as tightly as I could.

Line's mother had died on her way home from work at the Ministry of Religious Affairs where she was a departmental manager. A red Opel smashed into her on a pedestrian crossing and she was thrown high into the air before she hit the ground dead.

Line was at work when it happened. Her elder sister called her at the health food shop. The news of their mother's death knocked her for six and she left the shop without saying a word. Fearing she would have an accident if she rode her bicycle, she wheeled it through the city. The journey felt endless, but she didn't cry. Her face didn't crack until she arrived at her parents' house on Amager, where her three siblings and her father were waiting for her. There she collapsed and sobbed for hours, incapable of speech.

The feeling of guilt was the worst, she told me. Her grief at her mother's death was constantly disturbed by thoughts and memories of me and our evening, and she was ashamed to miss me in the midst of the tragedy. This made her feel even more upset. She hated herself for entertaining these feelings when she should be supporting her family and saying goodbye to the most important person in her life. That was why she couldn't make herself contact me, and if I hadn't appeared of my own accord, she would probably never have seen me again.

When she opened the door to her flat, I was probably the last person she had expected to see, but the one she wanted to find more than anyone. She accepted this coincidence as evidence of our shared destiny and didn't hesitate for one second, but pulled me inside.

I had never had any doubts and I still don't.

Wednesday

6

I left Rågeleje on Wednesday morning. The sun was shining and there was a mildness in the air that made it hard to leave the cottage during what was likely to be the last sprint before autumn handed over the baton to winter.

My black blazer hung from a hanger on the headrest of the passenger seat. I realized I hadn't worn it since last year's book fair when I found my old entry pass and programme in the inside pocket. On the back seat was a weekend bag with clothes for five days and a brown envelope with the beginnings of the first draft of my next book. It was untitled, but my editor had suggested the working title *By the Skin of My Teeth* as a joke and it had stuck. The plot was an offshoot of my research for *In the Red Zone*, where I had become intrigued by how easily people relate to a fear of dentists. I thought there was enough material for a separate novel and so far I had been proved right, even though I had only written about a third.

Before I reached Copenhagen, I pulled into a petrol station and bought a packet of cigarettes. I had quit smoking the first time Line was pregnant, but for some reason I always started again when I was going to Copenhagen, as if the fumes from the city traffic weren't bad enough or perhaps I believed the cigarettes would cancel out the smog. It was therefore a year since I had last smoked and it resulted in a couple of violent coughing fits and a feeling of dizziness as I inhaled my way through the first couple of cigarettes. But by God, they tasted good.

After one and a half hours' drive, I reached the hotel. Driving through inner-city Copenhagen for well over thirty minutes had been tough. I was far from used to that volume of traffic. My T-shirt was damp with sweat and I could feel a headache coming on. Once in Copenhagen I preferred to get around by taxi, or on foot if the weather and the distance permitted, and I was relieved when I finally parked the car in front of the hotel.

Marieborg is a five-storey white building with large windows overlooking the street. Behind those windows the interior of the restaurant was classic with dark wooden panels, wooden chairs, white tablecloths and dark pink carpets. Mirrors and brass lamps were mounted on the walls. The entrance to the lobby was situated on the right-hand side of the building, from where a lift and a staircase with the same pink carpet as the restaurant led to the rooms on the floors above.

The owner of the hotel, Ferdinan Jensen, was standing behind the reception counter when I walked into the lobby holding my weekend bag and the envelope in one hand and my blazer draped over my shoulder with my other hand.

'Welcome back, Mr Føns,' he said, flashing me a wide smile.

Ferdinan Jensen was Spanish by birth, but had married a Danish woman more than twenty-five years ago. He had Mediterranean skin, pitch-black hair and bushy eyebrows, which suggested he wasn't born in Denmark, but his Danish was impeccable and he was incredibly well informed about what was happening in the city. He was in great shape, probably as a result of his boundless commitment to the hotel where no job was beneath his dignity. I have seen him carry suitcases, change light bulbs and wait in the restaurant, always with the same wide smile on his lips.

'So it's the book fair again, is it?'

I set down my bag in front of the counter and heaved a sigh. 'Yes, it's that time of the year again, I'm afraid. The leaves are falling and it's raining books.'

Ferdinan Jensen laughed. 'Yes, and some of them are yours, am I right?'

I dug out a signed copy of *In the Red Zone* from the front pocket of my weekend bag and placed it on the counter.

'And now one of them is yours,' I replied and pushed it towards him.

His eyes shone. 'You shouldn't have, Mr Føns,' he said, and grabbed the book with both hands. 'Thank you so much. I'm starting this one tonight.' He studied the cover before carefully placing the book on the table behind the counter.

When he turned around again, he had a doleful expression on his face.

'I'm really very sorry about the mix-up with your room,'

he said, throwing up his hands. 'It's my fault. I could kick myself.'

'That's quite all right,' I replied. 'A change will do me good.'

He shook his head. 'That new computer is too clever for me,' he said, pointing to a screen on his left. 'It was my darling wife's idea, but I can't get it to work properly. That's why I couldn't reserve your usual room when you booked. I'm so embarrassed.'

'It really doesn't matter,' I assured him. 'As long as I've got a bed to sleep in.'

His face lit up. 'That you will have. I've got you a very nice room indeed.'

I got the key to room 501 and booked a table for two in the restaurant for the same evening.

'By the way,' Ferdinan exclaimed, bending down behind the counter. 'There's some post for you.' He reappeared holding a thick yellow envelope.

The size, the thickness and the sound it made when he placed it on the counter suggested it was a book. I picked it up and studied it. There was no indication of who the sender was, and my name was printed on an anonymous address label.

'Who delivered it?' I asked.

'No idea,' Ferdinan replied. 'It was left on the counter some time yesterday afternoon.'

I shrugged. 'My publishers, probably.' I stuck the envelope into the front pocket of my weekend bag.

Ferdinan offered to carry my bag upstairs but I declined and took the lift up to the fifth floor alone.

He was right. It was a great room, more like a suite,

in my opinion. In addition to a large bedroom with a king-size bed and a bathroom with a Jacuzzi, there was a spacious living room and an extra lavatory. The living room was equipped with a well-stocked minibar and the biggest flat-screen television I had ever seen. Two French balconies, one from the bedroom and one from the living room, overlooked the street and I discovered to my delight that noise from the traffic was perfectly tolerable on the fifth floor.

It was far too big for me. There was much more room here than in my cottage and I felt lost in the uncluttered surroundings. I'm used to a bit of mess – chaos some would probably call it – and the large living room with all that floor space and upholstered furniture not piled high with books, printouts or notepads was intimidating.

Having unpacked my clothes, which took up only a couple of hangers and one shelf in the five-door built-in wardrobe in the bedroom, I poured myself a whisky from the minibar and took the envelope from the front pocket of my bag. I carried it over to the living room and sat down in one of the armchairs.

My address in Rågeleje was secret so readers usually sent their letters to my publishers. From time to time fellow writers would send me signed copies of their books, as I would to them. It was an unspoken agreement and a way of announcing that yes, you had just had another book published. At times it felt like pressure, at other times gloating, especially if the book in question had been well received. I was rarely pleased to receive these trophies, and they were positively unwelcome if I was suffering from writer's block.

Please don't let it be from Tom Winter.

Tom Winter was a crime writer who had proclaimed himself to be my rival on several occasions. I wasn't terribly worried about his challenge, but it annoyed me that reviewers were always comparing us, as it was mostly to Tom Winter's advantage. We had never met and yet he insisted on sending me a copy of every book he wrote. So far, that amounted to five. I had never returned the compliment, but that didn't seem to worry him.

I ripped open the envelope and stuck my hand inside. As I expected, it was a book. I pulled it out and turned it face up.

It was a copy of *In the Red Zone*, my latest but not yet published crime novel. The cover was dominated by a close-up of a traffic light and, if you looked carefully, you could make out different figures and a single skull in the lamps.

I frowned. Who would send me a copy of my own book?

There was no signature on the title page that might reveal the sender. I checked the envelope for further information, but there was nothing.

I thumbed through the pages. Words and letters flickered before my eyes. A few sentences jumped out long enough to be decoded, but were soon overtaken by more words. The note had been inserted approximately halfway through. I went back a couple of pages to remove it. Perhaps that was the clue I had been looking for, an explanation from the sender?

It turned out not to be a note, but a photo.

A photo of Mona Weis.

7

The picture of Mona Weis was the size of a packet of cigarettes. She was leaning against a white wall, smiling, and her hypnotic blue eyes were aimed straight at the camera. I estimated it must have been taken around the time I knew her. Her hair was the same style and she looked very much like she did two years ago, which would explain why the colours had started to fade. The photo itself was slightly scratched, the corners bent and the back a little soiled as if it had been lying around someone's drawer for a long time.

I sat in my hotel room for hours staring at the photo. Slowly I drank my way through the minibar. When I reached the Baileys, I put down the photo and began studying the book itself. I examined the cover. It was brand new, no scratches or marks of any kind. I carefully went through the whole volume, page by page, and checked the text for marks or other signs. You can tell if a book has been read. It doesn't smell quite the same once its pages have been turned. Everything suggested this copy had never been opened.

To my regret, I had removed the photo without paying attention to where it had been inserted. Perhaps it was unimportant, but still I was annoyed at my carelessness. It had been in the second half, which was where Kit Hansen was murdered, but that was all I could be sure of.

None the wiser after examining the book, I looked at the envelope again. I turned it over, I sniffed it, I peered inside it and I poked my fingers right into the corners. There was nothing that revealed anything about the sender. My name was typed on a white label and stuck on the envelope a little askew, as if it had been done in haste or just indifferently.

Finally I leaned back in the chair and stared at the coffee table. The three objects – the envelope, the book and the photo – lay side by side, like an assembly instruction in reverse order.

Was Verner playing a joke on me? He had probably discovered the real nature of my relationship with Mona and he was the type who might decide to punish me by pulling a stunt like this. It would have been relatively easy for him to get hold of a photo from Mona's flat, had he wanted to, but I had no idea how he would have got his hands on the book. I had signed the copy I had given to him. But then again, he had contacts everywhere.

The thought was tempting, but I couldn't even convince myself. Verner simply didn't have the finesse to pull it off. My rejected-boyfriend theory wasn't very convincing either, and my earlier excitement at explaining the true facts of the case to Verner was replaced by a growing unease.

I felt nauseous, but not enough to be sick. No matter how hard I tried to relax, my breathing was laboured. My fingers tingled and my legs felt leaden. All I could do was sit there and stare at the three objects in front of me, but no amount of staring at them revealed anything.

The light faded until I sat in darkness.

Suddenly I remembered my dinner with Verner. I glanced at my watch. I was meeting him in the restaurant in half an hour. I forced myself to shower and change. The familiar movements helped me relax a little, but my hands were still shaking when I put the photo and the book back in the envelope and brought them with me down to the ground floor.

Roughly half the restaurant's twenty tables were occupied. Smaller parties, most of them American couples, from what I could hear. I was the only one sitting alone. Eating on my own has never bothered me and I usually bring my notebook so I don't get too bored.

I ordered a whisky, a 12-year-old Bowmore, a double. Verner never made an effort to be on time, so I settled in for a long wait.

I had met Verner through Line. We happened to be seated next to each other at a golden wedding anniversary in Line's family. I had dreaded the event, but when I found out the person next to me was a police officer, my mood improved considerably. Back then he had a mane of black hair and was only a little chubby, though he had already developed a significant double chin. A prominent nose combined with his small, deep-set eyes made him look anything but charming. Not that this prevented him from being loud-mouthed and drowning out most of the other guests at the table with his bragging manner. We talked for most of the dinner and he agreed to a partnership. He would help me with my research in return for the occasional dinner.

When I met up with Line later in the bar and raved about my new contact, she went mad and said I could forget about that. The man was a pig and I should stay away from him. I think I told her to relax, which had the opposite effect. We didn't meet up again until we left the party. On the way home, she said nothing. It wasn't until we got back that she explained her behaviour.

For Line's confirmation, at the age of fourteen, the whole family had gathered as they always did whenever there was something worth celebrating. The party was held in some function rooms on Amager with the obligatory speeches, songs and free-flowing alcohol. Line had her first glass of wine on that occasion, a family tradition her sisters had also experienced. Verner, too, stuck to tradition. He had knocked back quite a bit and became rather belligerent. After the dinner, the programme was less formal. Coffee was served and the guests mingled while the children played in the function rooms. Line had gone to the lavatory. She felt a little dizzy from the wine and had been looking at herself in the mirror. The clichéd speeches about coming-of-age and all the challenges she would be facing as an adult whirled around inside her head and she imagined what her face would look like in five or ten years' time.

She snapped out of her reverie, unlocked the door and walked straight into Verner's arms. At first she grinned and pushed him away, but he refused to let her go.

Instead, he tightened his grip and pushed her back inside the cubicle. He ran his hand over her throat and grabbed one of her breasts. She kept shouting and pushing him away, but he forced himself against her while trying to kiss her. His breath reeked of alcohol and his shirt was drenched in sweat. She managed to free herself and ran out, while behind her Verner muttered something about it all being a joke. Line keeping running until she was outside in the fresh air. When she had stopped feeling nauseous, she returned to the party. Verner had started singing drinking songs as if nothing had happened. She never told her family.

Her story made a deep impression on me, obviously. I felt physically sick and very angry and rather embarrassed that I had succumbed to his charm. Line calmed me down. It was a long time ago, but still she had no intention of forgiving him.

I assured her I would have nothing more to do with him, and yet, when he called some months later, I found myself agreeing to have dinner. It was with some disgust, a feeling I have always had in his company. There was something about the way he casually asked me how Line was that made my stomach turn. I tolerated him because, in my own clever way, *I* was exploiting *him*. However, Line would never be able to understand that, so I didn't tell her. She knew nothing about our dinners until some years later.

I had been sitting in the restaurant with my whisky for ten minutes when Verner appeared. He was flushed and I could see beads of sweat on his scalp through his thinning hair. He was wearing a crumpled grey suit and a white shirt stretched tight over his huge belly. His bulk seemed to swell with every meeting.

With a groan, he let himself flop into the chair opposite me.

'Hello, Frank,' he panted, wiping the sweat off his brow with a napkin from the table.

'Hello, Verner,' I replied and held out my hand.

He gave me a warm and moist handshake.

'Christ – that job will be the death of me.' He wriggled out of his jacket, which he tossed on a vacant chair at the next table.

We ordered our food. I had fish of the day and white wine, Verner a steak, rare, and beer.

'What a bloody mess, this murder, eh?' Verner said after some small talk about family and the weather.

I decided I might as well get it over with and told him about my relationship with Mona Weis two years ago. He listened with a lewd smile on his face.

'You're a dark horse,' he said. 'Was she good in bed?'

I ignored his question. For want of anything else, I introduced him to my theory about Mona's rejected boyfriend and his revenge on her and me using my script as his model. My lack of conviction must have been obvious, but I had nothing else to offer.

Verner shook his head. 'Everything is a mystery to you, eh, Frank? You're always looking for a complicated solution.'

He fell silent while the waiter served our food.

'It's far too elaborate to be a crime of passion,' Verner continued. 'Jealous men act on impulse. They don't go around planning something like that. Possibly the disposal of the body, but not the murder itself.'

'But . . . do the police know if she had a boyfriend?'

'They're working on it,' he replied. 'She would appear to have been single for some months, but there are rumours that she had affairs with older and married men so she might have had a secret lover.' He smiled. 'Your name came up.'

'I told you, it was several years ago.'

'I know, I know, but that kind of gossip has quite a life span. Affairs in a small town like Gilleleje, especially one that involves a famous writer, aren't easily forgotten.'

'Am I a suspect?'

Verner shook his head. 'No, not yet.'

'Not yet!'

'We're going to have to tell them about the book.'

'Are you sure? It was you who said we shouldn't.'

Verner heaved a sigh. 'It's no use,' he said. 'Once the book is published . . . when is it again?'

'In two days,' I replied.

'In two days,' he repeated and looked tired. 'Then we could be faced with an even bigger problem.'

I raised my wine glass and studied him as I drank. His smile had vanished and his small dark eyes were focused on the plate in front of him, but he didn't eat. He just sat there, staring at his steak.

In the Red Zone would be published on Friday, the first day of the book fair. It was all arranged. Interviews and talks had been scheduled, posters printed and stacks of books would be on display. If the police decided to stop the book, it would have serious economic consequences for my publishers and for me.

'It doesn't look good,' Verner said, looking up. 'If you had been upfront about your relationship, I could have told the Murder Squad straightaway. Now it'll seem as if we're hiding something.'

'What have we got to hide?' I protested. 'How could we possibly know how much Mona's murder resembles the one in the book? Very few details have been made public. For example, I haven't read anything about the diving gear or the marble bust.'

'Of course not,' Verner snapped. 'It's standard procedure to withhold that kind of information while the investigation is under way. The problem is I think I've drawn attention to myself by my considerable interest in the case.'

'That doesn't make us murderers,' I declared.

Verner scrutinized me. 'Well, at least I've got an alibi. I was in a bar with some colleagues. Police officers.' He spoke the last word in syllables.

'What are you saying?' I asked, a little too loud, unable to control my temper. Several guests stared. As we didn't say anything, but merely glared at each other, they turned their attention back to their food. Verner didn't reply.

'There is something else,' I whispered.

'Now what?' Verner asked. 'More secrets?'

I handed him the envelope.

'This was waiting for me at reception when I checked in.'

Verner pulled the book out of the envelope and studied

it. I watched his reaction. If he had something to do with it, I was sure I would be able to tell by his face, but he didn't move a muscle. He flicked through the book and found the photo. When he recognized the woman, he dropped the book as if he had burned his fingers.

He stared at me. 'What the hell is this?'

'I don't know,' I replied.

'Are you taking the piss, Frank?'

'This isn't a joke,' I replied. 'Someone left this at reception yesterday afternoon. I hadn't even checked in by then.' I paused, but when Verner didn't say anything, I continued. 'I think you're right, this is more than just an angry boyfriend.'

'Of course I'm right . . . but . . . how the hell did the killer get hold of the book when it hasn't even been published?'

Though I had been staring at the book for several hours, this question had never occurred to me. If it wasn't a rejected lover and the book wasn't Mona's, that made it almost impossible to answer. Unless . . . my heart started pounding and I had to drink some wine before I could tell Verner about my mental reckoning of the free copies and the fact that I was one short. I stressed that I could be wrong. Perhaps my publishers had made an error, but the possibility existed, the possibility that the murderer had broken into my home, and that scared me.

Verner was unimpressed. 'What about the picture?' he asked. 'Is that one of yours, too?'

I shook my head.

'Are you absolutely sure, Frank?'

A tinge of mistrust had crept into his voice, possibly out

of habit, a role he slipped into when he sat in front of the pushers he questioned every day. I gritted my teeth and made an effort to keep my voice down.

'I'm telling you I've got nothing to do with this. Do you really think I would commit a murder copied straight from my own book? And if I had, wouldn't I have made sure to have an alibi? I wasn't emotionally involved with Mona Weis any longer. She was history. Besides, I don't know how to sail and my knowledge of diving is purely theoretical.'

Verner looked as if he was briefly enjoying himself, which irritated me even more.

'Take it easy, Frank,' he said and held up his hands. 'I know you couldn't have done it. Yes, you've a sick and twisted mind when it comes to inventing these things, but you haven't got the guts to carry them out.' He laughed. 'You're far too weak.'

Something inside me was angered by his verdict. Who did he think he was? Why was I letting myself be talked down to by a meathead with paedophile tendencies? I wanted to hit him. That would teach him how weak I was. I should have done so a long time ago, the moment I first learned about his assault on Line. Beaten the crap out of him. Wiped that pathetic smile off his face. It might have made a difference. Perhaps I could have avoided the wounded look Line gave me when she finally found out I was meeting him in secret.

Greater than my anger, however, was my frustrating realization that I needed him.

My hands were trembling slightly. I grabbed my glass and downed its contents. With my other hand, I took the bottle and refilled my glass. Across the table, Verner was calmly drinking his beer. He placed his knife and fork together to indicate he had finished, though half his steak was left.

'Shit,' he said, exhaling heavily. 'Now how do I explain my involvement?' He closed his eyes and rubbed the bridge of his nose. 'I think it's best if I contact the Murder Squad right away.'

All I could do was nod.

'I'll take this,' he said, rapping the book with his knuckles. He stood up. 'How long are you in town?'

'I'm going back on Monday.'

'They'll want a word with you,' he said.

I nodded. I think we both knew this would be the last time we saw each other.

'Take care of yourself, Frank,' he said as he left.

I didn't reply, but pushed the rest of my food away and drank the wine while I wondered when they would come for me. Tonight? No matter when it was, it would be inconvenient.

When the bottle was empty, I got up and left the restaurant. As I staggered towards the lift I became aware of how much alcohol I had consumed. It took for ever before the lift arrived and when the doors opened I practically tumbled inside, nearly crashing into a young woman in a short skirt and a puffer jacket.

'Watch where you're going, idiot,' she said in a broad Copenhagen accent. She shoved me out of the way with surprising strength.

I started to apologize, but she had already left. The scent of her perfume lingered in the lift, a cheap smell of lilac. It was suffocating to be trapped with it during the ride up to the fifth floor.

My conversation with Verner churned inside my head. I was angry, but also relieved.

It was in his hands now.

I had told him what I knew and all I had to do was to wait.

Thursday

8

The police didn't show up at the hotel that night.

I slept badly. Not because I feared a bunch of uniformed officers might kick down the door at any moment; I always sleep badly in a new place. The first night in a strange bed I barely sleep a wink and tonight was no different. In my dozing state the thoughts whirled around my head and I kept seeing Mona Weis's blue eyes staring at me through the muddy seawater. When I finally nodded off, I had disturbing dreams about apes and cats.

Though I had little sleep, I felt surprisingly relaxed the next morning. It was as if my dopey state dulled the fear I had experienced the day before and I decided to carry out the new day's programme as if nothing had happened. That soon proved to be impossible, but I could always pretend. What other option did I have?

The day's programme included a hearty breakfast and I was starving. My discussion with Verner had ruined my appetite last night so there was plenty of room for an extra helping of eggs and bacon from the breakfast buffet. The thought that I might get picked up by the police at any moment undoubtedly hovered at the back of my mind and perhaps it contributed to my ravenous appetite. At any rate, I spent almost an hour at breakfast, reading the paper as plates from the buffet piled up on my table.

There was nothing new about the Gilleleje murder in the paper. It was now three days since the body of Mona Weis had been discovered and the novelty value had clearly worn off.

First on my agenda was a meeting with my editor, Finn Gelf. Finn published my first book, *In the Dead Angle*, and I had been with ZeitSign ever since. In those days, it was a very small firm and Finn was both managing director and editor. Since then the company had grown dramatically and Finn had increasingly delegated the editorial work to others, but not on my books. He insisted he was and always would be my editor. In a way, a great part of ZeitSign's success is down to me, so he owes me. My breakthrough novel, when it finally came, proved to be a goldmine for them and my subsequent books have provided both parties with a regular income.

In time, a friendship developed. Finn Gelf took a chance on *In the Dead Angle* and *The Walls Have Ears* and he continued to believe in me, despite the losses his company suffered in the early years. He later told me, once we knew each other better, that he saw in me a stubbornness and a hunger for recognition. Those two traits combined provided fuel; all I needed was direction. He judged I would discover the right formula at some point and he wanted to be there when it happened. Besides, the age difference between us – ten years – wasn't too big so he found it easy to empathize with the idealism I radiated the first time we met. Perhaps he saw himself in me a decade younger, or the man he hoped he once was.

My breakthrough novel also signalled the breakthrough for our friendship. Together, we travelled around Denmark and abroad and it was on these trips that we grew closer and started talking about other subjects than literature and the publishing industry.

Finn Gelf was the son of the travel publisher Gustav Gelf. Even as a boy, Finn was part of his father's business. When he was old enough he started packing books for mail order, a job that earned him extra pocket money and his father's respect. He was later apprenticed to a printer, but the printing works were owned by a brewery and he ended up producing beer labels, day in and day out. Finn, soon bored out of his mind, quit his apprenticeship and returned to his father's business. He was given an office job on the condition that he continued his education. He managed both some A levels and a business degree and soon became an invaluable part of the company.

The ageing Gustav had imagined that his business would be carried on by his son, but when Finn introduced plans to expand their list to include other types of books, such as fiction, they fell out to such an extent that Finn left and started ZeitSign.

Despite his young age, Finn had built up a reliable network within the industry and he managed to get his publishing house up and running through solid agreements with printers and buyers. It wasn't a highly profitable business, but he survived and was even able to make small investments in new writers. *In the Dead Angle* was one such gamble, and had it not been for Finn Gelf, I might never have been published at all.

I took a taxi from the hotel to Gammel Mønt. On the way, I wondered if I should tell Finn about the murder in Gilleleje. It would be right thing to do, but if the police hadn't turned up yet, it might mean they had already solved the crime. Perhaps there was no link to the book after all; ultimately I only had Verner's word that the details matched.

ZeitSign's reception lay behind toned glass doors. The floor and walls were covered with pale sandstone and a polished black counter lay like an overturned monolith in the lobby. The 45-year-old receptionist, Ellen, a noble-looking woman who never lost her composure, sat behind the counter. On the wall behind her, the name 'ZeitSign' was displayed in large black letters.

'Frank!' she exclaimed when I pushed open the heavy glass doors and entered. She got up, came towards me and gave me a big hug. I returned it with gratitude. It was a long time since a woman had hugged me, possibly not since last year's book fair, and that had probably been Ellen too.

'How are you?' she asked sounding overjoyed, and I mumbled that everything was just fine.

'You look a bit tired,' she remarked. 'Late night, was it?'

'Something like that,' I replied. 'How are you?'

Ellen started telling me about her most recent holiday with her husband and two children, who must by now both be close to twenty. I didn't quite catch where they had been or what they had done, but I went along with her excitement and the joy, all the reassuring and comforting stories of family life. I made appropriate noises to keep her chatting until the telephone rang.

'I had better . . .' she said, nodding towards the telephone. 'He's expecting you upstairs . . . And don't forget to pick up your post on your way out.'

I thanked her and went to the lift, which took me to the first floor.

In contrast to the light and open space of the lobby, the editorial corridor was narrow and dark. On either side were small offices where editors sat hunched over scripts or keyboards. A few of them looked up as I walked past and one or two even nodded, though I had never seen them before.

Finn's office lay at the end of the corridor. The door was open and he was just about to go out when I arrived.

'Frank, good to see you,' he said and we shook hands.

His hair had turned completely white since I last saw him a year ago. He had been going grey for the last five years, but now his hair had definitively given up and surrendered to the white invasion.

He showed me into his office, which was large enough to house an enormous desk, a meeting table seating six people and an old leather sofa that had followed Finn throughout his career. Framed covers of ZeitSign's greatest successes, including a couple of my books, hung on the walls. I left my blazer on a coat stand behind the door and sat down at the meeting table where coffee cups and pastries had been laid out. He poured me a cup of coffee without asking. I added a little milk and sipped it. Normally, I never take milk, but Finn made coffee strong enough to give me stomach ache. He sank one cup after another; he must have had his stomach galvanized.

'So, what do you say to that?' he asked.

'To what?'

Finn smiled and picked up something that looked like a sheet of cardboard from the table and held it up in front of me. It was a newspaper cutting, laminated in hard plastic as if he intended to display it on his wall with the other trophies.

The headline read: 'Young woman mutilated and drowned in Gilleleje Marina.'

9

'Sounds familiar, doesn't it?' Finn said. He looked at me expectantly while I read the article. It was from a tabloid and revealed nothing beyond what I had already read elsewhere.

I nodded. 'It *is* our murder,' I confirmed. 'I spoke to Verner yesterday. Everything matches, including the bust and the diving gear, though that information hasn't been made public.'

Finn snapped his fingers. 'I knew it!' he exclaimed, grinning. 'I said to myself, that murder, that's Føns. It has to be.'

'I haven't got anything to do with it.'

'No, no,' Finn said. 'I know that, but it has your name written all over it.' He reached out both hands as if to grab my head and place a big kiss on it. 'Imagine what this will do to the book sales.'

'Unless it's banned.'

Finn's smile froze. 'What are the police saying?'

'I've only spoken to Verner,' I replied. 'So far, we're the

only ones who know about the similarities, but Verner is very keen to tell the Murder Squad.'

'Oh,' Finn said. 'Can't you get him to hold off for a couple of days? The book is being published tomorrow, for God's sake.'

'He said he would contact them last night.'

Finn waved his hand. 'It'll be a close call,' he said. 'But if we can keep them at bay for twenty-four hours, we can still profit from it.'

Perhaps it was the coffee or the generous breakfast buffet, but I felt a churning sensation in my stomach.

'Perhaps we should pull the plug on it ourselves?'

'Are you crazy? This is far too good to miss out on.' He stared at me as if I had just insulted his closest relative.

'But . . . a woman has been murdered . . . are you sure that—'

Yes,' he said in a brusque tone. 'Stopping the book isn't going to bring her back to life.'

'Of course not, but what about her family?'

Finn looked annoyed.

'They might sue you,' I said.

He blinked at the prospect of spending money on lawyers and damages.

'We'll have to deal with that when it happens,' he said with resignation. 'We're not stopping anything until the police ask us to. Christ, Frank, if we're to base our decision on the information that has been made public, then there is no link.'

'Except that it has my name "written all over it",' I remarked.

Finn rolled his eyes. 'Only to those who know you,' he said.

I shrugged. 'So what do you want me to do? Lie?'

'No, no. Just act normally, stick to the programme and kindly refrain from going to the police.'

'That sounds like perverting the course of justice.'

'Not at all,' Finn exclaimed. 'If it wasn't for your friend Verner, no one would have made the connection until after publication.'

I shook my head. It was obvious that Finn had made up his mind, and somehow that was a relief. There was nothing left for me to do.

'Besides,' Finn said. He sliced through the air with both hands. 'Even without the additional twist, I have a really good feeling about this book.' He smiled and tapped the table three times. 'You've really hit on something this time. People get the whole phobia and fear theme. I've spoken to some of the newspapers today and they're reviewing it favourably. *Weekendavisen* wants your head on a plate as always, but otherwise it's good news across the board. It'll be a very busy book fair, I promise you. Our people have built a Frank Føns corner on the stand with large banners, "Face your fear" and so on. You'll love it.'

I was far from sure that I would. The book fair was a necessary evil for me and I was uncomfortable with all this attention. Especially now.

'Interviews have been arranged.' Finn's smile disappeared. 'TV3 is sending Linda Hvilbjerg.' He held up his hands. 'I know you don't like her, but we've no choice and she's popular.'

I nodded. 'It's OK. I'll just imagine her with a noose around her neck and I'll be fine.'

Finn laughed. 'I don't think she's forgiven you for *Media Whore* yet.'

Linda Hvilbjerg had hosted book shows on various TV channels for years and at one point I blamed her for the breakdown of my marriage. That was nonsense, of course. But I was so embittered in the years following the divorce that when I wrote *Media Whore* I put in so many similarities with Linda Hvilbjerg that any reader could see the character was based on her. In the book, the over-ambitious TV reporter, Vira Lindal, died suspended from a beam in the production suite with a script rammed up her vagina. Linda Hvilbjerg didn't review the book on her show and has never had a good word to say about my books since, if she even mentions them in the first place.

'I haven't put you on the guest list for the party on Saturday,' Finn continued. 'But if you want to go, just let me know. We can always get you in.'

I shook my head. 'I'm busy.'

I wasn't, but I knew that after a long day at the book fair, going to a party with the same people was the last thing I wanted to do.

We spoke for another hour. Mostly about the book fair, interviews and foreign interest in *In the Red Zone*. There had already been offers from Germany and Norway, a good indicator of further foreign sales. My breakthrough novel, *Outer Demons*, and its successor, *Inner Demons*, had sold reasonably well outside Denmark, but since then there have been no takers. The future prospects of *In the Red Zone* sounded promising, and the more Finn talked to me about contracts and expectations, the more hopeless it appeared to be to try and stop the huge machine that had been set in motion.

On the way out, I picked up my post from reception. Ellen had put a small stack of letters and a single packet in a black plastic bag with the company's logo.

'I hope it's a hit,' she said, smiling.

'So do I,' I replied and returned her smile. Ellen is one of those thoroughly decent people who do their job without complaint and is always kind. I have never heard her speak ill of anyone and she has an aura of authority and professionalism that is a great asset to the company.

'We need it,' she whispered, looking around embarrassed.

I leaned over the counter. 'What do you mean?'

'We need a bestseller,' she whispered. 'It's been a while since we've had one and I think money is a bit tight.'

'Finn didn't say anything about that.'

Ellen shook her head. 'He would be the last person to admit it,' she said. 'Or he's just pretending he isn't worried to protect the rest of us.' She heaved a sigh. 'If your new book doesn't sell, the future looks bleak. That's why he's making such a big thing of it. He would do anything to promote that book.'

Getting this far hasn't been easy.

My intention of switching off all emotion and letting the words flow unstinted has proved harder than I expected. There is nothing wrong with my memory, but my subconscious tries to manipulate the images that emerge when I add the words. The timing appears slightly better, the dialogue more polished or the mood lighter.

However, this kind of fraud won't go unpunished. I feel there is someone in the room with me, hiding in the shadows. A critic looking over my shoulder, constantly aware of the errors I make and upsetting my concentration every time I'm disloyal to the project. Then my body fills with dread, a nervousness that doesn't cease until I go back and rewrite the chapters where I was insincere, passages where I omitted details or toned down my behaviour.

It's not until I have corrected discrepancies and lies that I'm permitted to carry on, even more naked now and in the certain knowledge that it can only get worse.

10

When I was young, I had no intention of getting married. Marriage was an artificial construct that, at worst, was based on religion, i.e. a lie, and at best was a bureaucratic manoeuvre to improve your tax status, i.e. hypocrisy. This was the general attitude among us in the commune and we took every opportunity to voice it. Later, when I got married, it wasn't for rational reasons – I simply couldn't help it.

I remember the months after meeting Line as one long series of revelations. She surprised me again and again with her humorous nature and the convergence of our interests. When we made love it was with an intimacy and intensity I had never experienced before. I couldn't believe a relationship could be like this. We could talk about everything, and we did; we usually had the same attitude towards political issues, but on the rare occasions we disagreed we could have a debate without the mood turning ugly. We spent practically all our time together, interrupted only by our respective studies and work.

Line was the youngest of four siblings; she had two

sisters and a brother and it soon became clear to me that her family was very close-knit. Rarely a day went by without her being in contact with one of her sisters and at least once a week we'd have dinner with her father. I'd been invited over for dinner after only two weeks, and everyone welcomed me and treated me with the greatest kindness. The family was mourning for the mother, but they still had the generosity to include me in their group. Line's father, Erik, was an engineer who worked for the government. He designed motorway bridges, an occupation that had also become his hobby. In Erik's study in the villa on Amager were miniature models of over twenty bridges and he could tell the story of every single one of them – not without a certain amount of pride.

Line's sisters were also dancers and resembled her so much that I always felt a little awkward in their company. It was like being with three versions of Line at yearly intervals; I could tell how she would age and that certainly wasn't bad at all. Her brother had followed in his father's footsteps and worked as an engineer for a consultancy firm in Lyngby. The first time I met him he had just accepted a posting to Africa where he would build a water purification plant, but he had postponed his departure by a month following the death of his mother.

I recall get-togethers with Line's family as relaxed and yet lively and engaging. With so many children, their partners and grandchildren, there was an incredible maelstrom of people, but it never became superficial or meaningless. They accepted without question that I wanted to make my living by writing – something my parents never did – and when Line's family asked how my work was going, they were referring to my books and not to whatever casual job I happened to be doing at the time.

Unfortunately I was struggling with the writing and I produced little in the first few months. I only managed some editing of *In the Dead Angle* and the scathing reviews it received did nothing for my motivation. If I hadn't been with Line, I would probably have fallen into a black hole of self-pity and rage, but with her around, the negative feedback didn't matter all that much. It was impossible to be upset for very long in her company; she could always make me laugh with a remark or one of her smiles.

Bjarne was almost as fond of Line as I was. Line was a superb cook while I regarded myself as being something of a wine connoisseur and Bjarne benefited from both. The three of us would often eat together and sometimes our after-dinner debates would last well into the night.

Mortis didn't join in. He isolated himself, shut himself in his room to write, he claimed, and became increasingly sullen. His mood deteriorated to such an extent that even I, in my deep infatuation, couldn't help noticing, and it was at that point that I discovered it was Mortis who had invited Line to the Angle party in the first place. I tried to talk to him about it, but I was probably more concerned with describing how lovely Line was and ultimately only succeeded in making matters worse.

He must have breathed a sigh of relief when three months after the Angle party I announced I was moving out of the commune and into Line's flat on Islands Brygge. According to Bjarne, Mortis cheered up visibly after my departure. He resumed talking to me when I visited without Line, but the relationship between us was never the same again. My room was rented out and during the years that followed there was a high turnover of lodgers. They were all obsessed with writing, the original inspiration behind the commune, but the companionship was never as harmonious as it had been in the first few years.

The last lodger, Anne, fell in love with Bjarne's gentle nature, and he fell in love with her. Like Line, Anne was a fantastic cook and Bjarne had to admit there was some truth in the proverb that the way to a man's heart is through his stomach. You could tell Anne was rather too fond of food simply by looking at her. She was big, not obese as such, but because she was of medium height, her weight tended to look rather excessive and I think it upset her more than she ever let on. She was always happy and welcoming, one of those people who remembers what you told them and asks interested follow-up questions the next time you meet.

Anne's entry ticket to the commune was that she wrote poetry, like Bjarne, but she composed hers as riddles, made up of newspaper, cartoon and magazine cuttings. They were hard to decipher because the reader had to solve them first, but as a result you tasted every single word and were rewarded with a feeling of having uncovered a secret once the entire poem was clear. It wasn't until then that you could appreciate it in its entirety and, at that point, the meaning of the poem would change, like a thriller with a surprising twist. It was so satisfying that the reader would often start unravelling the next poem immediately.

The girls got on well and the four of us met up regularly for extravagant dinner parties where Bjarne and I were reduced to washing up and telling jokes.

With Anne's entry into Bjarne's life, Mortis once more found himself playing the part of gooseberry. He didn't turn his back on Bjarne as he had with me, and he was fine with Anne, but I think he found it hard to witness all this happiness from the sidelines. He had a tendency to compare himself unfavourably to others and he also resented the pity he detected from his two flatmates. After a couple of weeks he had enough and moved to a studio flat in Vesterbro.

It turned out that Anne was fairly wealthy, even though she tried to conceal it. Her money enabled her and Bjarne to take over the whole flat and stop looking for lodgers.

The Scriptorium had become a thing of the past, but I didn't miss it. It was only at dinner parties that Bjarne and I would retell the old stories and remember the special atmosphere that had reigned in the flat. Occasionally we might hanker for the inspiration, the free life and the parties, but we always knew that things could never be the same again.

With my invasion of Line's flat, it soon became too small for us. I was meant to write there and Line needed room to exercise. Fortunately we were able to swap to a four-room flat in the same block, but it stretched us financially. I earned nothing from my writing and very little from my casual jobs. Line worked in different theatres and was offered better and better roles, but at the start there were times where she had no work at all. For the first year we survived on Line's inheritance from her mother and even with that we both had to find extra jobs. However, having four rooms was a gift. I got my own study with books from floor to ceiling and we had a separate living room, dining room and bedroom. Apart from my study, all rooms were sparsely furnished with second-hand items we were given or bought cheaply at flea markets. This left plenty of room for Line to do her stretching exercises on the living-room floor with me as her always attentive audience.

Despite our modest surroundings I thought the flat was cosy. Line had a talent for getting a great deal out of very little and she never minded getting stuck in if she had to. If we needed a picture she would paint one herself, if a lamp needed hanging she would do it before I came home, even reupholstering soft furnishings posed no challenge for her. It was very much Line's home, but I enjoy it and felt settled.

I made only slow progress with my next novel, however. I juggled several jobs that left very few hours each day for writing. It took me more than two years to write my second book, *The Walls Have Ears*, and it was, to put it mildly, awful. It had a hopelessly constructed plot about a hotel room which told the story of the events that had taken place within its four walls, ranging from suicide to drunkenness and fornication. To this day, I have no idea why my publisher accepted it, but he did and was left holding most of the first edition. Only one hundred copies were sold across the country.

Still, I made some money out of it. It wasn't much, but the advance was big enough for me to take Line on a night out. We treated ourselves to a trip to Tivoli, dinner at D'Angleterre, the ballet and a club. All transport was by taxi until it was time for us to go home. At Line's suggestion, we walked. It was four o'clock in the morning, but it was summer so it wasn't cold and the sun was coming up. At Islands Brygge we sat down on the quay, embraced each other and looked across the water at the Copenhagen skyline. Line kicked off her shoes and snuggled up to me. Her breathing was steady and I thought she had fallen asleep. I was starting to get uncomfortable, but didn't want to stir for fear of waking her.

'Now would be a good time to propose,' she suddenly said.

I grinned, but soon stopped when I realized she was right and that I really wanted to. At that moment, I couldn't think of a single reason not to propose; on the contrary, I simply couldn't imagine life without her.

I gave Line a hug and pulled her to standing. Then I went down on one knee and told her how much I loved her. She said nothing, but she smiled. She knew perfectly well the effect her smile had on me and it gave me the courage to carry on, tell her all the things I loved about her, every part of her body I worshipped, every one of her actions I admired. It must have been a dreadful load of sentimental nonsense, but we were both tipsy and it felt right.

I had no ring, of course, but I pulled out the Penol 0.5 felt-tip pen I always carried and drew a ring directly on her finger. It tickled, she said, and giggled while I finished the ring with the outline of a large stone in which the letter 'F' was embossed.

Line accepted my proposal with the words, 'Of course, you idiot.'

*   *   *

Due to our hard-pressed finances, I had to borrow money from my parents to afford the wedding Line wanted. I had never liked asking them for help, but they were surprisingly willing. No doubt they were hoping I would finally get myself a 'proper' job to support my wife. I didn't care what they thought; I just wanted to give Line her dream wedding, a wedding fit for a princess, with a church, a wedding breakfast in a hotel and the whole shebang. The total cost was close to 60,000 kroner, but the result was perfection. Her family outnumbered mine by far and their cheerful presence rubbed off on the rest of the guests, so even the most vociferous opponent of the tradition had to admit they had enjoyed themselves. Bjarne clearly fell under the spell: a few days later he plucked up the courage to propose to Anne.

So much for our attitude to the institution of marriage.

After the wedding I was convinced we would be together for ever and everyone who knew us was of the same opinion. We suited each other, they said, and we were both invited whenever her or my circle of friends held a party. I wouldn't go as far as to say we were inseparable. We gave each other space and did many things independently of one another, but it was in the certain knowledge that at the end of the day there was always someone to come home to.

There was no jealousy between us in those days. Line's work was much more sociable than mine; she worked in practically every theatre and came into contact with countless people. Being a dancer is a very sensual profession and viewed from the outside dancers may seem more uninhibited than most people, but I never feared she might be unfaithful to me. A couple of times I forced myself to imagine it, mainly as an exercise to inspire myself to write about that very feeling, but had to shake my head every time. The idea of Line involved in a secret affair just didn't seem plausible. The wedding ring might have played its part. Even though I didn't believe in the ritual, I had to admit it made a difference. We had given ourselves to each other and this declaration of trust bestowed a certain serenity on our relationship.

If there was any kind of jealousy between us, it was rooted in money.

The bigger flat was more expensive and Line's income was the more reliable. I had various casual jobs, but I never earned enough to pay my fair share of the rent. It wasn't something we discussed or made a big thing of, but there were times when my vanity reared its ugly head. It didn't help that I found it very difficult to write in the years that followed our marriage. My jobs often involved antisocial hours or were physically so demanding that I didn't have the energy to sit down in front of my computer or think creatively in my spare time.

The failure of *The Walls Have Ears* lingered at the back of my mind and my frustration at not producing anything grew day by day. For the first time in my life, I started to doubt if I was cut out to be a writer. Perhaps I had burned out before I had even begun? When I wrote, it was at odd hours fitted in between casual jobs and doing things with Line. I would often be under the influence of alcohol, a habit that had followed me from the commune and did nothing to improve the quality of my work. The next morning I would frequently delete everything I had written in a whisky haze the night before and yet I still convinced myself that I needed alcohol to get started. The only effect it had was to make me so drowsy that I struggled to hold down my casual jobs and found it even harder to sit down at my desk.

By contrast, Line's career was taking off. She was in constant demand, she was cast in roles where she had solo performances and she was praised in several reviews. I attended as many of her performances as I could and I could see that she was good, not that I knew anything about dance. It provided me with an excuse to get out of the flat, away from my desk and it meant I visited theatres in Copenhagen I would probably not have gone to on my own. Sometimes Bjarne and Anne would come with me and afterwards the four of us would go out. Despite having danced the whole evening, Line was happy to carry on dancing and she always manage to drag me out on the dance floor, even though I often didn't feel like it. It was her smile that did it. She knew how to smile – and I surrendered.

Every time.

11

Finn had given me some complimentary tickets for the book fair.

Over time it had become a ritual that I would visit my parents and present them with two. They expected it. Not because they were short of money. They were both retired, had generous pensions and considerable equity in their bungalow in Valby and their holiday cottage in Marielyst. Even so, they refused to pay the modest entrance fee to the book fair and at times felt the need to remind me of this several months in advance. They also expected me to deliver the tickets in person as I was in town anyway, a tradition we had observed for many years. It was now the only occasion I saw them, once a year for dinner, red wine and conversations about books, the safest topic we could think of.

My father, Niels, used to teach and his interest in literature stemmed from that. My mother, Hanne, had carried on the family tradition and qualified as a doctor at a relatively young age. They read many books in her family. I remember my grandparents had a large library in their villa in Hellerup with hardback classics from floor to ceiling, deep-pile carpets on the floors and soft leather furniture we children weren't allowed to play on.

It was my parents' interest in literature that brought them together. They met at a poetry reading at Regensen Hall of Residence in central Copenhagen. They were both students and as far as my mother was concerned choosing my father was probably an act of rebellion. My mother's family were most unimpressed by Niels. They had hoped their daughter would meet a fellow doctor or a professor, an intellectual kindred spirit who could join in dinner party conversations. Niels was the first person in his family to have undertaken more than compulsory education and it took several years before his in-laws accepted him. His knowledge of literature helped, but the turning point was when he provided them with grandchildren.

My parents' interest in books didn't extend to mine. I always gave them a signed copy of every new book I wrote, but they never read it. 'Not really our thing,' they would say if I was dumb enough to ask if they had had a look at it. They had made an effort to read my early works, of course, but their only comment was that they thought they 'were a bit too old for that kind of thing'. They may well have been, but I think the rub was that they always regretted I didn't have a 'proper' job. As my first two books were so poorly received, they had hoped I would give up. This resulted in numerous clashes, and matters finally came to a head one evening some months after my wedding when Line and I were visiting. When my parents yet again hinted that a career change was long overdue, I stormed out in anger. I had no contact with my parents for a long time after that, despite Line's attempts at reconciliation. If she hadn't become pregnant and insisted on resuming the relationship for the sake of the child, I would probably never have seen them again.

I took a taxi to Valby. It was late in the afternoon and the sun hung so low in the horizon that the driver had to put on sunglasses. I always sit in the back. This usually signals to the driver that I don't want to talk, but this driver didn't take the hint and chatted away about the weather, sport and the latest headlines. I didn't need to say very much, he managed the conversation all on his own, but still I found it a little irritating. When I arrived at my parents' bungalow, I wasn't in the best of moods, and the prospect of spending an evening with Niels and Hanne did nothing to improve it. I didn't tip the taxi driver.

My mother's welcome was profuse and Niels handed me a very dry martini almost before I had time to take off my jacket. They had aged considerably in the past year. Hanne's hair was now completely white, the wrinkles around her eyes were more deep-set and the skin of her face looked slacker. My father's bald patch had spread. Only a band of hair at the sides and at the back of his head remained, but it actually suited him. It struck me that I might not have them for very much longer and I decided to make sure tonight was a good evening.

The reason for their ebullient mood turned out to be that they had booked their dream holiday to Thailand. Six weeks, leaving just after the New Year, with boat trips, temple visits and elephant safari all included. Since their retirement they had spent a considerable amount of their money on travelling. They had lived much of their lives through books and I was delighted that they now got to see the world for themselves while they still had the chance.

The most bizarre feature of visiting my parents is that they're still in contact with Line and their grandchildren, my children. I'm always stunned when I see photographs of them on the walls. I know their lives don't stand still either, but I sometimes forget and the sight of Line and the girls jolts me like an electric shock. It's unreal to see the change from year to year. People I had once been so close to are transformed. The girls grow with terrifying speed and Line ages with infinite grace. They always look so happy in the photographs and my heart feels heavy. Sometimes Bjørn, Line's new husband, features, and every time it makes me wonder if the girls call him Dad, a thought that feels like a punch to the guts.

The first few years after the divorce my parents would hide the pictures when I visited, but there were clear outlines on the wall where they had been. In time I think they forgot and later they might have expected me to have got over it. I suppose I did, but I always felt sad when I saw the photographs and wished that things were different.

And this year, too, they had new photographs, ones taken at their holiday cottage in Marielyst this summer, only a month or two ago. One photo was particularly successful. It showed the two girls with Line in the middle. All three wore white summer dresses and the younger, Mathilde, is crowning Line's head with a home-made garland. The older, Veronika, is grinning at the camera. She has grown so big. Thirteen, or is it fourteen now? She has her mother's smile.

'Great photos,' I said, taking a sip of my drink.

Hanne was in the kitchen preparing the dinner. Niels was sitting in his armchair.

'Yes,' he said, tentatively. 'I've got one of those digital cameras.'

'Are they all right?'

'Oh, yes, yes,' he replied. 'They're fine.'

I leaned towards a photograph to study Mathilde's face.

'Do they ever ask after me?' I asked as casually as I could manage.

'Oh, Frank, I don't know,' my father said, squirming. 'Why don't you ask your mother? I don't talk to them about that. I'm the one who reads stories or plays croquet with them.'

An uncomfortable silence descended until I asked about his new camera and then Niels spoke eagerly about his new acquisition and its many splendid features. I found it hard to take my eyes off the photographs and most of what he said went over my head.

Over dinner we talked about their forthcoming trip and about books. They had already planned which talks and interviews to attend at the book fair and they expected to buy their travel literature at the same time. We swapped recommendations of books we had read in the course of the past year and my father had a rant about the standard of literature teaching in schools today.

I was happy that books were once again an item for discussion rather than something that led to murder and mutilation in the real world. Along with the roast beef, my concerns about Mona Weis were washed down with a good Barolo, another one of my parents' retirement investments, and I think we all became rather drunk. A couple of generous brandies with the pudding only added to that.

My father cleared the table and started washing up. This had become the division of labour in their home and he seemed to enjoy it. They wouldn't hear of buying a dishwasher, not because they were stingy or wouldn't know how to operate it, but because my father actually looked forward to washing up on his own.

Hanne and I stayed at the table. We both had brandy left in our glasses and were too full to get up. The topics of travelling and books had eventually been exhausted and a pause in our conversation occurred.

'They look great, the girls,' I said, breaking the silence.

My mother smiled. 'Yes, they are lovely,' she said. 'They spent a week with us this summer at the Manor House.'

'Are they all right?'

'Yes, but they're so tall now.' She giggled. 'They grow up so fast.'

I sniffed my brandy. The alcohol tickled my nostrils. 'Do they ask after me?'

Her smile faded and she looked up. 'Please don't start that, darling,' she said with a pleading expression in her eyes.

I shrugged. 'I just want to know,' I said calmly. 'Have they forgotten me?'

'Of course they haven't forgotten you, Frank.'

'Do they ask after me?' I repeated in a slightly harsher tone of voice.

'Please don't.'

'Just give it to me straight.'

She gave me a searching look and I smiled back.

'Yes, sometimes they ask after you,' she said eventually, and sighed. 'Especially the older one. But surely you can imagine what it's like to be a teenager and have a stepdad . . .'

'Is anything—'

'Bjørn is a good dad,' Hanne interrupted me firmly. 'It's just the usual teenage rebellion.'

We both drank our brandy.

'So, what do you tell her?' I asked.

'Stop it, Frank.'

'I just want to know what you tell my daughter when she asks about her dad,' I said, raising my voice. 'You do answer her, don't you?'

'Frank . . .'

'Or do you just clam up?' My rage flared up, fuelled by the alcohol. 'Is Daddy someone you don't mention in polite society?'

Hanne shook her head. Her eyes were welling up.

'So what is it? Do you tell her I've gone away?'

'Frank, darling . . .'

'Am I dead?' I laughed bitterly.

'Take it easy, son,' said my father, who had entered from the kitchen. He was wearing a stripy apron and drying his hands on a tea towel. He looked like someone who wanted to get back to washing up as soon as possible.

I rose and threw up my hands in what I hoped was a disarming gesture.

'I just want to know what you tell my daughter.'

The tears were rolling down Hanne's cheeks.

I failed to see why. After all, she wasn't cut off from her children, as I was. She could see my daughters whenever she wanted to, play with them, comfort them, sing to them, spoil them rotten if she felt like it.

I banged my fist on the table and they both jumped.

'What do you tell them?'

'We tell them you're ill!' Hanne shouted.

I stared at her.

'What do you want us to do?' she continued. 'You *are* ill, Frank. You need help. What else do we say? She's old enough to know what a court order is.' She buried her face in her hands.

Niels placed his hands on her shoulders and gave me an accusatory look.

'Was that really necessary?' he said and shook his head.

I stared at my fists. They were trembling. I grabbed my glass and knocked back the rest of the brandy before I marched to the hall, snatched my jacket and the plastic bag from my publishers and left. Neither of them tried to stop me.

The road was dark and deserted. I walked briskly to the high street where I soon found a taxi. I threw the bag on the back seat and snarled the address of the hotel at the hapless driver. Wisely, he decided to keep quiet.

I looked through the window as the streets rushed past. The anger was still boiling inside me and I could feel tears pressing.

I turned my attention to the bag and peered inside it. There was a small pile of letters and a parcel. I pulled out the parcel and held it up to the window so the streetlight fell on it.

My heart started pounding.

In my hands, I held a yellow envelope with a white address label bearing my name. It was thick enough to contain a book.

12

The rest of the journey back to the hotel went by in a blur. Perhaps I said something to the driver before I went into the lobby and up to the lift, or maybe I just paid and walked away, I don't know, but I remember the sensation of falling even as the lift carried me up to my floor.

The envelope felt heavier the last few steps down the corridor to my room. Once inside I locked the door behind me and left the letters on the coffee table. Fortunately Ferdinan had made sure to stock up the minibar, so I poured myself a double whisky and sat down in an armchair. The envelope was identical to the one I had received earlier, yellow and anonymous, with my name written on a white label. The only difference was that this time my publisher's address had been added.

I swallowed a mouthful of whisky without taking my eyes off the envelope. There was plenty to suggest it was from the same person who had sent me the picture of Mona Weis, but I couldn't know for sure until I opened it. I put the glass down. My hands shook as they reached out for what I was sure would be the worst letter I'd ever receive. I turned the envelope over, but there were no other clues. With great care I eased open the flap. Once I had done that, I placed the envelope on my knees and stuck my hand inside. I got hold of the book and pulled it out.

It was a copy of *As You Sow*, a novel I had written five years ago, in which a murder is committed in the very hotel where I was now staying.

I placed it on top of the envelope. A dryness in my throat made me reach for my drink and take a large gulp.

The book cover was a photograph of a Copenhagen street by night. You couldn't make out which street it was, but it clearly wasn't a salubrious area. Dark doorways and grey facades combined with neon lights and cobblestoned alleyways to convey a dirty, raw atmosphere, exactly what the book promised.

The killer and main character, Silke Knudsen, was a Copenhagen prostitute who had seen most things and been screwed out of everything. One day she has had enough and takes revenge on everyone who has ever hurt her. Violent punters are dispatched with the same savagery they have themselves inflicted on the girls, pimps die a slow, painful death for every krone they have taken in commission and a vile, corrupt superintendent dies in a hotel room. The victims include a woman: a fellow prostitute who cheated Silke out of her share of the money they were paid for a threesome. Silke arranges for her to be gang-raped. Afterwards, as the woman lies bound, beaten and ravaged on a bench in a cold warehouse in Sydhavnen, Silke injects her with an overdose of heroin. The murder of this woman happens early in the book and it causes the woman's sister, Annika, to travel from Jutland to investigate. Annika is confronted with the dark underbelly of prostitution, but she doesn't give up. She uses her background as a lawyer to investigate the case, assisted by a young police officer who has a crush on her. The showdown takes place at a hotel in the red-light district where the two women finally meet. Their fight takes them to the top of the building while the lower floors go up in flames. Silke falls six floors from the roof – with considerable help from Annika – and smashes into the pavement in front of the hotel. Annika has avenged her sister, but discovers that she has prostituted herself in the process. She has no real feelings for the police officer and she has given legal advice to criminals in exchange for information during the investigation. At the end of the book, Annika's future is unclear; the reader doesn't know if she goes back to Jutland or becomes a prostitute.

As far as I could see the book was unread. It was a first edition, not surprisingly; *As You Sow* hadn't sold terribly well.

I turned the first ten or fifteen pages without finding anything. Then I flicked my way through the rest of the book.

It was a third of the way in, on page 124. A Polaroid. The image showed a man, slightly overweight judging from his face. At first I couldn't make out who it was. He had a broad strip of grey tape across his mouth. He was sweating and his small, deep-set eyes showed panic. Fear contorted his facial features, but eventually I recognized him.

It was Verner.

I turned the photo over. There was no information on the back so I focused my attention on the front. I tried to keep my emotions out of it by breathing deeply and concentrating on the details in the picture. Verner's short hair was soaked in sweat and his face slightly pink. He didn't appear to be wearing a shirt; I could see the top of his naked shoulders. Behind him was a brass frame of some sort.

I got up abruptly, tumbling the book and the envelope to the floor, and went to my bedroom. The bed was bigger than I was used to in hotels, but it was the same type – a sturdy brass frame with turned brass bars. I held up the photo to the bed frame to compare. There could be no doubt.

Back in the living room, I picked up the envelope and looked inside it. I hadn't expected to find anything, but this time it wasn't empty. A key nestled at the bottom. I turned the envelope upside down and scooped it up as it fell out.

As I had already guessed, it was the key to room 102, the room I normally stayed in, the room that was the crime scene in *As You Sow*.

I had a flash of inspiration. It could be a hoax. Perhaps Verner was setting me up. He was twisted enough to do something like that, but what would be the point? I looked at the photo again. The expression in his eyes looked like genuine terror and Verner was no actor.

There was only one way to find out.

It took two more whiskies before I summoned up the courage to leave my suite. On impulse I took the stairs, possibly because I didn't wish to meet anyone, least of all Ferdinan, but also because I felt queasy and didn't want to be trapped inside the claustrophobic lift.

I made sure no one saw me outside room 102. The corridor was empty. A 'Do Not Disturb' sign hung from the door handle. I inserted the key and let myself in.

The stench was overwhelming: a mixture of faeces, urine and a third substance I didn't even want to think about. I had to swallow a couple of times in order not to throw up on the spot.

It was dark. The blinds were down and the curtains closed. My hand found a switch inside the door and I turned on the light. I was in the small hallway with access to the bathroom, then the room itself, which was mainly occupied by the double bed.

Though I knew precisely what awaited me, I still gasped when I saw Verner.

He was resting against the headboard, naked, with his arms stretched out as far as they could go and strapped to the brass frame with black cable ties. On the wall above the bed, someone had written 'PIG' in what looked like blood. His chin rested on his chest as if he were staring down at himself. His large body was smeared in blood and vomit, and his legs spread and tied to the under frame with nylon rope. The weight of his body had caused the mattress to sink and a large pool of blood and other bodily fluids had formed around him.

I ran to the bathroom and reached the toilet bowl just in time to throw up. When my stomach was empty, I collapsed on the floor and sobbed. No one deserved what Verner had been subjected to, but I wasn't crying for him, I was crying for myself. I cried because I was powerless. I was the real victim here, punished for something I had yet to understand.

After some time, I don't know how long, I got up. I spat into the toilet bowl a couple of times, blew my nose, washed my face and tried to rinse away the taste of vomit with water.

Then I took a towel and wiped down the taps, the toilet seat and the door.

Back at the bed I spent a moment studying Verner. Everything seemed to match the description in the book: the way he had been tied up, the mutilation of his genitals and the deep cuts to his abdomen. However, in the book I had stated that his hands had turned purple like a pair of gloves from having been tied so tight, but in reality they had the same pale colour as the rest of his body.

Everything suggested Verner was dead, but I had to check. I bent over and pressed two fingers against his neck. He was cold and stiff. I withdrew my hand and wiped my fingers on the towel as if I had touched something contagious.

There was no need for me to examine him closely. If I wanted to know what had happened to him, all I had to do was reread my own book. There I would learn that his testicles had been cut off and stuffed into his mouth, and there would be blunt force trauma to his head from pistol-whipping. The scalpel should be lying on the floor somewhere, tossed aside like a lolly stick. I knelt down and leaned forward to inspect the floor. The scalpel lay on the other side of the bed. Next to it was the Bible, which had served as the chopping board during the castration.

I felt queasy again and ran to the toilet to be sick, but nothing came up. Only a dry cough rang out between the tiled walls. I was incapable of thinking clearly.

All the same I managed to retain my composure long enough to wipe down any area or object I remembered touching. Afterwards I let myself out into the corridor, gave the door handle the same treatment and stuffed the towel inside my shirt. That left the key. I briefly considered pushing it under the door, but for some reason I changed my mind and hid it in a flowerpot on the way back to my room.

There was no whisky or gin left in the minibar so I drank some brandy straight from the bottle. The taste of vomit was forced out by the alcohol, but the nausea lingered. I was sweating profusely and wiped my face with the towel.

The sight of Verner refused to leave me alone. With a photo of him in front of me, it was impossible to think of anything else. He had contributed much of the background for *As You Sow*. The superintendent murdered in the book was based on a specific person as far as Verner was concerned, but to me it was someone else. For Verner, it was his boss. For me, it has always been Verner himself. I have never liked him. When I wrote his murder, I felt that he was atoning for his racism, his offensive jokes and his lack of tact and empathy. He was being punished for all the snide remarks he had uttered about Line and for his pathetic paedophile tendencies. Line and I had been divorced for some years when I wrote the book, but I still had a feeling that I was exposing him for her sake. An act of penitence for contacting Verner after she had told me what a bastard he was.

If Verner ever suspected the victim in the book was him, he never said so. He was content to punish his own tormentor, the superintendent in his department whom he regarded as corrupt and greedy for power, characteristics which in time had come to define Verner as well.

The question of who was really murdered in the book had now been settled.

It *was* Verner.

Friday

13

I slept little that night. Instead I carried on drinking my way through the minibar, feeling increasingly sorry for myself.

I had no idea what to do next. Options whirled around my head, each one more unreal than the next. Several times I grabbed the telephone to call the police, but every time I chickened out before I had pressed all the numbers. What would I say? If I reported Verner's murder, I would have to explain how I had come to have the key to the hotel room, and thus the envelope. This, in turn, would bring up the subject of the murder of Mona Weis and consequently the question of why I hadn't contacted them earlier. I had no answer to this. It like an avalanche: impossible to stop it without someone getting hurt.

It was only a matter of time before the body in room 102 would be found. The smell in the room would soon spread and the staff would become suspicious. It would take Ferdinan seconds to recognize the method by which Verner had been killed. Besides, he was likely to remember Verner from the restaurant; other guests would testify we had dined together and that we had a row. It was only a short distance from there to the police knocking on my door.

I should have pre-empted them, contacted them immediately, regardless of the consequences, but something held me back. Verner had been killed before he had time to tell the Murder Squad that Mona's murder was a copy-cat killing; he had had our proof, the book and the photo of Mona, on him. I hadn't searched room 102, but I was fairly sure the killer had removed everything and left the scene precisely as in the book.

The irony was that this could work to my advantage – the book, I mean. There was a copy of *As You Sow* in room 102, and with a manual for the murder in the same room as the body there was no obvious link between the killing and me – if you ignored the fact that I knew the victim and was probably the last person to see him alive, apart from the killer.

My alibi was even more problematic. I didn't know exactly when the murder had been committed, but it must have been shortly after our dinner. The killer might have waited for Verner in the lobby and enticed him up to the room on some pretext. In the book, the killer was a vindictive hooker and Verner was just the sort who'd be susceptible to a honeytrap. He occasionally boasted of being paid 'in kind' when dealing with the local prostitutes so it wasn't difficult to imagine that he would let himself be tempted by a freebie.

The thought that I had left the restaurant, taken the lift and strolled to my room while Verner's life was ebbing away so close to me made my stomach churn. He was a bastard, but he didn't deserve an end like that, and certainly not on my account.

The bottom line was I had no alibi after our dinner other than an empty minibar, which would not necessarily help my defence.

My author brain had started working again after the initial shock. It examined the plot and the sequence of events, put the pieces together and built structures, but no matter how hard I pushed it, no solution was forthcoming. I needed more information. I needed time. I needed help.

The breakfast buffet opened at seven o'clock and even though I wasn't hungry, I left my room at five minutes to. Ferdinan was in reception, looking just as bright-eyed as he always did. It was bordering on inhuman to be that cheerful at this time in the morning when he had probably only had five hours' sleep.

'Good morning, Mr Føns,' he said with a song in his voice.

'Good morning, Ferdinan,' I replied with as much warmth as I could muster. I stopped at the counter.

'Can I help you with anything?' Ferdinan asked.

'Yes, I hope so,' I replied. 'Listen, my room is wonderful, but it's a bit too big for me.'

Ferdinan nodded.

'Any chance I could move to room 102?'

Ferdinan shook his head. 'I'm afraid it's not free yet,' he said. 'But I could find out when the guest is leaving.' He gestured towards the computer screen and added, 'If I can find out how to work the damn thing.' He stepped behind the screen and touched his chin. 'Let me see . . . hmmm.'

'Perhaps I can help you?' I suggested, and joined him behind the counter. 'I'm quite good with computers.' This was a lie – I have no technical qualifications at all. I use my computer purely as a typewriter.

'Yes,' Ferdinan said. 'Together we should be able to crack it.' He hit a key and a long list appeared on the screen. 'Look . . . this is supposed to be the rooms . . . No . . . looks more like bookings.' He stretched out his hands and mimed strangulation across the keyboard. 'Arrghh, it makes me so . . .'

I had spotted a button on the screen with the wording 'Room Deployment'.

'May I?' I asked, and Ferdinan stepped aside.

'Please,' he said with relief in his voice.

I clicked the button and the screen produced yet another list, this time sorted by room number.

'Oh, yes,' Ferdinan said. 'That looks like it.'

My eyes located room 102 before Ferdinan's did, and I had found what I was looking for.

'Oh, I'm so sorry,' Ferdinan exclaimed. 'The room won't be vacated until Monday afternoon . . . I can see the guest has asked for the room not be cleaned during his stay so it'll probably take longer to clean later.'

Luckily we were standing side by side so he couldn't see my reaction. The colour must have drained from my face. He was quite right: cleaning room 102 would take a lot longer than usual this time.

I thanked him and left the reception as quickly as I could without looking back. I had got what I wanted. One of those things was the check-out date – obviously relevant in respect of how much time would pass before

Verner's body was discovered – but just as important was the name in which the room had been booked.

That name was Martin Kragh, one of the characters in *Brotherly Love*, a disagreeable parasite of a man, who was based on my former friend and Scriptorium brother, Morten Due, known to us all as Mortis.

14

It couldn't be a coincidence.

Whoever had booked room 102 had obviously given a false name, but using Martin Kragh had to be significant. Did Mortis know something? Was he in danger, was it a red herring or was the killer taunting me? Another possible explanation was that the killer had simply picked a random name from the book; after all, it was very much an insider's reference, although Bjarne had spotted it immediately when he read the book.

The main character in *Brotherly Love* is Mark Nordstrøm, a 40-year-old managing director of a shipping company owned by his dying father. As well as running the company, Mark also nurses his father in his final days. Mark is a good son and attends dutifully at his father's deathbed in the knowledge that he is the sole heir to the family fortune. Or so he thinks. It turns out that his father had sired a handful of kids and they all appear at the reading of the will to claim their share of the estate. In Mark's eyes, they have never worked a day in their lives, but instead have been sponging on society and, worse, the family money that should rightly go to him. Even though there is enough money for everyone to live comfortably, Mark is so outraged that he decides to kill them all, one by one. Mark knows perfectly well that suspicion will fall on him so he takes care to make the murders look like accidents or suicides and to have a bullet-proof alibi ready for every one of them. And he succeeds beyond his wildest dreams; he dispatches all his new siblings in a variety of ways, but with the common denominator that it's their perceived laziness or lack of willpower that kills them, typically through some form of entirely unreasonable endurance test. Mark is never arrested, even though the sergeant investigating the case knows he is involved.

I considered various permutations while I ate a few mouthfuls of breakfast and drank some coffee, and I reached the conclusion that I had to get in touch with Mortis, if only to eliminate him.

From my hotel room I called Directory Enquiries, but they had no Morten Due listed in Copenhagen or surrounding areas. I called Bjarne. He was on his way to work at the sixth-form college where he taught.

'Hi, Frank,' he said when he heard my voice. He sounded out of breath and there was traffic noise in the background. 'What's up?'

'I wanted to know if you have an address or telephone number for Mortis?'

'Hmm . . .' I heard down the other end. A car horn beeped and Bjarne cursed. 'It's a long time since I've seen him. I might have an address somewhere at home. I think he lives in north-west Copenhagen.'

'Do you remember where?'

'No, sorry, I don't. Like I said, it's a long—'

'When will you be back?'

'This afternoon,' Bjarne replied. 'But we're seeing you tonight anyway. You haven't forgotten that, have you?'

Of course I had. Dinner with Bjarne and Anne in the old Scriptorium flat was normally the highlight of my trip when I was in town, but all plans had been upset now. I looked around as if I had just woken up from a nap. What day was it? Was it morning or afternoon? Suddenly I didn't know.

'Frank?'

I cleared my throat. 'Of course I haven't,' I lied slickly. 'Seven o'clock, was it?'

'Exactly.'

'OK, see you tonight.'

I hung up before Bjarne had time to reply. The clock on the wall showed nine. That meant ten hours before I could get the address. The dinner invitation prompted me to remember the rest of today's programme. It was the first day of the book fair and I was expected to promote *In the Red Zone* by signing copies. My editor's fear that the book might be stopped was so far unfounded. His words echoed in my head. Pretend nothing has happened. Stick to the plan.

But how could I when Verner lay murdered a couple of floors below me? Then again, neither could I stand being in the hotel any longer.

I took a taxi to Forum in Frederiksberg.

Forum was a large cube of concrete and steel, placed between proud old buildings with the finesse and sensitivity to its surroundings of a piece of rubbish tossed in a flowerbed.

The queue of visitors already stretched outside. I picked up my entrance pass at the information desk and entered the exhibition hall.

My first task was to sign books and even at a distance I could see people lined up clutching books outside ZeitSign's stand. It was ten minutes after the starting time stated in the programme.

ZeitSign's black and white colours dominated the stand, which was bigger than usual. Black fabric had been draped over one corner and this was where all my books were exhibited – with the exception of my first two, for which I was grateful. Hundreds of copies of *In the Red Zone* had been piled up around a small table and chair that were waiting for me. This was where I could look forward to spending the next hour signing autographs.

I toyed with the idea of walking on, losing myself in the crowds pushing and shoving in between the displays. Unfortunately I loathed being swept along by a constant stream of pushy book fanatics with plastic bags and darting eyes even more than I loathed signing books. I took a deep breath and forced my way to the stand and my table. There, at least, I would be able to sit down and no one would bump into me or step on my toes.

People shuffled closer and mumbled impatiently when I hung my jacket over the back of the chair and took my seat. I found my fountain pen, secured the cap, conjured up the biggest smile I could manage and turned to face the first person.

As always it was mostly women who wanted their books signed. This is obviously because more women read fiction than men, but I also think women want to see the person who wrote the book. They are curious to know something about the person behind it and the signature itself is less important. The female interest when I broke through with *Outer Demons* was huge. Women wanted to meet the monster who had dreamed up such explicit scenes of violence and torture. They searched for something dangerous or evil in my eyes to make them shudder. They may have been disappointed, but it has never prevented them from turning up in vast numbers for book signings to confess how affected they were when they read this or that passage.

'Oh, there you are,' a voice said next to me and I felt a hand on my shoulder. It was Finn Gelf. 'We were just starting to worry that you might not show.'

'Don't worry,' I said, giving a signed copy of *In the Red Zone* to a woman in her forties. She smiled gratefully and disappeared clutching her trophy. 'The circus horse is ready to take another trip round the ring,' I added, and smiled to the next person in the queue.

Finn patted my shoulder.

'That's good to know, Frank. Please would you pop by backstage when you're done?'

The backstage area was a small cubicle behind the stand. A couple of folding chairs let you to take the weight off your feet, a necessity for staff who had to stand up all day and a sanctuary for the authors. Though it was narrow and busy, it still offered some respite from the crowds and, most importantly, it featured a keg of beer. I was already looking forward to it.

The first thirty minutes I wrote dedications non-stop. My smile was set on autopilot while I listened to people's comments and thanked them, nodded and smiled again. Individuals turned into a blur of smiling, sweating, panting faces. The queue seemed never-ending and the only thing that kept me going was the prospect of an ice-cold beer in the backroom.

My gaze was fixed on the spot on the title page where I signed my name, but I was roused from my daze when someone put a book in front of me with a different title. The book was *Media Whore*, which I wrote seven years ago. I straightened my back and looked up at the reader. It was a man, which was in itself unusual, but even more unusual, he wore sunglasses and smiled in a bizarrely expectant manner as though he was waiting for me to recognize him, despite the glasses.

He wouldn't be the first weirdo to come to a book signing, but I must have been thinner-skinned than normal that day because I got a really bad feeling about him that I couldn't shake off. After I had signed his book, his smile changed to triumphant as he turned around and walked away from the stand.

I followed him with my eyes until the next fan placed their book on the table and demanded my attention.

The queue diminished only slowly. Some fans might even have given up waiting and gone away, but there was no escape for me. I rarely write by hand and my fingers were aching by the time the queue had almost gone. I

paused briefly and flexed my fingers while the next
female fan expressed her excitement at starting a new
Føns thriller. By now, I was exhausted and barely raised
my eyes. The books flowed through my hands as if I was
a checkout assistant in a supermarket, and the customers
were served with haste and indifference.

Suddenly my movements froze.

The last person in the queue placed her book in front of
me, opened on the title page, but it already had a dedication, and in my own handwriting, too:

> *Dear Line*
>
> *Another scalp. Hope you're well.*
> *Take care of yourself and the girls.*
>
> *Your F. Føns*

I looked up.

After a few seconds of disbelief, I recognized my older
daughter, Veronika.

15

The thought of having children had never really crossed my mind.

I had always imagined my books would be my legacy. With *In the Dead Angle* and *The Walls Have Ears* I had given birth to a couple of freaks that I could barely bring myself to acknowledge. They were rejects no parent could love, and it was in the light of this realization that I welcomed Line's desire to have children. Suddenly it was obvious we should start a family. Of course we should.

The joint project brought us even closer. We became obsessed with every aspect of how to bring up children, decorating the flat and dreaming about the future. We bought baby magazines and read articles on parenting methods and child psychology and our library of literary classics was supplemented with colourful self-help books about nappy changing and sleep training.

Sex acquired a whole new dimension. We enjoyed it more than ever before with the added awareness that tonight might be the night it happened. It made both of us conscious that everything should be just right. We wanted to be in the right mood and the bedroom must have the perfect romantic atmosphere with candles and soft music.

I will never know if this caused Line to fall pregnant as quickly as she did, but after throwing away the pill, we hit the jackpot very soon. Our families were thrilled. There were already plenty of children on Line's side, but she was nevertheless the object of extravagant attention and support from everyone. The child would be the first grandchild on my side and my parents were beside themselves. We hadn't seen them for nearly two years due to my disillusionment with their lack of support for my writing. Now they spotted an opportunity to become a family again.

Our greatest worry was financial. It was my idea to drop the writing completely for a while and focus on earning money until Line could return to work. It was the responsible thing to do and it lifted a huge weight from my shoulders. My frustration at not being able to write anything worthwhile vanished in an instant now that I had the world's best alibi. I no longer felt guilty about not contributing to our living costs; indeed, I relished becoming the breadwinner. I had hoped to achieve that status through my imagination, but now that my creativity had failed, my hands paid our rent. It didn't even feel like a defeat; on the contrary, I experienced a deep sense of satisfaction when I came home late in the evening after job number two or three and collapsed on the sofa or snuggled up to my sleeping wife.

Line had to stop dancing early in her pregnancy in order not to strain her body. She managed to get an office job in a theatre for a couple of months, but otherwise we depended on my income from whatever work I could find. In the period up to the birth, I had many different jobs including postman, delivering newspapers, assistant in a video rental shop and removal man for a kitchen fitter. None of these represented a huge intellectual challenge, but I think it ultimately helped make me a better writer. I mixed with people I wouldn't normally have met and heard stories from all levels of society and ethnic groups. It was all valuable experience that settled in my memory and gave me material from which I would later construct my characters.

I didn't touch my computer in that period. The only writing I did was filling in timesheets or making shopping lists. I enjoyed not having to think about anything other than where and when my next job began and how to get there.

Line's pregnancy went according to plan. She grew more beautiful with each day that passed and her stomach sat like a fully inflated beach ball on her slim body. Her friends envied her, and only a few months later Bjarne and Anne told us that she had thrown away her pills, too. When Line was eight months pregnant, they announced that Anne was finally eight weeks pregnant.

Anne miscarried a couple of days before Line gave birth. It was a monstrous coincidence, but not enough to mar our joy at our new baby girl, Veronika. Bjarne and Anne, however, took it hard and were unable to visit us in the first few weeks after the birth. When they finally did, the atmosphere was strained with awkward pauses where no one said anything.

No one except Veronika, that is. She was incapable of

shutting up. From the moment she opened her eyes to the moment she fell asleep, she would either be crying or babbling happily, and I listened in raptures to everything she had to say. I simply couldn't get enough and there was nothing I wouldn't do for her.

But it wasn't me she needed; it was her mother, which was fortunate as I had several jobs to hold down. It was tough to be away from home that much, but there was a point to it and I would always tiptoe into my daughter's room when I came back and just sit there gazing at her in her cot until I could no longer keep my eyes open. There is no better stress therapy than watching a sleeping baby.

The first four months flew by. I worked, Line breast-fed. She started exercising as soon as she was allowed. Even with three jobs I couldn't make enough money for us to live reasonably so it was essential that Line returned to work as soon as possible. With her income I would only need to do one job and I could look after Veronika the rest of the time.

In many ways this proved to be the turning point in my life.

My feelings for Veronika deepened with each day. She was now old enough to be aware of what was going on around her and she was easy to entertain and love. She was happy most of the time and she developed a special smile that knocked everyone who saw it for six. It was a slightly private grin as if we shared a secret or she had just made a sarcastic remark. Later it turned out to be one of her personality traits. Even as a baby we had nicknamed her Ironika.

Babies are creatures of habit and my new job as a father

meant I had to arrange my day to suit my daughter's needs. This was the second turning point. Her sleep pattern gave me time when she wasn't directly dependent on me. During those periods I started writing. First I just scribbled down everyday stuff I experienced with my daughter, the kind of naive observations that all parents probably make, but it soon turned into more coherent texts and stories. Ironika had forced me to organize my writing. I rose early to feed her and when she slept, I sat down in front of my computer and got to work. It became a routine that you could set your watch by and I discovered that it was an incredibly effective way to write. Before I had only written when I felt inspired, often at odd hours and mostly under the influence of alcohol or cannabis. Now I wrote with a clear head, keen to make the most of the time Ironika had deigned to grant me. These highly concentrated periods of writing produced surprisingly good results.

Whether it was my new responsibility that made the difference, I don't know, but what I wrote was more accessible than anything I had ever attempted before. Through my two previous books, both in some way a distortion of the crime novel, I had acquired a basic understanding of the genre, its clichés and literary devices, and it was that knowledge I now exploited. Rather than manipulate the genre this time, I embraced it and wrote a standard crime novel with all the components the reader would expect. I knew it would need a unique selling point to stand out from the rest, and I created the explicit torture and murder scenes that were to become my trademark.

I'm not exaggerating when I say that Ironika was

the reason I could write what I did. She rewarded my efforts with smile and gurgles when I was doing well and cried when she could feel I was frustrated at my lack of progress. Previously I hadn't shown anyone my work until it was finished, but my daughter was with me all the way. She sat on my lap when I proofread, I told her about the characters and their stories, about alternative complications or endings that she could reject or approve with a smile or tears.

Ironika and I wrote my breakthrough novel, *Outer Demons*, together. We were a team with set rituals and secrets known only to us. Not even Line read anything we wrote.

Finally the script was ready. A fat stack of 450 pages had slowly grown from our partnership. I remember feeling immensely proud because I knew I was on to something this time, something that would work. I also had a sense of loss. Even though Ironika couldn't talk yet, *Outer Demons* had been a joint project and the finished script was the end of an era.

At that point my editor, Finn Gelf, had almost given up on me. We hadn't spoken for a very long time and he was surprised, to put it mildly, when I turned up at his office with a buggy containing Ironika and the script.

'Bloody hell,' he kept saying as he flicked through the pages at random.

I handed over Ironika to cooing secretaries and female editors so we could have a conversation. I don't remember which I was prouder to show off that day, Ironika or the script.

'So that's what you've been up to?'

'That and changing nappies,' I replied.

He nodded. 'I can't promise you anything, of course,' he began, ever the salesman. 'But I'll have a look at it as soon as I can.'

It's possible he had a good feeling about the script from the start because he rang me the following day to tell me he had begun it the night before and had been unable to put it down. He was clearly excited and raved down the telephone about foreign and film rights. I stayed calm. Ironika sat in her highchair by the table, frowning. It was as if she didn't approve that I had handed over our project to a third party and she foresaw where it would lead. If I had shared her insight then, I would have snatched the script from Finn's hands and burned it.

Editing the script took hardly any time. The text was so carefully composed that there were very few corrections to make, either in language or structure. Finn bought advertising space, posters and special display stands for bookshops. Later I learned he had remortgaged his own house to finance the marketing campaign, but I also know that he got his money back and then some.

A week before publication, Line was finally allowed to read *Outer Demons*. Not that she had pestered me to read it, but she had dropped a few snide remarks along the way and acted a little offended when I denied her. There were several reasons why I kept it from her. First, I doubted she would think it was any good, and secondly, there was my exclusive partnership with Ironika, who didn't seem to want to share our work with others, not even her mother.

When she finally read the book, she was stunned. Mainly at the violence and the factual manner in which it was depicted. She said she couldn't recognize me at all. The words were mine, but the images they conjured up she could in no way connect to me as a person. I said it was the best compliment she could give me and I meant it, or I did at the time.

The publication was celebrated at Krasnapolsky, which ZeitSign had booked for the night. The bar was located in central Copenhagen and was at the time one of the trendiest places without being exclusive. It was a huge change from the Scriptorium parties. This time we had bartenders, bouncers and waiters. Black banners promoting the book hung from the walls all the way around the rectangular room and stickers were scattered across the tables. At the bar guests could buy the book at a reduced price, which a lot of people did. In fact, more copies of *Outer Demons* were sold at Krasnapolsky that night than of my two first books put together.

All my friends came, as did all of Line's family and even my own parents turned up. ZeitSign's staff were present as well as a fair number of journalists, whom Finn plied with drinks. I got drunk very quickly, both on my editor's visions for my future and a couple of strong cocktails called Demons, which had been invented for the occasion, so my speech was a tad more improvised than I had planned. But the mood was jubilant, except that Mortis was in his usual changeable frame of mind and kept fiddling with the free copy I had signed and given to him. I knew he disapproved of my writing a typical genre novel and he was only waiting for an opportunity to voice his disgust.

I managed to avoid him all evening and at some point he left. Bjarne and Anne were there too, obviously. They had given me a gold fountain pen, 'to sign autographs' as Bjarne had joked, and done their best to recoup the cost of it in Demon cocktails.

The party at Krasnapolsky ended and I remember very little of the rest of the night. I know that at some point we went to Café Viktor, a place I had never been to before – I wouldn't have been seen dead there – but the flattering attention from my guests, the Demon cocktails and the success of the book went to my head and convinced me that I was the most important man in the whole world, or at least in this bar. I enjoyed rubbing shoulders with famous cyclists and wannabe celebrities, who were all suitably impressed when they learned who I was. I couldn't get enough of it. I wanted all of them to come and meet me, and I made sure I spoke to as many people as possible.

My guests slipped away quietly, even Bjarne and Anne. I think they said goodbye to me, but I'm not sure. I was probably deep in conversation with some television presenter.

That was my first, but by no means my last meeting in Café Viktor.

When I surfaced the following morning, I could taste Demons in my mouth. I swallowed half a litre of water. I was alone, but Line had bought all the papers and arranged them on the coffee table next to a thermos flask of coffee.

Armed with coffee and my duvet, I sat down to read the reviews. They were mixed, but even the worst ones were to my benefit. The critics queued up to express their outrage at the explicit violence and the scenes of torture and murder, but there was fierce disagreement whether this was art or exploitation. These mixed reactions were precisely what Finn Gelf had predicted and he had assured me that both points of view would boost sales. Regardless of which review people read, they would be intrigued by the critics' disgust and revulsion. Everyone would want to read a book that induced nausea in several critics and a few had refused to finish.

After writing in isolation for so long, being on the receiving end of this kind of attention was very strange.

At the bottom of the newspaper pile, I found a note from Line. She had taken Ironika to her family so I could have a lie-in. She didn't say whether she had read the reviews, but she added a PS that she had unplugged the telephone.

I got up from the sofa, a little wobbly, and walked over to the windowsill where the telephone was. I had barely plugged it in before it started ringing. It was a journalist from *Politiken*, the first of countless reporters to call that day. When Line returned home four hours later, I was still sitting on the sofa with my duvet wrapped around me, cold coffee in my cup, talking on the telephone. Everybody wanted to speak to me and I let them, until Line pulled out the plug later that night. It was like coming out of a state of intoxication. I realized that I had eaten nothing all day. Ironika refused to talk to me, but Line made some food, which we ate on the sofa with the reviews spread across the coffee table.

Initially, after reading the reviews, she had no idea what

to think, but the huge interest did convince her I was on to something.

She was proud, she said, and that was the best review I could have hoped for.

16

'It's a bit early to be drinking, isn't it?'

Ironika gave me a reproachful look as I poured myself a glass of beer from the keg in the backroom behind ZeitSign's stand. She had shoulder-length hair, dyed black, and wore slightly too much eyeshadow over her blue eyes. A tight black blouse emphasized her teenage breasts and a red gingham miniskirt over black tights with 'random' holes revealed her long, pretty legs. She was Line's daughter all right, and it was becoming more obvious the older she got.

'I had an early start,' I replied and drank nearly half the beer before topping up my glass. 'Besides, it's been a bad day.'

'Great, thanks,' Ironika said and sipped her mineral water, the only thing she wanted from ZeitSign's bar even though it was lukewarm.

'Yes, until now, of course,' I said, by way of a save, and smiled. 'It's good to see you.' That was a lie. I would have preferred her not to see her father hungover and on the verge of a nervous breakdown. It was more than seven years since I had last seen her, apart from the photographs on my parents' walls.

'I'm here with some friends,' she said. 'And I thought I would stop by and get myself an autograph.' She waved the book.

'Of course,' I exclaimed and grabbed it while I set down my beer and fumbled in my inside pocket for a pen.

'Have you read it?'

'Not yet,' Ironika replied. 'But I've read a couple of the other ones even though Mum hides them.'

'She hides them?'

'Yes, she piles them up in her wardrobe, like that would stop us or Bjørn, but I always find them.'

'Yes, you've always been bright,' I said and smiled to her.

'I don't like them . . . The books, I mean.'

I tried to maintain my smile, but she must have seen that it grew somewhat rigid.

'But that's probably just because I don't understand them,' she added.

I shrugged. 'They're not really suitable for children.'

Her eyes hardened. 'Frank, I'm not a child any more.'

'No, you're not,' I said quickly. 'It's just so long ago . . .'

At that moment Finn Gelf burst into the cubicle.

'Frank, are you ready . . .' He spotted Ironika. 'Oh . . . you've got a visitor,' he said with a sideways smile.

'This is my daughter, Veronika,' I said. 'You've met her before.'

'Of course,' Finn exclaimed and stuck out his hand to her. 'But the last time you can only have been . . . three years old, I think, so you probably don't remember me.'

Ironika shook her head, but she still took his hand and pressed it.

'So your dad brought you along to the book fair?'

'Nah, he's at home,' Ironika remarked dryly.

I swallowed a mouthful of beer to hide my irritation. Judging from the expression on Finn's face, he wished the ground would open up and swallow him.

'I'm here with some friends, Stine and Anna. We're going shopping afterwards.'

'Uhu, that sounds expensive,' Finn laughed. 'But if you fancy some books, just let me know. On the house.'

'Thanks, but I don't think so.'

'OK,' Finn replied and nodded. A small pause arose. Finally, Finn turned his attention to me. 'Frank, the interview starts in fifteen minutes and I've got something I need to show you first.'

'OK,' I said. 'Give me a couple of minutes.'

'Of course,' Finn said and held out his hand to Ironika. 'Good to see you again. Give my best to Line.'

'I will,' Ironika replied.

Finn Gelf exited and left us alone.

'Is she all right?' I asked.

'Mum? Yes, she's fine. Sometimes she overreacts for no reason, but she's OK as far as I know.'

'And Mathilde?'

'She's started secondary school. Teacher's pet, she is.'

We laughed. I drank my beer. Ironika sipped her mineral water.

'Tell me, why did you two really split up?' she asked me out of the blue.

I nearly choked on my beer.

'I think she still loves you,' Ironika carried on. 'She cuts interviews and reviews of your books out of the newspapers, and sometimes I hear them arguing about you.'

'Eh, that's a long story,' I stuttered.

'Was it because of me?'

'No, absolutely not!' I set down my beer and grabbed her by the shoulders. 'Please don't ever think that. Everything that happened was my fault, no one else's.'

Her face took on a frightened expression, so I let go of her instantly and took a step back. 'I'm sorry.'

Ironika shook her head. 'It's OK.'

'Listen . . . I've got to go now,' I said, my voice filled with regret. 'But perhaps we could meet some other time?'

'Maybe,' Ironika mumbled and looked down at her hands.

I reached into my jacket. 'But I want to subsidize your shopping trip,' I said, rummaging through my wallet.

'No, it's OK, Frank, you don't have to do that.'

'Yes, yes, I want to,' I said and pulled out all the notes I could find. Three one-hundred kroner notes and a crumbled fifty. It wasn't much, but it was the only cash I had on me. I offered it to her.

'No, please don't. It's all right. Mum has given me some money.'

'Take it, for my sake,' I said. 'It would make me happy.'

She shrugged and accepted the money.

'Take care of yourself,' I said and gave her an awkward hug.

'You too,' she replied.

'And let's meet up soon, properly, OK?'

'I'm not sure. I don't think Mum would like it.'

'OK, but if you change your mind, you know where I am. Any time.'

Ironika nodded, opened the door and slipped outside and into the crowd. She glanced back and raised her hand by way of goodbye. I waved eagerly. When she had gone, I closed the door and flopped down on one of the folding chairs.

I cursed myself to hell. Just how pathetic could I be? I hadn't seen my daughter for seven years and the first thing I do is drink in front of her, call her a child and then try to bribe her. What a crap dad I was! I knocked back the rest of my beer and stared at the empty plastic cup. The anger surged inside me. I crushed the cup and got up with a sense of purpose.

Finn Gelf always had something stronger than beer and mineral water at the book fair, so I went through the boxes until I found a bottle of Smirnoff. I took an empty cup, half filled it with vodka and swallowed a large gulp. The acrid taste made me grind my teeth, but I forced down another mouthful. It nearly came right back up again, but I managed to wash it down with what was left of Ironika's mineral water.

At that moment, Finn opened the door to the cubicle.

'Are you OK?'

I nodded and he entered and closed the door behind him.

'Christ, she's grown tall, hasn't she?' His eyes registered the bottle I had left on the table. 'Listen, I'm really sorry I said that stuff about—'

'It's all right, Finn,' I said and swallowed the last vodka in my cup. The alcohol was starting to take effect. A pleasant sense of lethargy spread through my body. 'What did you want?'

Finn straightened up and a broad grin transformed his face.

'The reviews,' he exclaimed. 'You've got to see the reviews!' He took out a pile of newspapers with yellow Post-it notes sticking out. 'Not at all bad . . . I mean compared to what we're used to.' One by one, he placed the newspapers on a small camping table and found the reviews of *In the Red Zone*.

Four newspapers in total had decided to review the book on the date it was published, which was fairly rare. Literary editors had been allocated extra column inches on account of the book fair, but it had happened to me several times that a few newspapers completely failed to review my books or did so several months after they had been published and then by some random trainee. The four reviews were critical, but not downright repelled as I had expected. One called the book 'the best Føns since his breakthrough' and another 'vintage Føns' and practically everybody agreed that fans of the genre wouldn't be disappointed.

'What have you got to say to that?' Finn said when he could no longer keep his excitement at bay. 'Great, isn't it?'

I nodded, but failed to be carried away by his exhilaration. Neither his words nor the reviews could penetrate into my consciousness after the meeting with Ironika, and the knowledge that my moderate success had cost one woman her life made it impossible for me to celebrate. Instead I poured more vodka into my cup.

'Party time!' Finn roared and helped himself to a dash of vodka to which he added plenty of orange juice. 'Congratulations, old boy!'

Near the stage where I was going to be interviewed, I was met by Linda Hvilbjerg, who gave me a polite hug and we exchanged pleasantries. She looked great. We were roughly the same age, but she looked younger. She was still slim and stylish in a grey suit with a black shirt and high-heeled shoes. Her dark hair was gathered in a bun and she wore a pair of glasses with a square steel frame that gave her a strict secretarial look, straight out of some sexual fantasy. We hadn't spoken since *Media Whore* had been published, which was understandable, but she wasn't even slightly frosty. On the contrary, she seemed positively forthcoming, though it's possible my level of intoxication clouded my judgement, or she might have helped herself to her own medicine. It wouldn't be the first time we got high together. In fact, it was something of a tradition.

Two upholstered leather armchairs had been placed on the stage, angled so they faced each other and the audience. Behind the chairs was a blue background on which a flat screen displayed today's programme. *Next: Linda Hvilbjerg in conversation with Frank Føns.* In front of the stage were seats for around fifty people and every seat was occupied when we made ourselves comfortable. Sound engineers rushed over to help with our microphones. I wondered if all those people had come to hear about my book or to see this TV darling. The billing on the screen suggested the latter.

Linda Hvilbjerg introduced both of us and described me as one of the genre's loyal contributors. She was witty and charming, avoided fawning excessively, but kept a good, sober tone.

'If this interview had a title it would be "Fiction and Reality",' Linda Hvilbjerg began. 'Frank, many of your fans explain their passion for your books by describing them as real and authentic, despite the very colourful depictions of murder.'

I smiled and nodded while I tried to work out where she was going with this. I knew for certain that she had an agenda and her initial politeness was merely camouflage.

'To what extent is it important to you that your stories seem real?'

'It matters a great deal to me,' I replied immediately. 'Even though my stories are scary, even terrifying and repulsive some might say, then it's of the utmost importance that the reader will think, this could happen, and if it were to happen, then this is exactly how it would be . . . it's often the realism in my books that my readers find most shocking.'

Linda Hvilbjerg nodded. 'It was certainly shocking to read the newspaper the other day.' On the screen behind her a newspaper headline flashed up: 'Woman murdered in Gilleleje Marina'. 'I can tell those of you who haven't read *In the Red Zone*, without revealing too much of the plot, that a woman is mutilated and drowned in Gilleleje Marina.'

My scalp was sweating and itchy and I was suddenly aware of the heat from the spotlight above the stage. The audience was murmuring.

'Now the police haven't released much information about the murder yet, but it seems like an incredible coincidence. How do you feel about that?'

I took a sip of my vodka and cleared my throat before I replied.

'I read that article too,' I replied. 'It's awful that something like that can happen in a lovely place like Gilleleje, but it proves that evil is everywhere, that we're never safe, no matter where we are or how secure we feel . . .'

'But doesn't the similarity upset you at all?'

'Of course it does,' I said and I think I might have snapped at her. 'But you also have to be careful about jumping to conclusions just because you've recently read a book.' I paused. 'If you've got a hammer, all problems look like nails,' I quoted. 'I can't imagine that every detail of that murder matches the book. It must be a coincidence.'

I hated lying so brazenly and I didn't think for a moment that I was fooling anyone, certainly not Linda Hvilbjerg. She fixed me with her eyes and I could see that the reporter part of her brain battled with the entertainer part over which one of them would be allowed to continue. Fortunately, the entertainer part won.

'As I mentioned, your fans regard the realism as the appeal of your books, while your critics claim you've written the same book ten times over,' she said. 'What have you got to say to them?'

'That they can't have read them properly,' I replied and was rewarded with a few laughs from the audience and a brief smile from Linda. 'I get numerous letters from my readers stating precisely the opposite. Many look forward to the next book and express how they're surprised time and time again at the imaginative plots and range of characters . . .'

'But, Frank . . . is it correct to say that every single one of your books follows a particular template, a model you have used since your best-known work, *Outer Demons?*'

It was a reasonable question and I had no reason to think she was trying to provoke me, I just objected to *Outer Demons* being referred to as my best-known work yet again. It was as if I would never improve on my breakthrough novel in the eyes of the critics. It had dragged after me like a ball and chain ever since; it rattled every time I tried to move and drowned out my voice, no matter what I did.

'It's correct, Linda, that my books have a unique style and that the tension builds up according to a pattern, but that's also my strength. The reader recognizes a Føns thriller when they read it, just like you recognize a song by Depeche Mode, even if you haven't heard it before.' I shrugged. 'All my books are about murders and the detection of them, so in that sense they're identical. However, if you look closer, you'll see that it's not entirely true.'

Linda nodded. 'So you're saying that if I read a passage from one of your books, you'll be able to tell me which one it is?' She pulled out a piece of paper and the audience greeted the challenge with scattered laughter.

I held her eyes for a second. She smiled at me with a cheeky expression around her lips. I wasn't entirely clear what she was up to, but it was too late to back down. My day was already ruined: how much worse could it get?

'OK,' I replied. 'Any children present?'

The audience tittered, but Linda peered across them,

temporarily wrong-footed. Nevertheless, she must have decided that it was acceptable to carry on and coughed before she started reading:

The girl squeezed her eyelids together as hard as she could. Her face was bathed in sweat and tears and the gaffer tape had started to peel off her cheek. She whimpered.

'Look!' he ordered her. 'Look, or the eyelids will be next!'

Reluctantly, she opened her eyes. They were filled with tears and terror. He held up the severed nipple in front of her. She tried to scream and she fought against the cable ties pinning her to the chair, but they only dug themselves deeper into her flesh.

He moved the nipple to his lips and sucked it as if he were a nursing infant. The woman thrashed her head from side to side spraying sweat, tears and snot around.

He laughed and lifted the shears to her other breast. She froze at his touch and he smiled while he fondled the breast with the cold metal. Slowly, the nipple hardened.

'Look, she likes it,' he exclaimed and leered again.

With his thumb and index fingers he pinched the nipple, rubbed it a little and pulled it. He opened the shears and placed the steel jaws around the nipple.

The flesh quivered . . .

Linda stopped reading. The audience had fallen silent, completely silent.

She was good at reading aloud; I had to give her that. Her stresses were accurate, the pauses precisely measured and the characters brought to life despite the brevity of the passage. Personally, I didn't like reading my own books aloud. There was something revealing about reading to others. It was proof of what I had written, an open declaration that I stood by it. Consequently I carefully selected the sections I read aloud, unless I could avoid it altogether. The choice itself would expose me. How would it reflect on the author if I read the most bestial passages? After all, the mood should ideally remain pleasant and, for that reason, I typically chose the more subdued chapters, preferably those with a little humour that wouldn't offend anyone and which had no direct link to me.

However, it wasn't Linda Hvilbjerg's plan to let me get away with that.

'*Inner Demons*,' I replied. 'Not exactly a bedtime story.'

The audience laughed with relief bordering on gratitude.

'Correct,' Linda declared. Some members of the audience applauded. 'What this passage doesn't mention is that the woman is heavily pregnant – otherwise we would have made it far too easy for you.'

She smiled and I laughed briefly.

'*Inner Demons* was the follow-up to your breakthrough novel, *Outer Demons*,' she explained to the audience. She turned her gaze back on me.

'Is it true that you wrote it while your then wife was expecting your second child?'

153

17

'That went great,' Linda Hvilbjerg said, having checked that the microphones had been switched off. The interview was over, but I didn't have the energy to get up from the armchair. She had grilled me for forty-five minutes, pursuing her 'theme' of fiction mirroring reality by bringing up examples from my earlier books and linking them to events in my private life. From *Nuclear Families* she had drawn parallels to my divorce from Line; she viewed *You Don't Have To Call Me Dad* as a book that criminalized decent step-parents and which, as Linda pointed out, had been written after Line moved in with Bjørn and their shared children, including mine.

I hadn't tried very hard to defend myself. All I could do was refuse to discuss my private life and argue that the best stories take as their starting point experiences that are familiar to us all or which we can easily imagine. In order to describe the horror that had made me famous, I had to explore every detail of it, no matter how revolting it might be. If it meant using my own experiences and feelings as a springboard, then that's what I did. It improved my motivation, the book and, ultimately, the reader's reaction.

All in all, I was quite pleased with my performance. After the shock start with the Gilleleje murder, I had quickly spotted in which direction the interview was heading and, though alcohol coursed around my body, I felt more sober than I had for a long time. Not once did I lose my temper or reply in anger, even though it required enormous restraint not to react emotionally. I knew that was what she wanted, an outburst that would reveal the monster who produced what she could never bring herself to refer to as literature. If she was disappointed at her failure, she didn't show it. Perhaps muddling up fiction and reality and presenting it as her 'evidence' had been enough for her?

'You failed to mention *Media Whore*,' I sniped. 'That would have proved your point.'

Linda Hvilbjerg shrugged. 'That's water under the bridge, Frank. Let's call it quits?'

'Quits? So this was payback?'

'Payback?' Linda exclaimed, smiling. 'Not at all. I've just given you forty-five minutes of free publicity. Your books will carry on selling, don't you worry.'

I snorted. 'Possibly, but you also made sure that no one will ever speak to me again because they think I'll end up killing them in a book.'

She gathered her papers and stood up. 'Can you blame them, Frank?'

I shot up and was about to inform her just how little importance I attached to her opinion, but the words never came out of my mouth.

'Take care,' Linda Hvilbjerg said and hugged me as if nothing had happened. 'Good luck with the book.'

I had no time to reply before she had turned around and stepped down from the stage. She attracted a fair amount of attention; the crowds moved out of her way and let her glide through as if an invisible force was parting them for her. Behind her, the crowd filled the vacuum and, after a few seconds, I could no longer see her.

'What a bitch!'

Finn Gelf was standing in front of the stage, holding out his hand to me. I took it and stepped down to him.

'I saw most of it,' he said sympathetically. 'She really managed to open up old wounds, eh?'

I nodded.

'But don't worry about it,' Finn said, patting my shoulder. 'It can only boost sales. Including the back catalogue.' He rubbed his hands. 'People will read the books she mentioned to gain an insight into your writing process.'

'And my private life,' I added.

'That too,' Finn Gelf admitted. 'But then again, you don't give many interviews, so where else can they look?' His face took on an animated expression. 'People want to know how the famous and mysterious Frank Føns is put together, what makes him tick. It's perfect. It couldn't have happened at a better time.'

'I really don't think—'

'Yes, yes, it all fits.' He leaned into me. 'And linking it to the murder in Gilleleje . . . it's going to be massive,' he whispered and nodded conspiratorially. 'And when they've read all your books, we'll launch the biography.'

'Biography?'

'Yes, we'll have no choice,' he carried on, now in a normal voice. 'The true story of your life in murder and mutilation.'

'Sounds like a death sentence,' I declared.

Finn Gelf snapped his fingers. 'That could be the title – *Death Sentence*!' He nodded, pleased with himself. 'Bloody hell, it'll be brilliant.'

We were interrupted by a middle-aged woman pressing a book in between us with a request for an autograph. I grabbed my pen and signed the book without looking at it, but kept my eyes fixed on Finn Gelf.

He looked like he really meant it. His eyes shone with a passion I hadn't seen in him for a long time. Once he got that look in his eyes, it was hard to talk sense to him. I remembered what Ellen had told me about the company's finances. ZeitSign was Finn's life. There was nothing he wouldn't do, and – in many cases – hadn't already done to keep the company afloat, and when there was money at stake, he could be very convincing.

'I'll think about it, Finn,' I said.

He smiled. 'Super,' he exclaimed. 'It's going to be great, just you wait.' He checked his watch. 'I've got to go, but I'll be seeing you tomorrow as arranged.'

I nodded and we said goodbye.

I wanted to tell Finn about Verner, but I didn't want to do it at the book fair, and Finn *was* the book fair. He breathed it for the three days it lasted, moving between the stands and the crowds such that no one could keep up with him and he heard everything, despite the noise level. He seemed indefatigable. Everyone knew him and he knew them, but he wasn't there for the small talk.

157

His brain was set on business, making new contacts and nurturing his existing network. I was tempted to believe he had a filter that would remove Verner's murder, if I tried to talk to him. Everything but publishing would be white noise to Finn.

To some extent that was why I had indulged his idea of a biography, but part of me was just as excited as he was. I wasn't keen on exposing my private life, but I was intrigued by the premise, and I discovered that my brain was already working on possible angles for the story, not least – I'm ashamed to admit – how I could use the murders of Mona Weis and Verner to spice up the narrative. They might have been murdered to harm me, but now it looked like it could have the opposite effect. However, it would only work if I could play the hero, the detective who uncovers the plot and catches the killer at the end.

Now that would be a biography I'd want to read.

18

After Finn had left, I stood there for a moment not knowing what to do with myself. The idea of the biography refused to leave me alone and everything else faded into a distant humming.

I wandered around aimlessly. I skimmed books and back-cover blurbs without really registering what I read. I stopped at some of the small makeshift platforms where authors answered questions with clenched fists and shaking voices, mercilessly amplified by microphones and speakers. But I didn't listen to what they were saying and I didn't notice where I was going. Eventually I found myself in a corner of the exhibition hall with a small bar in the style of an old English pub, quite unlike the other refreshment outlets at the book fair, which consisted mainly of plastic chairs and canteen tables.

I ordered a dark beer, which was drawn from a brass tap, and sat down in a corner on a bench upholstered in red velvet. It was the last free seat and I had to share the table with two raucous men in their fifties discussing the bookseller trade. Judging from their accents, they were from Jutland. This was probably their annual trip to the capital, which was spent on books, beers and hookers. One of them nodded to me as if he recognized me. I nodded back, but took out my notebook in order not to encourage further conversation.

I had to rein in the ideas buzzing around my head, write them down while I still remembered them. In a short space of time I had written four pages of notes without having drunk my beer. To reward myself, I raised the glass to my lips and drank half the contents in one go.

'Someone's thirsty,' one of the booksellers remarked, but I ignored him, picked up my pen and carried on writing.

The murders would form an important part of the biography, but that required that they were solved, and what would be better than if I myself contributed to the detection? The possibilities made my head spin. For years I had written about ordinary people who found themselves in extreme situations where they were forced to act. Sometimes they took on the role of detective to solve the mystery. I could easily imagine the resulting publicity if somehow I helped capture the killer of Mona Weis and Verner. In the past few days I had been a paranoid nervous wreck, but now it was the thrill of having a mission that made my heart beat faster.

The only real clue I had was the name Martin Kragh in which room 102 had been booked, and it raised more questions than it answered. Nevertheless it was a start. It meant something – to me at least – and, I had to presume, to the killer. Mortis might be involved, he might even be in danger, but as I couldn't get hold of his address until later tonight, I couldn't progress any further down this route.

The image of Verner's body in the hotel bed haunted me, but I forced myself to imagine what had preceded it, what he had done after leaving me at the restaurant.

He was probably worried about our conversation, knowing that he would get a dressing down when he told his colleagues he had withheld information from them. Perhaps they would freeze him out? Or he might be transferred to another department, a station in the provinces where nothing ever happened? He leaves the restaurant, walking briskly. In the lobby he spots a familiar face. It's Lulu, or whatever they call themselves in that profession, and a smile forms at the corners of his mouth. He tells her she must have got lost, that this is a respectable hotel which doesn't rent out rooms by the hour. Lulu looks frightened or she pretends to be and shows Verner the key. She isn't doing anything wrong and has a right to be here, she says. Verner doesn't believe her, mainly because he sees a chance to get into her knickers, and he threatens to take her down to the station.

'Frank!'

The voice shattered my reconstruction of the meeting at the Marieborg Hotel. The booksellers had gone and David Vestergaard, editor-in-chief of the publishing house Vestergaard & Co., sat down next to me with a broad smile and two freshly drawn beers. He pushed one in my direction.

'Good to see you again, Frank.'

We had spoken a couple of times before; in fact, he inflicted himself on me every year at the book fair, but I always ignored his ill-concealed offer to jump ship. Now I found myself trapped between him and a column of imitation mahogany. Besides, my glass was empty and I was in need of a refill.

I nodded by way of a thank you and we drank.

'Have you started your next novel?' he asked, glancing at the notebook in front of me.

There was no risk that he could read my handwriting, but I shut my notebook all the same and put it in my pocket.

'Something like that,' I replied and attempted a smile.

David Vestergaard grinned. 'That's just like you,' he said. 'Always busy, always productive.' He nodded to himself. 'That's what I like about you, Frank. You're a proper grafter. Nothing airy-fairy about you. No, it's the product . . .'

His flattery would lead to the inevitable offer so I stopped listening. Instead I drank the beer he had bought me and nodded in the right places. David Vestergaard was the third generation of the publishing house Vestergaard & Co. He was considerably younger than me – in his early thirties – but he spoke like a much older man and used expressions such as 'airy-fairy' and 'not inconsiderably'. His short haircut and trendy horn-rimmed glasses made people wonder if he was sending himself up or if he genuinely spoke like that, but having met him several times and talked to others who knew him, I had concluded that his manner was the product of private education and the literary tradition of the Vestergaard family.

David Vestergaard leaned into me and caught my attention again.

'Just between us,' he said. 'ZeitSign is in serious financial difficulties.'

'I don't know anything about that,' I replied.

'I don't imagine it's something Mr Gelf acknowledges if he can help it,' said David Vestergaard, and briefly looked as if he felt genuinely sorry for Finn. 'Nor does he appreciate the necessity of developing his writers.'

'Well, I can't really—'

'Not that you're not a good writer,' David Vestergaard interrupted me, holding up his hand as if swearing an oath. 'But with the right guidance and publicity, you could sell twice as many books, at least.' He drank his beer and so did I, mainly to hide my growing irritation. 'When did he last inspire you?'

'Inspire me?'

'Yes, a good editor doesn't just criticize and correct commas,' David Vestergaard said.

'Listen,' I said, putting down my glass a little too hard on the table. 'I'm not interested, OK? Whatever you're offering, I'm staying with ZeitSign, no matter what happens.'

'Suit yourself,' David Vestergaard sighed. 'But when Gelf goes bankrupt, you know where to turn.'

'What about Tom Winter?' I said. 'You already have a crime writer, one who regards me as his biggest rival.'

David Vestergaard's eyes flickered for a moment. 'That's not going to be a problem,' he replied. 'It's simply a question of timing publications properly and, as far as the rivalry goes, that's just playing to the gallery.' He smiled and raised his glass.

I refused to join in. He shrugged and emptied his glass in solitude.

'See you, Frank,' he said as he left the bar.

His seat was quickly taken by two women with sore feet and plastic bags bulging with books.

I fished out my notebook again. The conversation with David Vestergaard had interrupted my reconstruction of the meeting between Verner and Lulu, the hooker who lured him to room 102, and I tried to pick up my train of thought. Verner had just threatened to arrest her for soliciting in the hotel.

Lulu suddenly becomes more cooperative; perhaps she puts her hand on Verner's bull neck? There is no need to get angry. Why doesn't he come up to see for himself?

I knew Verner well enough to know he wouldn't refuse an offer like that, but there was something in my reconstruction that didn't hold. It wasn't the hooker, Lulu, who was out to get me and who had murdered Verner. Her job was simply to deliver him to the room, after which she would have left.

And then I realized that I might have seen her myself. After the meal, on my way into the lift, I had almost knocked over a small, slender woman. Verner frequently held forth about the type of women who turned him on. They had to be petite, slim and most importantly Danish. 'I don't mind them being seventeen as long as they look like thirteen,' he had said once and roared with laughter. Anyone who wanted to ensnare Verner would send a girl like that, I was sure of it. Petite, slim and Nordic; a description that fitted the girl in the lift perfectly.

Someone must have hired her and this person had to be the real killer.

So where was Lulu now?

19

I was completely shattered after the first day of the book fair.

Every year the hordes of people came as a total surprise to me. After living for so long in the cottage where I could control who I saw, walking through the exhibition hall felt like a constant infringement of my personal space. It was a relief to leave Forum and inhale air that hadn't already been breathed by tens of thousands of book fair visitors. I hailed a taxi and I may have jumped the queue. I heard someone shout out after me as I flopped down on the back seat.

At the hotel reception, Ferdinan was busy typing on the computer.

'Arrghh, useless thing,' he exclaimed, oblivious to my presence. He tapped the keyboard hard and clenched his jaw. 'Come on, you stupid machine.'

I cleared my throat and he straightened up, startled.

'I just can't work these . . . machines,' he said and smiled, embarrassed. 'How can I help you, Mr Føns? A table in the restaurant?'

I shook my head. 'No, thanks. I'm dining with a friend tonight,' I replied.

He nodded. 'Another time perhaps.'

'Definitely.'

I did a Columbo: I pretended to leave, but turned around when I remembered something.

'Listen, Ferdinan,' I said, casually. 'Do you remember my guest on the first day? Big broad man with thinning hair?'

Ferdinan looked up at the ceiling, but soon lit up in a smile.

'Oh, yes, a large gentleman, I remember him well. I directed him to the restaurant on his arrival.'

'Did you see him when he left?'

No,' Ferdinan replied immediately. 'The kitchen was busy so I helped out there most of the evening. Sometimes we all have to muck in.' He smiled. 'Has your friend gone missing?'

I sighed. 'He wasn't entirely sober. I wanted to know if he asked for a taxi or if he drove himself.'

'I'm sorry,' Ferdinan said. 'The last time I saw him was in the restaurant with you.'

'How about a slim woman, petite, wearing a short skirt and puffer jacket?'

Ferdinan shook his head. 'Not her either.'

I thanked him and went up to my room. I was due at Bjarne and Anne's in an hour and I had just enough time to kick off my shoes and splash some water on my face. Their flat was less than half an hour's walk from the hotel and I needed some fresh air so I decided to go on foot. It was windy. Large clouds drifted across the sky and there were crests on the water in the Lakes. Quite a few people had braved the weather; joggers darted between puddles and pedestrians as though they were on an obstacle course.

I wondered how much I should tell Bjarne. I desperately wanted to leave as soon as I had got Mortis's address and spare Bjarne and Anne my problems, but I also needed support. I couldn't get that from Finn, that much was obvious, and I had no one else. This realization made me feel very alone. The years in the cottage had protected me to some extent, but also narrowed down my circle of friends to very few people I trusted completely, and I didn't feel I could burden even them with my troubles.

Bjarne never changed. In the last ten years he had let his hair grow and wore it in a ponytail. Combined with his round, horn-rimmed glasses and casual clothes, he looked like an ageing hippie.

He gave me a bear hug practically before I crossed the threshold and I could feel that he certainly hadn't lost any weight in the past year. Anne, too, embraced me and we exchanged greetings.

Since giving up his dream of being published, Bjarne had worked as a teacher at a sixth-form college. With Anne's financial resources and her job as a social worker, they could still afford the large flat overlooking the Lakes, although the area had been greatly gentrified since our Scriptorium days. Inside the flat the second-hand furniture had long since been replaced with Danish design classics and the kitchen extended to include a breakfast bar and a dining area. The bookcases no longer held tattered, dog-eared books we had nicked or scrounged; now attractive hardbacks and special editions covered the walls in the two connecting reception rooms. In the absence of children, they had discovered and been able to afford good taste twenty years too early.

It wasn't long before Bjarne and Anne's hospitality had banished my dark thoughts and we chatted and joked like we always had, over a wonderful meal of coq au vin with generous quantities of an excellent red wine. I needed to relax, take my mind off things, and it was astonishingly easy in their company. You couldn't tell it was a year since we had last seen each other. The conversation flowed effortlessly, like a brook in an old forest running over stones long since polished smooth.

When we left the table, I realized just how drunk I was. I struggled to keep my balance and found it hard to focus. Bjarne took me by the shoulders and led me into the reception room where we sat down with brandy while Anne cleared the table. There was a moment's silence, and my thoughts flew back to the gravity of my situation. Bjarne must have detected a shift in my mood because he asked if anything was wrong.

Even though I wanted to confide in him, I found it almost impossible to know where to begin. My brain was a massive knot with countless ends you could tug at, most of which would either snap or simply tighten the knot if you started pulling them. Moreover, the alcohol had given my tongue a will of its own, so it took a while before I was capable of replying.

'Someone has copied my murder,' I said at last and groaned.

'Not to worry,' Bjarne said casually. 'You've got plenty of them.' He swirled the brandy around his glass and inhaled

169

the bouquet. 'It might not be a conscious imitation.' He sipped his drink. 'By now you must have murdered hundreds of people. No wonder someone has accidentally repeated one.'

'That's not the—' I began, before Bjarne interrupted me.

'Surely there is a limited number of ways in which to kill people? You must know that better than anyone. Being innovative is difficult. Even you find it hard not to repeat yourself these days.' He shrugged. 'Forgive me, but some of the most recent murders you've committed seem a tad elaborate, if you ask me.'

'Elaborate?'

'Yes, I know that graphic violence has practically become your trademark,' Bjarne said. 'But you're trying too hard. The execution of the murder, the description of every detail of the act overshadows the rest of the story.'

'You don't understand,' I muttered.

'I'm speaking as your friend, Frank,' Bjarne continued and placed his hand on my knee. 'The explicit torture and murder scenes have taken over. The plot has been reduced to a weak glue that connects the murders and the characters are all stereotypes. Your stories have no bite these days.'

We had always been honest about each other's work. At the time of the Scriptorium, we could be merciless in our verdicts, at times so harsh that objects were thrown and doors were slammed, but Bjarne's words didn't upset me. What irritated me was that he didn't understand.

'Bjarne . . .' I caught his eye and he seemed to realize that I was trying to tell him something important. At any rate, he shut up. 'Two people, *real* people, have been murdered. They were killed because of me . . . or in ways which I have described.'

Bjarne stared at me as if he expected or hoped that I would start to laugh. When I didn't, he cleared his throat.

'Is that why you want to get hold of Mortis?'

I nodded.

'It makes no sense,' he said. 'Mortis couldn't kill anyone. Don't you remember how thin he was? Nothing but skin and bones.'

'And hatred,' I added. 'If the police were to ask me if I had any enemies, Mortis would spring to mind. I think he hated me with all his being.'

Bjarne shook his head. 'He was jealous. There's a difference.'

'One thing can lead to another,' I said. 'I stole his woman and I was successful with—'

'He wasn't jealous of your books,' Bjarne interrupted me. 'On the contrary, he felt sorry for you. You know what he's like, utterly uncompromising when it comes to literature. In his eyes, you had lost your way, you had strayed from the light and were on the road to hell. That was enough of a punishment for him.'

'When did you last speak to him?'

Bjarne drank his brandy before replying.

'Only a couple of months ago, actually. He called to ask if I wanted to buy some of his books.' Bjarne closed his eyes and massaged a temple. 'I declined. It's not as if we need any more books, but . . .'

'But?'

'Well, it sounded as if he was in trouble.' Bjarne sighed.

'It didn't occur to me until afterwards. I've tried to push it from my mind . . . until now.'

'When did you last visit?' I asked.

'It's been a long time. He lived in north-west Copenhagen then, 43 Rentemestervej, I looked it up, but I don't know if he still lives there.'

'I'll find out,' I said.

I have a sense of being halfway there.

Perhaps I'm being optimistic. Though I can see the road ahead, I know I will face further temptations in the second half. It will be difficult to resist shortcuts and leave out painful interludes, but I must persist, focus on the next step all the time.

My resolve is stronger than ever. I'm writing with greater confidence and I can work for longer periods without getting lost or taking breaks. Could it be that the critic is approaching? He has stepped out from the shadows and I sense him by my side, like a guide or a travelling companion.

But I'm alone.

I realize this when I look up from the screen and stare into the darkness. I listen out, but there is no advice or directions. My route is already determined and I must follow it if I'm to ever arrive.

So I turn my eyes back to the screen and take another step.

20

The weeks that followed the publication of *Outer Demons* went by in a blur of interviews, meetings and appearances. I was expected to have an opinion on anything and everything from school bullying to prison sentences and – surprise, surprise – violence as entertainment and means of artistic expression. I was invited to parties, gala premiers and talk shows and I went to most of them.

Book sales soared. Translation rights to some territories were sold by auction and several companies expressed an interest in the film rights.

Soon the sales figures and the hype were so colossal that even the arty television book show *On the Bedside Table* had to admit defeat and feature me in an interview. The host was Linda Hvilbjerg, a journalist I had seen several times at Café Viktor, Dan Turèll or one of the other bars where I had been partying in the wake of publication. We hadn't spoken very much, but I got the impression she was a cold-hearted bitch. However, she was a stunningly attractive bitch. Dark, curly hair, brown eyes and a wide smile that almost blinded you. In the spirit of the programme she was discreetly dressed in a pale skirt and black blouse, which still managed to hint at a trim waist and a pair of firm, medium-sized breasts.

We met in the studio one hour before the start of the programme, which would be broadcast live. I was nervous. It was an important interview and I was intimidated by her. As I sat in make-up, my goal was just to get through it without her actually wiping the floor with me, so I was very surprised when she entered and greeted me profusely. She gave me a hug, praised my work and generally came across as open and approachable.

When the make-up artists had finished, Linda Hvilbjerg proceeded to offer me some of her own beauty powder, as she called it. She prepared four lines of white powder on a pocket mirror and quickly snorted two. Gripped by the mood and hoping to get my nerves under control, I took the other two. It didn't take long before my anxiety had gone and I actually started looking forward to the interview.

We chatted and joked before we went on. I felt safe. It was as if we were sharing something important and I could tell her everything.

The studio consisted of two partitions with bookcases filled with fake book spines, a red velvet sofa for the guests and an armchair for the host. The style was elegant and subdued, with a deep carpet, standing lamps and dark colours. We sat down and while she reviewed her notes one final time, I took the opportunity to study my surroundings. Two cameramen were doing focus checks and beyond the cameras' range there were cables everywhere and clusters of lights suspended from a grid in the ceiling. The crew seemed almost indifferent to us; as far as they were concerned we were merely part of the set.

The interview began and Linda Hvilbjerg opened by congratulating me on my success and the huge interest. Had I ever expected it? I replied – as I had done in the countless interviews I had given recently – that it was probably something you could never really prepare yourself for, but that I was enjoying it after having worked for it for a long time. We talked about the furore the book had caused and violence in the media in general. These were all questions I had been asked before and I knew the answers to them blindfolded, but even so, Linda, the atmosphere and – let's not forget – her beauty powder made it resemble an intimate conversation rather than a hard-hitting interview. I gave more of myself than usual and felt good about it. She also flirted a little, which probably did no harm.

Halfway through the interview, she asked me how I managed to come up with all that horror and describe it in such detail that the images evoked were almost unbearable. I had answered that question before, but this time I didn't fob her off with the standard answer.

This time I told her the truth.

Ironika was a huge part of my life when I wrote *Outer Demons*. My day revolved around her and, in her own way, she had been my inspiration. I would often carry her around the flat; she liked that. While she lay there, defenceless and filled with trust and love, I explored my greatest fear: what was the worst thing that could happen to her? Parenthood had changed my outlook on life, there was nothing I wouldn't do for my daughter, and it was this total surrender that paved the way for an even stronger emotion: fear. What if anything happened to her? I conjured up my worst nightmares and examined my reaction. If I couldn't bear to think about it happening to my daughter, I would use it in my book; otherwise I would dismiss it and carry on searching. To this end, I would wander around the flat rummaging through drawers for suitable instruments of torture and explore the most terrifying scenarios inspired by my fear.

The victims in *Outer Demons* were teenage girls, not infants, but the ideas behind what they were subjected to were rooted in my days with Ironika.

This was roughly the answer I gave Linda Hvilbjerg. A moment of silence followed and I detected a change in her eyes. Not revulsion or distance, but a kind of admiration or ecstasy. She carried on her line of questioning and asked about other sources of inspiration, which authors I read and who my role models were.

When the interview was over, I felt very pleased. Linda Hvilbjerg was downright elated. She claimed it was one of the best interviews she had ever done and she thanked me warmly. Her eyes had taken on a relentless aggression, a hunger that made me feel a little uneasy.

Intoxicated by her beauty powder and flattering attention, I was persuaded to go to a party with her. She had her party clothes in her dressing room and used the studio's facilities to get ready. In the meantime I was installed in a sofa with a gin and tonic and a pile of magazines.

When Linda Hvilbjerg came out from make-up, she was transformed. The discreet bluestocking was gone and in her place there stood before me a red-carpet beauty in a clinging dark dress, white earrings and her hair piled up.

Embarrassed, I apologized for my own appearance, but she wouldn't hear of it, grabbed me by the arm and led me to a waiting taxi.

The party was held in Nørrebro in a large artist's studio that had been taken over by an advertising agency and turned into their offices. There wasn't a desk in sight. The floor had been cleared and lights mounted on the ceiling beams high above us. Professional DJs created an impenetrable wall of electronic music. Linda knew many of the people there, and I could make out a few familiar faces, but it was impossible to have a conversation.

We knocked back a couple of green cocktails and tried to dance, but we soon agreed that we were in need of something stronger. Linda gestured towards the lavatories and we made our way through dancing guests and conversations being shouted between frocks and suits.

The party covered both floors of the building, so we went downstairs where the noise level was lower and there was no queue for the lavatories. A few clusters of people who had escaped the pandemonium were hanging around. They stared hungrily after Linda as we passed them by.

The lavatory was newly renovated with black wall and floor tiles and large mirrors over square sinks with brass taps. There were three cubicles, all vacant, and we chose the furthest. I locked the door and Linda took out her pocket mirror from her handbag. She set up four lines while I rolled a one-hundred kroner note into a tube. We took turns snorting the lines.

As I snorted the last one, Linda threw back her head, closed her eyes and inhaled deeply with a huge smile on her lips. She giggled, opened her eyes a little and looked at me through the narrow cracks.

'Do you know something?' she said, resting her hands on my shoulders.

'You're really a man?'

Linda Hvilbjerg giggled again. 'You'd like that, wouldn't you?'

'Not at all,' I replied quickly and placed my hands on her hips. 'What a waste that would be.'

'Your book is crap,' she stated boldly.

'OK,' I replied and removed my hands as if I had burned myself.

She merely laughed. 'But you know something?' She took my hands and put them back on her hips. 'It made me so horny.'

I let my hands glide around her back and over her buttocks. They tensed slightly as I grabbed them. I could feel through the flimsy fabric that she wasn't wearing any knickers.

'And what did you do about it?' I asked in a thick voice. The drugs were starting to work; Linda seemed to glow and my penis strained against my trousers.

'I took the book with me to bed.' She started unbuttoning my shirt. Her hands found their way in and brushed my chest before moving down to the waistband of my trousers. 'I lay down completely naked,' she carried on, while her fingers undid my belt buckle. 'And read the best sections while I touched myself.'

I started pulling up her dress, inch by inch.

'I imagined it was me who was lying there, tied up.' She sighed when she finally released my penis, which willingly jumped to freedom. 'Me being fucked . . . everywhere . . . and not being able to stop it.'

Her dress was now up so much so that I could reach her groin with my hand. Her body twitched when I touched her labia and she grasped the root of my dick with a grip that threatened to cut off the blood supply.

'I came like a fucking train,' she whispered, lifting up one leg and placing her foot on the cistern to give me better access. 'This is my way of saying thank you.'

It may have been the drugs, but sex with Linda Hvilbjerg was the kinkiest I had ever had. It was not passionate as with Line, but wild and demanding as if the world was about to end. The sweat poured from us and we gasped for air when we finally came. I collapsed on the toilet seat with my trousers around my ankles and she sat astride me, with my penis still inside her.

Linda laughed quietly between her heavy breathing.

'That's going to hurt in the morning,' she said.

Morning. Suddenly it dawned on me that there was a tomorrow, a day with a wife, a child and work. A life with people who meant the world to me. It was as if my body expelled me and I floated up above the cubicle where we were sitting and observed the tawdry scene below. The attraction vanished. My penis shrivelled and withdrew from Linda's body. The bile rose in my throat and I felt so woozy I had to close my eyes.

When I opened them again, Linda was fixing her hair. Her face and throat were still a touch flushed.

'I'll see you upstairs,' she said, leaning forward to give me a quick kiss before she left the lavatory.

All I could think about was getting out of there. I stood up, my legs shaking, and pulled up my trousers. My shirt was soaked in sweat and my trembling hands could barely button it. I gave up trying to stuff it inside my trousers and went outside. It was cold and I skulked along the buildings until I found a taxi. I wished the trip would last all night and delay the meeting with my real life, but I was home in an instant.

I hesitated. My heart pounded and sweat was dripping from my forehead again. It was just after midnight and Line had probably gone to bed. I inhaled deeply a couple of times, slipped the key in the lock and carefully opened the door. It was dark, but I refrained from switching on the light. Having closed the door behind me, I stepped out of my shoes and peeled off my jacket. I sneaked over to the door to Ironika's bedroom and peered inside. Despite the darkness, I could see she wasn't in her bed. When I wasn't at home, she would sometimes sleep in the double bed with Line, so I tiptoed to the master bedroom. I held my breath and listened out. There was no sound. Slowly, holding out my hands, I walked through the darkness towards the place where the bed was.

It was empty.

I switched on the bedside lamp and realized that my hands hadn't been mistaken. The bed hadn't been slept in. A wave of relief washed over me. Perhaps there was still time for me to take a shower and wash off the smell of Linda? But my relief soon turned into worry. If they weren't here, then where were they? I entered the living room and switched on the light.

Line was sitting in the armchair by the window, her arms folded across her chest and an insistent gaze directed at me. She wasn't smiling.

'How could you do it, Frank?'

Her eyes didn't leave me and I felt like cowering. My palms grew sweaty and my cheeks felt hot.

'What do you mean?' I managed to say, but it sounded low and hollow.

Still it was a fair question. Line couldn't possibly have known that I had been with Linda. Yes, people had entered the lavatory while we were at it, but I couldn't have been so unlucky that it was someone who knew me and Line – that was *too* improbable. My remorse at my infidelity vanished temporarily.

I straightened up and flung out my hands. 'What have I done?'

While I waited for her to reply, I scanned my brain to retrieve any event that might have made her angry, things I had said or done or failed to do, but I couldn't find anything.

'How could you have such thoughts about our daughter?' Line said at last.

The interview! It was the interview. At that point in time, I was so full of my success that I failed to see the connection between the television interview and Line's reaction. How could I? It seemed to me that the interview had been a triumph, and that was also the impression Linda Hvilbjerg had given me.

I took a step towards Line. The right thing would have

been to go to her and hold her in my arms to reassure her and convince her, but the smell of sex and Linda Hvilbjerg still lingered on my body and in my clothes, so I stopped. She must have interpreted it as hesitation because she looked away and her face took on a resolute expression.

'So it's true,' she said. 'You fantasized about mutilating and murdering my daughter.'

'That wasn't what I meant,' I protested. 'Or, I mean . . . I would never . . .'

'Don't you think it sounds a little bit sick, Frank?'

I shook my head. 'I would never hurt her,' I said. 'I love Ironika more than anything in the world.'

Line's eyes bored into me again. They were filled with distrust.

'I've read the book, Frank,' she said slowly. 'I can't even begin to imagine how you can think like this and certainly not in the presence of Veronika.'

I looked around, searching for the object of the discussion, who had been here while I wrote the book and approved every line. Perhaps she could come to my rescue, deflect this row.

'She's with her granddad,' Line said.

I felt torn in half. One part was consumed with the most profound guilt at having been unfaithful to Line, the other with righteous indignation at being treated unfairly. The two halves couldn't agree and their opposite qualities cancelled out any decent course of action. The result was that I simply stood there, gawping at my wife without defending myself or apologizing to her.

Line stared at me for a while, but as I didn't react, she got up with a sigh.

'It's no good,' she said. 'I need time.'

I stepped forwards, but she held up her hand to me.

'Alone,' she said as she walked to the door.

I retreated slightly as she passed me. The smell of Linda was still very fresh on me, but to Line it must have looked as if I was giving up on her. I still couldn't think of anything sensible to say and she got dressed in silence and left the flat without looking at me. From the window I saw her wheel her bicycle in the direction of Amager. At the corner, she turned around and looked up at the flat.

Away from Line's accusing eyes, the half of me that felt victimized got the upper hand. I went over the interview and replayed the exchange in my mind. I hadn't lied, this was how *Outer Demons* had been conceived, but to think . . . it was precisely because I loved my daughter that I had been able to write such dreadful things. They were my worst nightmares, the most revolting things I could imagine ever happening to her.

The anger surged in me until I could no longer suppress it. I punched the sofa, kicked cushions and furniture, howled at the door through which Line had left.

I was upset and I felt betrayed. Of all people, Line ought to understand me.

When I had finished punishing the furniture, I collapsed from exhaustion.

My guilt slowly returned. If I didn't deserve to burn in hell because of the interview, then I deserved it for my disastrous mistake with Linda Hvilbjerg. The whole episode had been so grotesque that I could hardly describe it as infidelity, but of course that was what it was. I was a bastard, a terrible father and a rotten husband. My anger with Line had disappeared – she was right. I was a bad person who hurt the people around me. I cried, raged and beat myself up as the pathetic loser I was. I ran around the flat, slammed my palms against the walls and door frames, threw myself on the floor. At one point I drank gin straight from the bottle and my fits of rage ebbed away as my blood alcohol percentage increased. My vision blurred and the light faded until at last everything around me grew dark.

I woke up in a foetal position on the bathroom floor. It stank of vomit and urine. The stench made my nausea worse and I just managed to raise myself to the toilet bowl before the bile poured out of me. I could have saved myself the trouble. The floor was already swimming in vomit and piss.

I struggled to stand up and I looked at myself in the mirror. It was cracked from when I had headbutted it at some point during the night and I had a split eyebrow to show for it. My clothes were wet, lumps of vomit were stuck to my hair and the whites of my eyes depicted a fine, intricate river delta of blood. I stood like this for a couple of minutes, studying the wreckage in what remained of the mirror. Slowly I undressed and threw my clothes in the bath. I poured water and detergent into a bucket, found a cloth and started cleaning the floor.

It was over.

From now on, I would pull myself together.

I had to get my family back. No more alcohol or drugs, no more benders, no more parties or receptions and definitely no more Linda Hvilbjerg.

21

Though I had never been there before, I knew that Rentemestervej hadn't changed. I have always imagined north-west Copenhagen as grey, gloomy and neglected, and it didn't disappoint when I arrived in a taxi straight from Bjarne and Anne's flat. Once I got Mortis's address, I made my excuses and left. Bjarne was clearly worried. He almost certainly knew I'd go straight to Rentemestervej, but he said nothing and he didn't try to stop me. Perhaps he believed that seeing Mortis would clear up the situation for me and finally convince me I was on the wrong track.

I started having doubts myself as I stood outside number 43. It was a yellow brick building, but over time sunlight and exhaust fumes had given it a sickly grey hue, like a chain smoker's fingers. Cheap aluminium balconies had been screwed to the brickwork outside every flat in the three-storey building, but most of the residents used them to store rubbish or junk they had no room for inside. It was hard to imagine anyone in this block could plan or manage anything other than basic survival.

On the ground floor I studied the list of residents and

found Morten's name. Morten Jensen. Of course. That was the reason I had been unable to find him through Directory Enquiries. Mortis's real name was Morten Due Jensen, but in the Scriptorium days he refused to use Jensen and called himself Morten Due. 'Jensen is the name of the bog-standard Dane,' he said if anyone asked. He wanted to stand out from the crowd. He wanted to be someone. It would appear he had changed his mind.

The communal light switched itself off, so I switched it back on and headed up the stairs. I hesitated once I reached Mortis's door. I didn't really know why I had come. Perhaps it was to check he really existed, now confirmed by the white plastic letters on the letter flap.

There was no doorbell, so I knocked on the door, three hard knocks that echoed in the stairwell. It was quiet behind the door. I waited a few seconds and knocked again, but there was still no response. Irritated, I squatted down, pushed open the letter flap and tried to peer inside. It was completely dark.

'Morten?' I called out, my lips close to the flap.

I refused to accept I'd come in vain. It couldn't be a dead end. There was too much at stake.

I lifted the doormat to check if there was a key. Of course there wasn't, but the idea wasn't that far-fetched. Mortis had a tendency to lose things when he went out, so back in the Scriptorium days he had always kept a spare key somewhere. I got up and traced my fingers along the top of the door frame, but all I got out of it was a cushion of dust. Perhaps he had got better at looking after his keys? I pushed down the door handle, just to make sure he hadn't given up on keys altogether, but the door was locked.

The communal light switched itself off and the light from the moon shone on me from a window between the floors. I walked up a few steps to the window and opened it. My heart started racing. Mortis's balcony was only two or three metres from the window and I could see that the balcony door was ajar. The balcony itself was only a couple of metres square; I could see that it was littered with empty bottles, leaving a small area clear around the door.

My eyes sought out the building across the road. It was only eleven o'clock, so there was still light coming from most of the flats. Televisions glowed in some of them, others had candlesticks on the windowsills or tea lights in saucers. But there were no people to be seen, no one who would notice an intruder on the balcony.

I rested my forehead against the window frame and closed my eyes. How badly did I want to do this? If I fell from the second floor, I could break both arms and legs, and if I was very unlucky, I might end up dead. The image of Verner in the hotel bed surfaced in my mind. Mortis was my only real clue. Admittedly only in the form of a pseudonym from one of my own novels in which room 102 had been booked, but nevertheless it was a clue, it was a name.

I opened my eyes and pushed up the window. The sill outside was fairly wide. The pigeons had discovered this too and it was covered in pigeon shit. I held on tight to the window frame, climbed up and out on to the sill. I knelt down, like a runner on a starting block, and concentrated on the balcony diagonally below. The blood was pumping around my body as if I was preparing for a parachute jump rather than a leap of a couple of metres. The hand that was gripping the window frame was starting to get sweaty.

I checked the building opposite and I set off.

My feet slipped in bird poo, my arms reached out, my eyes focused on the balcony. I felt the wind against my face as I moved through the air. It wasn't elegant or graceful, more like a diver jumping from the three-metre board and suffering a heart attack halfway. The balcony rushed closer and my chest banged into the railing followed by the rest of my body. It sounded very loud to my ears and all I could think about was getting inside the balcony and out of sight. I climbed over the railing and slid down on a sea of empty bottles. The clinking sound rang out between the blocks.

The impact had knocked the air out of me and I inhaled greedily until a sharp pain in my left side made me stop. I tried to breathe more calmly, but it still hurt. Had I been able to swear or scream I would have done so, but all I was capable of was gasping. Carefully I lifted a hand and touched my ribs. My body contracted as my fingers explored the left side of my chest. More bottles on the balcony toppled. I gritted my teeth and closed my eyes.

It took me a couple of minutes to get my breathing under control. I heard someone call out and a door nearby being closed; apart from that, it was quiet. The bottles underneath me felt like a pile of stones, but I didn't dare move even though my body ached all over. The crash might have woken up the whole block, but I prayed that no one had seen me and that the noise had echoed around the walls so its origins couldn't be identified. I lay there for another five minutes to make absolutely sure.

The door to the balcony couldn't be opened immediately. The bottles had rolled everywhere and in order to make room for the door, I had to move several of them while remaining unseen. My ribs hurt with every movement and I was forced to pause to catch my breath. At last I had cleared enough space to open the door and sneak inside.

When I could lie down on my back on the living-room floor, I allowed myself to moan loudly. I examined my ribs again, but could find no sign of fracture.

The flat was quiet. All I could hear was my own laboured breathing. The place smelled stuffy and close. The balcony door might have been ajar, but not enough to air the room. I was lying on a parquet floor and a short distance away from me was a dark leather sofa, an armchair and a coffee table. Empty bottles and cups of cold coffee and cigarette butts were scattered across the table. What appeared to be big frames of some sort were lined up against the walls and it wasn't until I had closed the blinds and switched on the light that I realized the frames were bookcases, empty bookcases.

I was taken aback. Mortis loved books and a home without books would be anathema to him. The TV stand was also empty. A black square in the dust revealed that a television had sat there until very recently.

In the hall lay a huge pile of newspapers and post, mainly bills. They had been pushed to one side behind the door so you could just about open it. I found what I was looking for: Mortis's spare key hanging from an elastic band right next to the letter flap so you could pull it out with a finger, if you knew where it was. My ribs protested and I cursed loudly.

I found the most recent newspaper and checked the date. It was over a month old. Had Mortis moved, done a runner or was he just too lazy to sort his post?

The bottle collection carried on into the kitchen and the fridge was just as empty as the bookcases in the living room. Plates, glasses and pizza boxes littered the work-tops and the sink. Only a few clean plates were left in the cupboards.

I pushed open the door to the bathroom. The light was already switched on and revealed walls of yellow plastic with rounded corners, which were probably easy to clean, but reminded me of a passenger ferry. It stank of urine and the toilet bowl was brown from limescale and muck. An empty gin bottle lay in the sink. The shower curtain was mouldy and pulled across.

I was just about to switch off the light and close the door when something made me stop. As I was there I might as well make sure I hadn't overlooked anything. I went back, grabbed the shower curtain and prepared to fling it aside. I held my breath. My brain and my heart had already told me what I would find, the biggest horror film cliché of them all, a body in the bath, naked, pale and staring at me with accusing eyes.

With a brisk movement, I opened the shower curtain.

Mortis lay curled up in the shower tray. His long body was folded up in the small space, but he wasn't naked and he wasn't staring at me with dead eyes. He looked like he was asleep. His hair was shoulder length, wispy and had acquired streaks of grey since the last time I saw him. He wore a white shirt with yellow stains; a pair of black jeans concealed his skinny legs. His feet were bare and practically ashen.

I squatted down and held out a hand to him.

'Morten.'

His shoulder was scarily fragile and I took care not to shake it too violently. I pressed a couple of fingers against his neck. There was a pulse; it was weak, but it was there.

At that moment Mortis's body jerked, he opened his mouth and threw up all over my hand in an odd mechanical movement. I leapt up and took a step backwards.

'Bloody hell, Mortis,' I cursed. I washed my hands while keeping an eye on him. My concern had turned into irritation.

He didn't move, but started to snore, loudly and regularly. Nor did he react when I straightened him up in the shower cubicle. His head lolled from side to side and he coughed once, but he accepted being moved into an upright sitting position. He stank of vomit though he clearly hadn't eaten for a long time.

I swore again, took the showerhead and hosed Mortis's stomach contents down the drain, before directing the jet of water at him. Eventually the water soaked into his greasy hair and flowed down his face and chest.

He tried to move his head away from the water, but I followed him and turned up the cold water. He spewed bubbles and rambled some swear words.

'Morten!'

His eyelids twitched and deep furrows emerged on his forehead.

'It's me, Frank!'

His lips appeared to repeat my name and the furrows grew deeper. Suddenly his eyelids sprang open and he stared directly at me.

'What the hell,' he muttered.

I turned off the water. 'Are you OK?'

His gaze was swimming and his half-open eyes looked around the bathroom and down his clothes before returning to me. 'Frank?'

'From the Scriptorium.'

'Yes, yes . . . what an honour.' Mortis swallowed a couple of times before expelling a long belch. 'I don't remember . . . I don't remember inviting you.' He shut his eyes for a moment, but then he glared at me. 'Why can't a man be allowed to party in peace?'

'Party?'

'Yes, for Christ's sake, party . . . you know . . . it's . . . what day is it?'

'Friday.'

'That's right!' He had barely spoken the words before his head slumped on one shoulder and his eyes closed.

22

Bjarne arrived at one o'clock in the morning.

I called him from Mortis's mobile and he hadn't sounded surprised. Anne drove the car, a Volvo of a square design, spacious and with seatbelts everywhere. She parked right outside the entrance door so Bjarne and I could easily lift Mortis on to the back seat.

He was still unconscious. Occasionally he would mutter to himself, but he hadn't opened his eyes or spoken coherently since the shower cubicle. None of us said anything on the way back to their flat. Anne made up a bed in the spare bedroom, my old Scriptorium room, and Bjarne and I took off Mortis's clothes, dressed him in an old pair of Bjarne's pyjamas and put him to bed.

'Just like the old days, eh?' Bjarne said, as we watched our sleeping Scriptorium brother.

I laughed briefly, at the same time thinking this was nothing like the old days.

Bjarne promised to keep Mortis indoors for a couple of days. He didn't want to know the reasons for my request; to him it was enough that our mutual friend needed help.

I think he felt ashamed at his failure to respond when Mortis contacted him a couple of months ago. He ought to have known, he said over and over.

Once Mortis was safely installed, I left Bjarne and wandered down to the Lakes. I sat down on a bench and stared across the water. Neon advertisements reflected in the surface of the water, but numerous little waves broke up the images into smaller, sharper stripes of light, blinking in an infinite variety of patterns. I was mesmerized by this dance of light for a long time. I can't remember what, if anything, was going on behind my unfocused eyes.

What I do remember when I stood up again was a sense of resolution. I had a feeling that everything was up to me. It was impossible to know if Mortis was part of the killer's plan, but if he was, I had just saved his life. I had thwarted the killer's game plan, refused to play along and therefore won this round. This meant, I felt, that I wasn't fighting a losing battle. There was hope. The time had come to take action and apply all of my criminal imagination to getting out of this mess, like a fighter, stronger than before.

The problem was that my only real clue hadn't lead to a breakthrough. All I had to go on now was my instinct, but then again, why wouldn't that be enough? If the killer was really trying to get me, he must have made an effort to get inside my head, understand my thinking, and I could exploit that as a kind of double bluff.

My reconstruction of Verner's last moments might turn out to be quite near the truth. All I had to do was find Lulu – that is, if she really existed. My contact with the police had ended with Verner's death and I couldn't start asking them questions without attracting unnecessary attention.

If I was going to find Lulu, I would have to do it on my own.

I knew I stood no chance of getting information out of the prostitutes in Vesterbro if I was on foot. They would think I was a policeman. However, there was no risk anyone would take my old Toyota Corolla for a police car, so I fetched it and drove towards Halmtorvet.

Urban regeneration had improved the old red-light district considerably and initially the hookers had been scared off. Nevertheless the area's reputation had been hard to shake off and a few years later the prostitutes returned to their old haunts because that was where the punters came looking for them.

I drove down Søndre Boulevard. The girls were lined up at fifty-metre intervals, some in pairs, others alone. They were mainly foreign, dark like the night or pale with angular, Russian features. When I slowed down, they would walk up to the car with a frozen smile and their eyes fixed at a spot behind me.

'We have sex?' they asked in a voice that sounded like a recording.

I was looking for a white girl. Verner had nothing but contempt for East European or African women and I knew they would never have been able to lure him anywhere.

The sad and bleak expressions in the women's faces failed to move me. My brain had switched to survival mode and the feelings and predicaments of others were lost on me. I was on a mission: Mission Frank Føns.

I turned down the women's offers, but asked if they knew a Danish girl who had worked the Marieborg Hotel last Wednesday, and described the girl from the lift. Most of them didn't understand me or knew nothing about it. One of them suggested I went to Istedgade, a street favoured by the Danish prostitutes, and I followed her advice.

Istedgade had more traffic, better lighting and was indeed more popular with the Danish girls. There was a greater degree of presence with them and their approach seemed more genuine, or at least better rehearsed.

After only a few enquiries, I struck lucky with a tall slim woman with jet black hair, enormous breasts and a huge firm bum. The whole package was poured into a tight-fitting black catsuit and a white jacket.

'You're looking for Marie,' she said with the accent of a docker, never letting her chewing gum rest. 'That was the easiest job she has ever had.'

'Do you know where she is?'

'What do you want with her? You a cop or something?'

'No, no,' I said quickly. 'Someone recommended her.'

'Right,' the black-haired woman said, still staring at me with distrust. 'And what's wrong with me,' she said, opening her white jacket to give me a better view of the inflated breasts.

'Perhaps some other time,' I said and smiled. 'I'll give you two hundred if you tell me where she is.'

She looked around and held out her hand. I found my wallet and fished out two hundred kroner, which quickly disappeared down her cleavage.

'Try Saxogade,' she said, nodding further down the

street. 'But she has the decorators in so she's only up for French and hand jobs.'

'Decorators?' I asked, but interrupted myself. 'Oh, I get it. OK.'

'Are you sure you wouldn't prefer a filly whose equipment is in full working order?'

I declined and drove on to Saxogade.

'Ask for Monica next time!' she called out after me. 'Monica!'

I found Marie sitting on a doorstep in Saxogade. She was small and thin, just like I remembered her when I bumped into her in the lift. Her hair was blonde and her skin pale, where she hadn't covered it with blusher. Her make-up was slapped on as if she had applied it going down the stairs. Her vacant eyes registered that I stopped the car and she forced the corners of her mouth into something that resembled a smile but only made her look worse.

I asked if she had been to the hotel two days ago.

She closed her eyes as if it took all of her concentration to remember what day it was and where she had been. When she didn't reply, I thought she might have fallen asleep. I got out of the car and went over to her.

'Lulu,' I said, prodding her. 'Did you go to the Marieborg Hotel last Wednesday?'

She opened her eyes. 'My name's not Lulu.'

I shook my head. 'Did you meet Verner, the police officer, there?'

I spotted a flicker of recognition in her eyes.

'Oh, Paedo? Yes, yes.'

My heart began to pound and I could barely control myself.

'What happened?' I asked. 'Who contacted you?'

Marie stared at me. 'Who the hell are you?'

I straightened up and glanced around. 'I'm a friend of Verner's. I need to know what happened.'

'How much?'

'What do you mean?'

She rolled her eyes. 'How much do you need to know?'

I reached for my wallet. 'What do you want?' I asked.

She wiped her nose with her hand. 'I need a hit,' she said. 'And I need it now. Business is bad when you're on the rug and I need something now.'

'OK, Lulu,' I said. 'How much is it?'

'Why do you keep calling me Lulu?'

'Sorry. Marie,' I corrected myself and looked up and down the street again. 'How much is it?'

She peered at me through half-closed eyes. 'Eleven hundred per gram,' she said.

I only had five hundred in cash, but I nodded. 'Deal.'

'That's twenty-two hundred,' she added quickly. 'I need two grams.'

I protested, but she interrupted me.

'Do you want to know what happened or not?'

'OK,' I said. 'Tell me what you know.'

Marie shook her head. 'Oh, no, that's not how we do it. Drugs first.'

We both stood up and got into the car.

'OK, where we going?'

'Just drive to Enghave Plads and I'll direct you from there.' Her eyes stared straight ahead at the reward waiting for her.

I stopped at a cashpoint in Istedgade to get some more

money. At Enghave Plads she directed me through some side streets before telling me to stop outside a 7-Eleven.

'Here?' I asked.

'No, it's a bit further down the street,' she replied. 'But you'll wait here. If they see a strange car outside the flat, they'll shit themselves.' She held out her hand.

'How do I know you'll come back, Lulu?' I asked as I counted out the twenty-two hundred kroner.

'Cut that Lulu crap, OK?'

I held up my hand in a conciliatory gesture. 'How do I know you'll come back, Marie?' I repeated.

'I'm not shooting up in there again. Once I woke up with no knickers and spunk all over me. I'm not doing that again.' She snatched the notes from my hand. 'And get me some water.'

Marie left the car and walked down the street. I watched her and wondered if I had just waved goodbye to twenty-two hundred kroner and the last real clue I had.

23

Fifteen minutes later, Marie returned.

I had been into 7-Eleven to buy cigarettes and a bottle of water. I spent the rest of the time smoking and regretting that I had allowed myself to be duped so easily. Again. I knew perfectly well what people would promise in return for a hit, a drink, a beer or some dosh. Consequently I was both surprised and relieved when I saw Marie stroll casually towards the car, her hands deep in the pockets of her puffer jacket and a small smile on her lips.

The car was thick with smoke from the two cigarettes I had managed to get through.

'That took you long enough,' I said as she flopped down on the passenger seat. I handed her the water bottle. 'OK, out with it.'

She shook her head. 'You'll have to help me,' she said, passing back the bottle to me. 'I can't do it on my own.'

I looked around. 'Here?'

She pointed to a place somewhere behind us. 'We can drive to the railway if you're shy.'

I started the car and drove from her directions to an

area bordering the railway tracks at Enghave station. It was a site for storing railway sleepers and old rails, which shared the plot with piles of gravel and building waste. I switched off the engine and turned on the light inside the car. The yellow light made Marie looked even sicklier.

She took out two tiny home-made envelopes and passed one to me along with a white beaker as she wriggled out of her puffer jacket. Her arms were scarily thin and I wondered how such a small body could cope with her line of business. Having removed her jacket, she took back her drugs and prepared them with practised motions. Her withdrawal symptoms had gone, exorcised at the mere prospect of a fix.

'Who hired you?' I asked while she worked away.

'I've never seen him before,' Marie replied, never taking her eyes off the beaker. 'It might sound like a big fat lie, but he wore a hat and sunglasses and he had a beard.'

Sunglasses. In a flash, I remembered the man from the book signing, but I couldn't remember whether he had a beard. All I could remember was the sunglasses and the smile he had given me, but I was fairly certain he hadn't been wearing a hat and he didn't have a beard.

'Could it have been false beard?'

'What do I know? His money was real enough.'

'What did you have to do?'

'And he was speaking in a weird way, spooky.'

'You mean he changed his voice?' I asked.

'I think so,' Marie replied.

'What did he say?'

'He showed me a photo of the bastard, Paedo, I mean, and told me to wait for him outside the hotel. When he came out, I was to make him come up with me to room 102, that was all, the easiest money I've ever made.' She snorted. 'Though he was creepy . . . intense, like. I'm good with numbers, but he insisted I repeated it ten times at least. 102, 102, 102 . . . psycho.'

The heroin was ready and Marie sucked the fluid into a syringe and handed it to me.

'Wouldn't it be better if you did that yourself?' I asked.

'Nope,' Marie replied. 'Almost all my veins are messed up so it's got to go in the neck. I'm not bloody doing that myself.' She tilted her head and bared her throat. Her artery stood proud on her fragile neck, like a crease in a white tablecloth. There were already a couple of needle scars.

I swallowed even though my mouth felt dry. I took the syringe. 'Are you sure?' I said.

She nodded. 'Quite sure.'

I grabbed hold of her neck with one hand and tried to work out where to insert the needle. 'And what happened then?' I asked.

'After some time Paedo came out of the hotel, just like he had said. The bastard even grinned when he saw me, said he was just in the mood for meeting me. Wanker. He was so horny he didn't even seem surprised when I told him I had a room ready where we could find out how much in the mood he really was.'

I held her neck with one hand and aimed the syringe with the other. The artery eluded my attempts at piercing it and Marie started to twitch.

'Come on, man.'

The needle found its destination and Marie smiled.

'What happened in the room, Lulu?'

'Well, he was . . . you called me Lulu again,' she protested.

'Sorry, go on.'

'Paedo was dead impatient and snatched the key from me to unlock the door. The lamp on the bedside table was lit, but apart from that it was dark. He pulled me inside and I closed the door like he told me to. I was scared shitless, man. Where the hell was the guy? I thought all I had to do was deliver Paedo and then get out of here. I hadn't reckoned on being screwed by that disgusting pig.'

I pressed the fluid into the artery and pulled out the syringe. Marie responded with a sigh. A drop of blood trickled from her neck and I wiped it away with my thumb.

'Carry on.'

'Right, when Paedo passed the door to the toilet, he finally came forward, the guy. He looked exactly like he did the first time I met him, dressed in a coat, a hat, sunglasses and everything. And he had a gun.' Marie giggled. 'You should have seen Paedo. Got the shock of his life. Almost made it worth it. He started stuttering and sweating and his face went all red.' Her voice had started to soften.

'In his scary voice, the guy told Paedo to sit down on the bed. He did, nearly pissing himself. He was shaking all over and held up his hands as if he could stop a bullet with them.' Marie laughed again. 'I got my money. The guy stuck his hand into his coat pocket without taking his eyes off Paedo and pulled out an envelope and gave it to me. A big fat one. It was my payment plus a bit extra, he said, so I would keep my mouth shut.' Marie sent me an embarrassed look. 'But a girl's gotta live.'

She smiled and her eyes took on a floating expression so I raised my voice.

'What happened then?'

'I left like he told me to,' she replied.

'Was that everything?' I asked. My voice sounded high-pitched and agitated inside the confined space.

Marie shook her head and smiled again. 'Mmmm,' she whispered.

I grabbed her by the shoulders. 'Tell me!'

Her eyelids were half closed.

I shook her gently. 'Marie! Did you notice anything about the guy?'

She opened her eyes again. 'You can call me Lulu now,' she said, and smiled, while her eyes swam away again.

'Anything!'

I shook her a little more forcefully and she widened her eyes with a hurt expression.

'Did you see anything else?'

'There was . . .'

'Yes?'

'A key,' she mumbled. 'He dropped a swipecard . . . when he pulled out the envelope . . . number 87.'

'A hotel keycard?'

Marie nodded at first, but then she shook her head.

'Not for the Marieborg,' she said. 'For the BunkInn.'

'Hotel BunkInn, are you sure?'

She nodded slowly and with every nod her eyelids lowered. I shook her again, but she didn't react. A small smile formed around her lips and she sank into the seat as if she could pass through its molecules.

I pulled away from Marie and stared at her. Now what? Should I leave her or wait? She had given me something to go on, but perhaps she knew more? Could I be sure that her memory was accurate?

I switched off the light in the car.

It was now very dark, but I could still see the outline of her. It started to get cold so I leaned over to put her back in her jacket. Her thin arms were limp and only reluctantly agreed to being stuffed into the sleeves again. It reminded me of the last time I got someone dressed. My daughters, oblivious in sleep and completely floppy as if their bones had dissolved. In this state they were helpless, trusting, at the mercy of those around them.

Having fumbled with the zip, I pulled it all the way up to Marie's neck. She muttered to herself and shifted in the seat until her head rested against the window. Part of me wanted to stay there, watch her sleep, but another part urged me to move on. I had got what I came for. I had no idea how long she would be out of it and I felt a growing sense of impatience.

Marie didn't react when I started the engine and drove back to Istedgade. The windows kept steaming up and I had to wipe the windscreen several times until the car had warmed up again. I drove up and down Istedgade a couple of times before I found Monica. She was getting out of a car, a small red Seat, and stretched her long body as the car accelerated and disappeared.

I drove closer and rolled down the window. 'Monica!'

'Hey, take it easy,' she said, trotting towards me. 'There's plenty to go around.' It took a moment before she recognized Marie and then me. 'What the hell, it's you again?'

'Hello, Monica.'

'You found her, I see.'

'Yes, thanks,' I replied. 'But she needs some help getting home.'

'What the hell have you done to her?' Monica's voice hardened.

'Nothing, she shot up in my car.'

Monica grunted and looked at Marie then back at me. 'And why is that my problem?'

I tried to smile. 'Because you're a good person and I'll give you five hundred kroner.'

'You bet I'm a good person,' she replied and held out her hand.

I gave her the money and Monica pulled Marie to standing as if it was a daily occurrence. As soon as they were out of the car, I shut the door and drove off. In my rear-view mirror, I could see the two girls clinging to each other as they staggered down the pavement.

It was almost half past three in the morning when I parked the car in front of the hotel. No one noticed me. The hotel was deserted and quiet. Exhausted, I walked through the lobby and straight to the lift. It started moving and I looked at myself in the mirror. My face was red and shiny with sweat running from my forehead. My eyes were bloodshot. It was a pathetic sight of a pathetic man. I had just helped a girl take heroin and then abandoned her to a life more horrifying than anything in my books.

The ping of the bell snapped me out of my trance and I stumbled out on my floor.

Back in my room I drank tap water until I couldn't swallow any more. Then I dumped my clothes in a heap and collapsed on the bed. I realized how tired I was, but in a sudden flash of panic I got up and went over to the coffee table. There I found a pen and wrote 'Marie – 87' on a scrap of paper. I stared at it for a long time before going back to my bed and burrowing under the duvets with the note in my hand.

How old was she? Twenty? Eighteen? Younger? When had it started? When she was Ironika's age?

24

The days after Line had left me were terrible. As I couldn't get to talk to her by telephone or by turning up at her father's house, I wrote to her instead. I was taken back to my school days when we'd conquered girls' hearts with our poetry, and though I never spoke to her directly, I sensed my letters had some effect. I had never written anything so straight from the heart; never before had I bared my soul the way I did in the missives I sent to her every day.

I told her how much I missed my little family, why I had said the things I had, and what was going on in my mind and in my now very empty life.

At the same time I worked on getting my apology through via Bjarne and Anne. They spoke to Line several times and I pleaded with them to pass on my feelings to her. Even though they too thought I had messed up, they soon started feeling sorry for me. I think they made it their mission to reunite us.

My life was still turned upside down because of the book. There were interviews and events I had to attend, but I hardly touched alcohol or drugs in that period, and I made sure I was at home as much as possible in case Line called. I passed the time doing all the little jobs I had put off in the last couple of years. DIY jobs around the flat, clearing out the basement lock-up, sorting out paperwork.

The breakthrough came after ten days of silence from Line. I was invited to dinner at Bjarne and Anne's and Line would be there too. 'We'll be able to enjoy the girls' cooking, just like the old days,' Bjarne declared. I was overcome by enormous relief, which was almost instantly replaced by anxiety. How would I make her take me back? I had been thrown a lifeline and if I didn't make the most of it, I would never forgive myself.

In the two days before the dinner, everything revolved around preparing for seeing Line. I had my hair cut, I bought new clothes, a blazer and a blinding white shirt, and I memorized questions to ask her, neutral questions that weren't about me, my books or what had happened, but questions about her and Ironika. I even took up running, which was rather silly as I only managed one run and nearly injured myself in the process. But it felt good. My aching body after my first run in seven years was proof of my commitment to this enterprise.

On the day itself all I did was get ready. I ironed my shirt, styled my hair and doused my body with scent. I left home in plenty of time, bought flowers on the way and tried to cycle at a sedate pace to avoid sweating. But it wasn't the bike ride that made me sweat, it was my nerves. I took off my jacket and stood outside the stairwell for a couple of minutes to cool down.

'Someone's had a makeover,' Bjarne exclaimed,

grinning. He was wearing jeans and a T-shirt, his usual uniform, and I suddenly felt like an idiot. In my shirt and blazer I looked like a cake decoration. I quickly took off my jacket and rolled up the shirtsleeves, while Bjarne enthused about tonight's menu.

'The girls are in the kitchen,' he said eventually, glancing at my bouquet.

I thanked him and walked through the living room and out into the kitchen with a dry sensation in my throat. I was met by loud laughter, and the sight of Line made me stop in the doorway. She was standing sideways, leaning against the kitchen table with a glass of wine in one hand. Her teeth showed as she laughed heartily and a small tear trickled from the corner of her eye and down her cheek. The girls carried on laughing until Anne noticed me.

'Hallo, Frank,' she exclaimed and raised her glass to me.

Line turned to face me. She seemed to be studying my shirt briefly, but then she smiled.

'Oh, are they for me?' Anne asked, reaching for the flowers.

I cleared my throat. 'Actually, they're for my wife,' I stammered.

'Really,' Anne huffed, pretending to be offended.

Line set down her glass and came over to me. She looked at the flowers and then me.

Hallo, Frank,' she greeted me quietly, snuggled up to me and hugged me. I held her tight and felt my eyes well up.

Anne coughed and reluctantly we let go of each other.

'These are for you,' I said, offering the flowers to Line.

She smiled and held them while Anne found a vase. An awkward silence descended on the kitchen.

'It's a little hot in here, isn't it?' I said and we all laughed.

'I think what you need is a glass of cold white wine,' Bjarne said and poured me a glass that disappeared far too quickly.

The dinner was almost like old times, we told stories and silly jokes. Bjarne and I baited each other and the girls teased Bjarne. I spoke less than usual, but I could barely take my eyes off Line. She seemed even more beautiful than I remembered her only twelve days ago and my infatuated glances were reciprocated when she didn't look away, blushing.

'It'll be fine,' Bjarne said when we sat in the armchairs, each with a whisky while the girls washed up.

'I don't remember ever feeling so nervous,' I confessed, glancing in the direction of the kitchen.

'Don't worry, the two of you will work it out, I just know it.' Bjarne stuck out his big paw of a hand and patted me on the shoulder. 'You two are made for each other.'

'I nearly ruined everything.'

Bjarne shook his head. 'Rubbish, what the two of you have can't be wrecked just by an interview.'

I hadn't told anyone about my one-night stand with Linda Hvilbjerg. As far as everyone else was concerned, the interview had been the tipping point, while I kept factoring in the episode with Linda in the lavatory. That was what I truly repented and Bjarne's words failed to assuage my guilt.

'I knew it right from the start,' Bjarne continued. 'The perfect couple.'

He had had a lot to drink, more than we normally did at this stage, and it showed.

'The successful author.' He pointed to me with his whisky glass, swirling the liquid around and nearly spilling it. 'And the world's loveliest dancer.' He raised his glass in a toast and we drank. 'Who have the most beautiful daughter in the universe.'

'May we live happily ever after,' I added and took another sip.

Bjarne leaned closer to me with a grave face.

'It's not a joke,' he said. 'I mean it. What the two of you have is special. Never forget that.' He drank his whisky and pulled a face. 'You have won life's lottery, hit the jackpot, got a hole-in-one, struck gold, your ship has come in—'

'I think I get it,' I interrupted him, grinning.

'I don't think you do,' he said, staring at his drink. 'I envy you and I'm embarrassed by that. Your book is a success, you have a lovely wife and an even lovelier kid.' He drank the rest of his whisky.

'You have Anne,' I pointed out. There was something in Bjarne's voice I had never heard before, something melancholic inconsistent with his normally jovial manner.

He nodded. 'I'm very fond of Anne,' he said. 'I think I love her. That's why I want to give her what you can give Line. I want to give her a successful husband, but more importantly, I wish I could give her a child.'

We had never talked about Anne's miscarriage, but I assumed it was one of those things and that they were still trying.

'It'll happen,' I said, placing my hand on his. 'Give it time.'

Bjarne shook his head and picked up the bottle.

'It's my sperm,' he said, half filling his glass with whisky. 'Something's wrong with it. The little fellows are sick.' He drank his whisky and topped up his glass. 'Anne is perfectly healthy. That's why she miscarried. Her body rejected the freak I had implanted in her.'

I reached for the bottle and, reluctantly, he let it go.

'Surely you can find a donor? Or adopt?'

Bjarne made a face. 'Somehow it just doesn't feel right, eh?'

'What doesn't feel right?' asked Anne, who had just entered the living room.

We straightened up in our chairs and exchanged looks.

'That Frank and I get married and moved to Samsø,' Bjarne said.

'Now, why on earth would you want to move to Samsø?' Line asked.

'Precisely,' Bjarne said, nodding. 'Precisely.'

The conversation carried on for a couple more hours, but Bjarne grew more and more drunk and unintelligible, so in the end Line and I thanked them and left. We had also drunk quite a lot and practically stumbled down the stairs, giggling at our clumsiness. I asked if I could see her home. She would like that, she said, but only as far as the garden gate. We cycled slowly through the city. I asked about Ironika and her, all the questions I had prepared but hadn't yet had the chance to ask. She replied that they missed me. When we reached Amager and Line's father's house, we ran out of things to say and we looked at each other.

I took her hand. It was cold, but she gave mine a small encouraging squeeze.

'Won't you come home soon, please?' I asked.

Line looked straight into my eyes and nodded. 'We'll come home tomorrow.'

She leaned towards me and kissed my lips. I closed my eyes for a moment. When I opened them again, she had got off her bicycle and was wheeling it up the garden path.

'I had a lovely time,' she said as she disappeared around the corner of the house.

'Me too!' I called out and my voice echoed between the buildings. I could hear her giggling. Then I stepped on the pedals and cycled home to the flat.

In the months that followed it was like our relationship had been reborn. We were together all the time. We talked about everything, laughed a lot and flirted at every opportunity. We rediscovered sex. We couldn't keep our hands off each other and it happened more than once that we were late for appointments because there was 'something' we just had to take care of before we could leave the flat.

Ironika enjoyed having a father again and I realized how much I had missed her small secretive smile. Fortunately she was oblivious that she had been the subject of our crisis.

It was also during this period that I developed the idea for *Join the Club*, which I believed would be my next project, a 'proper' novel, the one I would be remembered and admired for. Line was in favour. She supported and encouraged me almost to the point of excess. I suspected that some of her enthusiasm was sheer relief that I would be writing something far removed from *Outer Demons*.

Join the Club would be my effort at the great contemporary novel I had always imagined I was destined to write one day. The book would capture the age and the world we inhabited, a kaleidoscope of scenes from the everyday lives of a dozen different Danes and their experiences alone, in company and with each other. The stories would unfold with clockwork precision and eventually converge with pinpoint accuracy, although the reader wouldn't realize this until the final page. *Join the Club* centred on our common need to belong: the immigrant trying to access the Danish community, the workman who wants to write books, the gay man seeking acceptance from his family, the nerd who desperately wants a girlfriend, the engineer who would rather run a bar than build bridges, the disabled person who wants to be noticed, the model who wants to be admired for more than her looks, and so on. No one was mutilated or tortured to death, no one would be murdered by psychopathic killers or perverted kidnappers. It would be a book everyone could identify with, a book its readers could admit to having read; the book that would be my epitaph.

Ironika didn't like the idea. She had been there while I worked on *Outer Demons*, guiding me with smiles and grunts, but she cared little for *Join the Club*. Every time I whispered the story to her or read her samples, she burst into tears. This worried me a little, but I brushed it aside. After all, it was very early in the creative process.

Meanwhile, the momentum of *Outer Demons* was unstoppable. All the Nordic countries and most European ones bought it, the film rights went to a British company at an auction, but the really big prize was when we sold the book to the US market. The advance alone enabled us to buy a house in Kartoffelrækkerne and the subsequent royalties financed our holiday cottage in Rågeleje. Property prices were much lower back then, but the houses still represented considerable investments and for the first time I sensed that my parents believed I might actually be able to provide for their grandchild.

I let myself be dazzled by the money that poured in, and when Finn talked me out of writing *Join the Club*, the loss of potential earnings was a major argument. A contemporary Danish novel would never achieve the same sales figures as my breakthrough book, he claimed, and foreign sales were more or less out of the question. We discussed it on the plane to New York where I was meeting the American publisher, a small round man by the name of Trevor, who had an eye for European culture, especially literature and music. The music was mainly a hobby, but we always discussed music rather than books when we were together. It was on the way to meeting him for the first time that Finn buried *Join the Club*. During our eight-hour flight he convinced me it would be in my best interests to carry on writing horror stories. In his view, it was important to give the public what they wanted, and when they bought a Føns, they wanted to be scared. They expected to be shocked, outraged and possibly repulsed, but if an author didn't meet their expectations, his readers would turn their backs on him.

I was angry as well as disappointed when we reached New York, but our stay there changed my mind. We were treated like royalty. Trevor took us to all the right places and parties, got hold of the best tickets for the hottest shows and supplied us with everything we could eat, drink and snort. Our trip to New York was one big party, and after such treatment I was easily persuaded to carry on the party, even though it would require me to write another thriller.

It was weeks before I told Line that our shared project would have to wait due to image and financial considerations. She wasn't happy at all. In fact, she was so upset that she was willing to give up both the holiday cottage and the new house if necessary. I assured her it would only be for a short period, that the sacrifice would enable us to determine our own future. The words coming out of my mouth were Finn's. They were the very arguments he had used on me. I couldn't help feeling a touch of sadness when Line finally gave in and agreed that *Outer Demons* would be followed by two more books of the same genre. But after that no more splatter stories, as she referred to them.

When everyone had sworn to accept the plan, all I had to do was sit down and write. Only it wasn't as straight-forward as that. I felt like a cow that had been allowed to graze outside for some months, but had now been herded back to the darkness of the cowshed for the foreseeable future.

Moreover, there were plenty of other distractions. I was still invited to take part in interviews and talk shows. I had become the guy they called whenever there was a discussion of violence in literature, on television, in films or in computer games. I agreed to participate in anything from Saturday evening entertainment to writing columns in the local paper. The interruptions were welcome. They provided me with an excuse for not writing, because I had nothing to write. Every time I sat in front of the computer, the ability to express myself coherently deserted me. I was incapable of thinking of plots or structures. As my frustration rose, I invented more and more displacement activities. I always found time to go out with Bjarne, carry out domestic duties or simply let myself be swallowed up in the bosom of my family with Line and my daughter.

I opened up socially, but I shut down in terms of work. I told no one, not even Line, that I wasn't producing anything at all. She had sufficient delicacy not to ask too many questions and I sensed her tacit acceptance that I would complete the splatter trilogy without her, as long as I was present in the family. And present I was. I was the superdaddy who always had time to play with his daughter and I was the attentive husband who supported his wife in her career as a dancer.

All the things I failed to do as a writer, I achieved as a father, and fathers make babies, so when Line told me she was pregnant again, I was overwhelmed not only with joy, but also relief. Now I had yet another reason for not working, a project that no one would ever blame me for investing all my energy in. The best excuse in the world.

I'm fascinated by how the subconscious works. Sometimes I think there is a tug of war between the two halves of the brain, a battle between will and intuition. If one lets go, the other wins. When I tried to force myself to write or plot a story nothing happened, but when I adjusted to being a full-time father and postponed my writing, the story appeared effortlessly.

The idea for *Inner Demons* came shortly after Line got pregnant with our second daughter. We lay in bed, naked and sweaty after making love, and I rested my head in her lap while she ran her fingers through my hair. She wasn't showing very much yet, but her breasts had grown and were a little tender – to my great irritation, because she was quite hysterical when I handled them and I, in turn, couldn't get enough of them. Line's breasts weren't large, but when she was pregnant they grew to the size of a good handful and they hung perfectly.

I don't know how we got on to the subject, but we started talking about childbirth in earlier times, how tough it must have been without anaesthetic and how many maternal and infant deaths must have occurred. How would it affect a child to have been subjected to a traumatic birth where its mother had died, and the child had to live its life knowing it had caused its mother's death? It was this idea that started fermenting inside me and it would later form the premise for *Inner Demons*.

Line stopped dancing, but maintained her contacts to the profession through her job as an assistant at the Bellevue Theatre. This meant that I was alone with Ironika during the day and could focus on writing and looking after my daughter. It was almost like when I wrote *Outer Demons*, a father–daughter collaboration that brought us closer together.

Perhaps Line felt marginalized? One day she claimed I

was shutting her out and she was scared I was becoming too involved with my work. She didn't know precisely what I wrote, that was between me and Ironika, but she was aware that it was affecting me. I didn't share her view and couldn't understand her concern at all. The script grew day by day and with it my self-esteem as a writer returned. I had forgotten my ambitions with *Join The Club* and got a kick out of seeing the number of pages for *Inner Demons* increase, so perhaps she was right, I might have seemed a little distant and tired when I had written that day's quota of words. She considered taking early maternity leave, but I persuaded her to carry on for the benefit of her own career. Not because I couldn't work when she was at home, but I treasured the fixed routine of taking Ironika to and from nursery, and the pleasure of playing with her when she couldn't entertain herself. Line probably envied our closeness. It was as if Ironika and I shared a secret. We'd exchange private glances during dinner that went completely over Line's head. I felt a bit sorry for her, but we enjoyed our little game and I attached no further importance to its effect on Line.

Meanwhile Line's stomach grew and I followed her body's development closely. When Line had been pregnant with Ironika, I had been too busy with the various jobs I needed to do to pay the rent, but this time I had front-row seats. Apart from the fascinating study of how the female body changes, I had a secondary motive: it was of the utmost importance that every detail about pregnancy and birth was correct in the book. It's possible I may have been a little too curious. One evening when I was exploring her stomach and groin as usual, she pointed out that it would be nice if I could talk to her face rather than to her genitals for once.

A few days later something happened for which Line never forgave me.

Ironika had been in a sulk all morning and refused to go to nursery. This irritated me. I had hoped to be able to write four or five pages that day, but my daughter had now reached an age where she demanded constant attention. I tried to strike a deal with her. She would be allowed to stay at home if she could look after herself. I made myself a cup of coffee and sat down at the computer to work. The agreement with my daughter lasted ten minutes, then she appeared in the doorway with her plastic kitchen equipment and insisted we bake a cake. I tried very hard to control myself, but eventually I got rather angry. In a stern voice I told my daughter to go downstairs to the living room, play on her own and be quiet. If she didn't do that, I would take her to nursery and leave her there until the next day. It was an empty threat, of course, but it worked, and a crestfallen Ironika left my study and padded downstairs.

Not long after there was a crash from the kitchen followed by clattering sounds and a scream from my daughter.

I leapt up, ran downstairs and into the kitchen. Ironika was lying on the floor, sobbing. She was surrounded by knives, forks and other cutlery. She must have decided to bake a cake on her own and could just about reach the kitchen drawer, which she had pulled out, causing the utensils to rain down on her. To my horror, I saw a dark puddle of blood under her thigh and it was spreading with alarming speed. I lifted her up on the table, pulled down her trousers and spotted a deep cut to her inner thigh. It was a clear cut from one of the carving knives and the sight of blood pouring from it made me dizzy. I got hold of some tea towels and tied one around her thigh and closed the cut itself with another. Ironika was still howling, but she was also turning disturbingly pale.

I took her in my arms and ran out of the house. If necessary, I would run the two kilometres from Kartoffelrækkerne to the Central Hospital, but our neighbour, Kaj, had a car and was usually at home. Fortunately, he was in and took us to the hospital in the back of his old Saab. All the way I could see Ironika grow whiter and whiter, though I pressed against her cut as hard as I could. Her screaming had been reduced to a whimper and she could barely keep her eyes open.

The only thought I remember was: what have I done?

We were seen immediately when we arrived at A & E. Ironika was taken from me by people in white coats and moved directly to theatre. I called Line at work and told her what had happened. There was complete silence from the other end. I couldn't even hear her breathing. When she finally spoke, her voice was shaking and she announced she was on her way.

Even though it probably only took half an hour, it felt like days before they rolled Ironika out of theatre. They assured me that everything had gone well. She had received a blood transfusion and they had sutured the veins.

Line hadn't had turned up yet so I sat alone at Ironika's side while she slept. It was horrible to see her tiny body in the huge hospital bed, but she also looked so peaceful lying there, completely unaffected by the mayhem around her. When Line arrived she barely looked at me, but headed straight for the bed and took Ironika's hand. She cried very quietly, interrupted only by a sniff. I handed her a tissue and she blew her nose without looking at me.

When she finally spoke, it was in anger.

'Where were you? Why weren't you looking after her? Why wasn't she at nursery?'

The questions came one after the other, far too quickly for me to reply when a yes or a no wouldn't suffice. I took her in my arms and pulled her towards me. She resisted to begin with, but slowly relaxed and, at last, she embraced me and sobbed. I cried a little myself.

Line stayed with Ironika while I went back to the house, which we had left with no thought of locking the door or closing the windows. Adrenaline was pumping around my body. I couldn't help imagining how much worse it might have been; I was probably the luckiest man alive. In attempt to calm my nerves, I carried out all the housework I had planned to do that day. I washed clothes, tidied up the kitchen, carefully scrubbed the bloodstains off the kitchen floor and washed the cutlery and put it back in the drawer. I binned Ironika's bloodstained trousers. I didn't want them reminding me or others about the incident so I carried them all the way out to the bin in the street. When I had finished, the only trace of the accident was a dent in the kitchen floor where the knife had embedded itself after cutting my daughter's inner thigh.

When there were no more practical tasks to occupy my thoughts, I returned to the hospital to give Line a break.

I could see that she had spent the time thinking and she sent me a searching look when I arrived. I had to tell her the whole story again, where I had been when it happened, what had taken place in the moments leading up to the accident and how we had got to the hospital. Eventually she ran out of questions, but I could see that something was nagging her – a thought she couldn't or didn't dare to voice.

Ironika woke up and felt fine. Her vocabulary was still limited, but we understood that she had little recollection of what had happened. With some help from me she could remember being in the kitchen, but not the reason why she was now in hospital. However, she soon adjusted. We spoiled her with sweets and stories and made sure one of us was by her side constantly.

The next day all three of us came home.

Ironika was excited to see her room again and insisted on having a nap before we had even taken her coat off. Line and I stayed by her bed, watching her until she fell asleep. When we tiptoed downstairs, Line asked me to show her where precisely it had happened. I suppose I grew a little irritated. We had already talked about it and I thought it was over and done with, but Line insisted and I showed her the drawer and the mark in the floor from the knife. She thought it was strange that I had thrown away Ironika's trousers. They could easily have been mended and perhaps it wasn't such a bad idea to be reminded of the incident every now and again. I felt I was being attacked, forced to explain a simple accident as if it were the plot of a novel.

Finally I'd had enough. I stormed out to the bin to

fetch Ironika's trousers. It had started raining, naturally, and I had to rummage through the rubbish for a long time getting soaked in the process before I gave up looking for them. The trousers weren't there. Litter lay scattered around me on the pavement and I was aware of our neighbours' curtains twitching. Either the bin had been emptied or someone had taken the trousers. I started clearing up while I cursed myself for having thrown away the 'evidence'. Wet and filthy, I returned to the house, where I tried to account for the missing trousers. Line followed me into the bathroom, where I took off my smelly clothes and showered. When she wasn't asking questions, she would scrutinize me, and when I went to embrace her after my shower, she wriggled free. She didn't speak to me for the rest of the day, but the following day she was her usual gentle self. It was as if nothing had happened. I breathed a sigh of relief.

That same day Line took early maternity leave from her job to be at home. I didn't think it was necessary, but she insisted, and we could afford it so there was little to discuss. It meant I could focus on my writing, but my partnership with Ironika changed. Now it was the girls who had secrets and me who didn't understand their private exchanges.

Slowly we grew accustomed to the new rhythm. I worked more and more in isolation and Line and Ironika looked after each other while Line's stomach grew. We never discussed the knife incident again, but I was aware of an increased vigilance in Line every time I played rough and tumble with Ironika. She tried not to let her daughter out of her sight, and her lack of trust exasperated me.

As I was also struggling with the pivotal chapters of *Inner Demons*, I might have been rather prickly in the weeks leading up to its completion. We had a couple of minor arguments, nothing serious, but enough to oppress the mood in the house. When it got too bad, I would shut myself away in my study.

The book was finished around the time Line gave birth to our second daughter, Mathilde. The birth went without a hitch. Line came home only two days later and in the meantime her father looked after Ironika. When we were all home again, it was as if the air had been cleared. We were a family once more. I had submitted *Inner Demons* for editing and could devote myself to my girls, and Line had nine months more leave, during which we could have a nice time together.

Everyone was happy and content, until the book was published.

Saturday

25

I must have been overcome by tiredness in the end because the next morning I was woken up by the sound of the telephone ringing. I had kicked off my duvet during the night and I was cold.

'It's Finn,' a voice said down the other end.

'What time is it?' I stammered.

'Take it easy,' Finn said. 'You've got plenty of time to get to the book fair, I just wanted to make sure you were awake.'

I muttered something to that effect.

'I didn't have time to remind you yesterday,' Finn continued. 'So I thought I would just—'

'That's great, Finn. I'm on my way.'

I hung up before he had time to reply.

It was only Saturday.

I felt I had been in the city for months. The prospect of again sitting for hours signing books held no appeal at all. I dragged myself into the bathroom.

A deathly pale face with black rings round the eyes observed me from the mirror. A huge purple bruise spread across a couple of ribs under my left nipple and it hurt if I breathed too deeply. I shuddered and stepped under the shower, turning up the water as hot as I could stand it. Even so, I couldn't get warm. It was as if the events of last night had planted a chill in my body that had taken root while I slept. I pushed aside the memory of Marie and concentrated on my morning ritual. The familiar routine of trimming my beard, combing my hair and applying deodorant helped keep my thoughts at bay.

Breakfast was reduced to a cup of coffee and a crusty roll, which I wolfed down while I flicked through the newspaper. Reading the news had become a nerve-wracking experience. Every moment I expected to see Verner's eyes staring out at me from one of the pages, though I knew that once he was found, I would hear about it before the newspapers did.

'Will you be checking out tomorrow?' Ferdinan asked as I walked through the lobby.

Suddenly I was unsure. I desperately wanted to leave the city as quickly as possible, but I had a case to solve and I couldn't do that from the cottage in Rågeleje.

'I might be staying a couple more days,' I replied.

Ferdinan's face lit up. 'Ah, a woman perhaps?'

I shook my head vigorously. 'No, nothing like that. I want to visit some friends.'

'If so, you can get your old room back,' Ferdinan said and smiled.

My heart galloped. The thought of staying in that room made me feel sick. I was sure no one would ever sleep in there again.

'No, that's not necessary,' I replied and tried to smile. 'I'm slowly getting used to the luxury suite.'

'OK,' Ferdinan replied. 'Just let me know.'

I thanked him and hurried outside to my taxi.

I told the driver to take me to Forum, but once we were in motion I had second thoughts. How could I sign books as if nothing had happened? Shouldn't I go to the police instead? Shouldn't I do what I had put off for far too long, try to fix it all? I cursed myself. If only I had contacted the police straightaway everything would be different. Even though I now had a concrete clue, room 87 at Hotel BunkInn, I couldn't pass on this information to the police without getting Marie in trouble and I didn't want that.

I grew increasingly frantic, but I was also aware that it really was up to me to solve the case. It was no longer about an ingenious angle for an autobiography or research for my next thriller, this was about survival.

It looked hopeless. All I had to go on were the words of a drug-addicted hooker, the name of the hotel and a room number. However, it was the first time since the body of Mona Weis was discovered that I felt I had caught up with the killer. No matter how devious he was, he couldn't have predicted that I would find Marie. Unless he had actually been following me last night, he couldn't know I was breathing down his neck.

A plan was starting to take shape. I didn't delude myself that I could overpower the killer physically, that was too risky, but I might find evidence in the room at the BunkInn, something that pointed straight to the real killer, something I could take with me and place in the room where Verner lay murdered. In this way I wouldn't be directly implicated. It was simplicity itself. However, it required that I gained access to room 87 soon. When the booking of room 102 expired, it would be too late.

When we had almost reached Forum, I told the taxi driver to take me to Copenhagen Central station instead. Finn and his autograph-hunters would have to wait.

Hotel BunkInn is near the station, but I had to buy a couple of things first. Marie had told me that the man who hired her, Verner's killer, had a beard and wore a hat and sunglasses. I already had the beard, but was lacking the hat and sunglasses. A quick visit to a shop took care of that. Of course, I couldn't know what kind of hat he had worn or what his glasses looked like, but in my experience people don't pay much attention to such details. Not if they staff a busy hotel reception, and especially not in Vesterbro where a hotel receptionist's best qualification is a short-term memory.

I put on my disguise and headed for the hotel. It was a strange feeling. I thought people were staring at me, that they saw through my disguise and I was attracting more attention to myself rather than less. This made me walk faster, which in turn only made it even worse.

The hotel was much smaller than I had expected. Only a small facade fronted the street, and the reception was the size of a parking space. The dark red carpet and brown wallpaper did nothing to make it seem bigger. A young man appeared behind a reception counter of imitation mahogany and black marble. He was pale, gangly and wore jeans, a checked shirt and glasses with a strong steel frame. A pair of half-open eyes behind them registered my presence without noticeable reaction.

'Room 87,' I said in as calm a tone of voice as I could manage.

The young man turned to the board with keycards and found number 87.

'You're that author, aren't you?' he said when he faced me.

I was too flabbergasted to reply.

'Johnny told me he had checked you in when he was on duty last Tuesday. We share the job, you see. I'm a student, so—'

'What else did he say?'

'He said that you were a writer and that's why you had asked not to be disturbed.' He winked at me. 'Don't worry, we haven't been in there.'

I nodded. 'Keep it that way.'

'But I could give you a couple of fresh towels. And some clean linen,' the receptionist said, crouching behind the counter. 'Since you won't let us come in and change it.' He sounded a little wounded. 'Just leave the dirty linen outside, I'll come and pick it up later.'

I accepted the stack of towels and bed linen he gave me and walked up the stairs. They squeaked and the red carpet was worn through in several places. Large patches of wallpaper had come loose and only seemed to be attached by the nails that held reproductions of classical motifs. In contrast to the Marieborg, I could easily imagine that a girl like Marie was a regular here.

Room 87 was on the second floor. It had a white panelled door with the number in brass letters. I glanced around to make sure there was no one in the corridor. I knocked softly. My heart seemed to have swollen and was beating against my ribcage, which hurt. I held my breath and bent forward to hear if there was any response on the other side, but I could hear nothing.

The lock buzzed willingly when I inserted the key-card. I entered and quickly closed the door behind me. It smelled of dusty carpet and stagnant air. The curtains were closed, which left most of the room in darkness.

I walked over to the window and opened the curtains.

Light flooded into the room and revealed a wicker chair with a matching round table, a standing lamp with a rice paper shade and a double bed with a thick, floral bed-spread. Posters by Arnoldi and a few amateur drawings of the hotel hung on the walls. The bed didn't appear to have been slept in, the bedspread hadn't been disturbed and there was no sign that someone had even sat on it.

Apart from the table, it looked like the room was unoccupied. The wicker table had a glass top, and a newspaper, a map and a pair of sunglasses lay on it. I checked the bathroom. It was empty and the towels and soap were unused.

The wardrobe too was empty, only some flimsy metal coat hangers clanged into one another when I tore open the door.

I concluded there was nothing of interest anywhere and focused my attention on the table again. I approached it like an archaeologist about to start an excavation. Without touching anything I noted that the newspaper was from yesterday, the map was of Copenhagen and surrounding areas and was opened up on Frederiksberg and Valby. I looked for any marks that might reveal what was special about those places, but found none. Carefully, I lifted up the map from the table and put it on the bed. I did the same with the newspaper.

When I turned to the table again, I got a shock.

The newspaper had concealed a book.

It took me only a moment to find the photo between the pages.

The book was *Media Whore* and the photo was of Linda Hvilbjerg.

26

Perhaps Linda Hvilbjerg was already dead, I couldn't know, but I hoped that – for once – I was one step ahead of the killer. Not only had I found his hotel room, whatever he used it for, but I had also come a little closer to discovering his identity: the copy of *Media Whore* bore my signature and it was very likely to be the same copy I had signed the previous day.

The killer had to be the man from the book-signing queue.

Even though I had nothing but a signature and a pair of sunglasses to go on, I was convinced I was on the right track. There was nothing to indicate a specific person, so my scheme to plant evidence in room 102 had come to nothing, but I wasn't disappointed.

Now, at least, I knew where he was staying and my first thought was to wait for him. I wanted to surprise him and catch him myself. For a moment I considered contacting the police so they would be here when he returned, but I couldn't cope with explaining everything to them, including how I had found the room. I would obviously have to answer questions if I overpowered the killer, but then at least I could produce the perpetrator and my story would sound more convincing.

However, I couldn't wait for him. There was too much at stake. The killer might already be on his way to Linda Hvilbjerg. If I didn't exploit my advantage, I might not able to prevent her murder. She wasn't exactly my favourite person, but she didn't deserve to die, and certainly not as described in *Media Whore*.

Media Whore is about a serial killer who kills female TV presenters. The killer hates TV personalities for the adulation they get and the way they behave as if they're superior to everyone else and above the suffering of ordinary people. It's the killer's self-appointed mission to make them understand they are real like the rest of us. He wants them to experience the pain of being ordinary, a real physical pain that will be enough to kill them. One of the victims is the host of the literature programme *LIX*, a carbon copy of Linda Hvilbjerg in every respect, except her hair colour, which I did change. She and the other victims are tortured to death in a way that is appropriate to the programmes they front. A TV chef is boiled, the presenter of a gardening programme is mutilated with tools before being buried in a vegetable plot, and the host of *LIX* is murdered in the cutting room after being raped with a book. As the story progresses, the killer's pattern is detected and the TV personalities are put under surveillance. However, this only serves to enrage him. Now that TV hosts have become so precious that they need protection from the public, it becomes more pressing than ever for him to bring them back down to earth. In the last scene, the killer hijacks an entire TV studio and murders two studio hosts on live TV at peak viewing time. However, the hero, a quick-thinking production assistant, manages to ambush the killer, who is roasted alive in a tangle of cables.

Before leaving the room at the BunkInn, I carefully returned everything to the way it was. I surveyed the room from the doorway. It looked just as I had found it half an hour earlier. I left the bed linen and towels I had brought upstairs outside one of the other rooms, after which I crept away.

The receptionist sat with his back to me watching football on a small portable television. I tiptoed over to the counter, put down the keycard and disappeared out of the door without him noticing.

It had started to rain outside. Grey clouds tumbled across the rooftops and powerful gusts of wind forced pedestrians to stagger or lean into the wind using unfurled umbrellas as shields. I ignored the drops lashing my face and walked to Copenhagen Central station and through the vast hall with its shops, sandwich bars and people making it their mission to block my way.

I rang Finn from a payphone. I was fairly certain Finn would have Linda Hvilbjerg's number. He didn't answer. I imagined him talking to some bookseller, glancing at his mobile and ignoring the call because he didn't recognize the number.

I slammed the phone down and headed for the main entrance. There I jumped into a taxi and told the driver to take me to Forum. I must be the only person in Denmark not to own a mobile, something everyone I know reminds me of at every opportunity. Even Bjarne had succumbed years ago and, though he hated to admit it, he could no longer manage without it. For some reason it has never appealed to me. I wanted to be unavailable. I didn't care for interruptions and constantly having to account for where I was the moment I answered it, or share my conversations with random passers-by or fellow passengers. There had been very few times when I really needed a mobile, but one of them was now, as I sat in the taxi on my way to Forum.

I found the drive torturous. The city centre traffic was heavy and the car was stationary more often than moving. I couldn't know if Linda Hvilbjerg would be at the book fair and I wondered what I'd say to her if she was, or what I'd say to Finn if I needed to get her number from him.

The crowding in the book fair hall was worse than the city traffic. Faces paraded endlessly by and I registered none of them, other than that they didn't belong to Finn or Linda Hvilbjerg.

At ZeitSign's stand, Finn was in conversation with three men in suits. He waved me over as soon as he spotted me and introduced me to them. They congratulated me on the good reviews. I didn't catch their names or where they came from, but mustered a smile, a sweaty handshake and a 'thank you'. With a nod of the head I signalled to Finn that I wanted to talk to him. He nodded back and gestured he would be with me in two minutes.

The stand was packed with visitors. Some glanced at me and I feared they might pounce at any moment. My only friend in this mayhem was Finn, so I was loath to move too far away, but nor could I cope with hanging around while people stared at me.

I edged my way to the cubicle where I was alone, thank God. The beer keg was empty, I realized, when foam spluttered into the empty beaker with an angry hiss. There was an extra keg under the table, but I couldn't work out how to replace it and instead hurled my beaker into the bin with such force that it shot out again and vanished in a corner. Having paced up and down the tiny area for a couple of minutes, I sat down on a chair and buried my face in my hands. I tried to ignore the constant hum of voices, imagining what a boon a hearing aid that you could switch off must be. It helped if I closed my eyes and focused on the spots that danced behind the lids. My thoughts began to drift and eventually the noises around me disappeared from my consciousness.

I don't know how long I had been sitting like this when I felt a hand on my shoulder.

'Are you asleep?' Finn said, laughing. 'Well, I never. If you can sleep through this din without being knocked out by a hammer, you must have a special gift.'

'No, I was just nodding off.'

Finn laughed again. 'OK, let's call it that.' His smile disappeared. 'You're late, Frank. In fact, you can't even call it late, you failed to show up altogether. You had a signing session this morning, remember?'

I nodded drowsily.

'That's why I called you,' Finn continued. 'You told me you were on your way. We had an agreement, dammit.'

Anger started to rise in me. How could he think about

book signings when people were dying around me as if I was the carrier of some deadly virus? I stood up abruptly, a little too quickly it would appear, as I felt dizzy and my body swayed.

'Hey, watch it, mate,' Finn said, grabbing my arm. 'Take it easy.'

'I need to get hold of Linda Hvilbjerg,' I said, staring at Finn. 'Now.'

Finn studied me for a moment. 'Are you sure that's wise?'

'She's in danger,' I said.

'Yes, my point exactly,' Finn replied. 'You should get some sleep. You look like you need it.'

'You don't understand. Linda Hvilbjerg is in danger.'

Finn sighed. 'Honestly, I thought you'd got over that. She's a bitch, no argument there, and she crossed the line in that interview, but please don't make it worse by confronting her. That's exactly what she wants. She would love it if you lost your temper and did something stupid that would land you on the front page.'

'It's not me,' I said. My throat was dry and I could barely produce the words, possibly because they sounded like something from a potboiler. 'Someone . . . someone else is trying to kill her.' I grabbed Finn's shoulders. 'Murder her.'

Finn stared at me for a moment, then he erupted in a broad grin, which soon froze when he saw that I wasn't returning it.

'Someone is trying to kill Linda Hvilbjerg,' he repeated slowly. 'It wouldn't be the same person who was at work in Gilleleje?'

I nodded and let go of his shoulders.

'I have to warn her.'

'And what makes you think she's in danger?'

'It's too complicated to explain right now,' I said. 'Do you or don't you have her telephone number?'

Finn held up his hands. 'I still think you ought to get some sleep, Frank. I understand you're upset at the murder, but you've got to get a grip.'

'The number.'

He stuck his hand inside his jacket and took out his mobile. 'You didn't get it from me,' he said as he pressed buttons on the mobile.

Finn Gelf dictated the number, which I wrote down in my notebook.

'Why don't you just get some sleep and come back tonight?' Finn suggested as I tried to leave the cubicle. 'Linda always comes to the party. You can talk to her there and sort it out over a beer in the bar. We're all grown-ups, for Christ sake.'

I looked into his eyes. 'You don't believe me, do you?'

'Isolating yourself up there in the north is making you increasingly odd,' he replied, turning away from my gaze. 'Try to get used to being around people. Get out a bit more, but for God's sake take it easy, Frank.'

'I'm trying to prevent a woman from getting murdered and you're telling me to take it easy?'

'But you've already killed her, Frank. In *Media Whore*. That's why I indulged your little therapy project. I paid for you to vent your frustrations, even though I knew the book would be a flop. Let him get it out of his system, I thought, and all will be well again.' He took my arm. 'And it worked.'

I was outraged.

'You're saying you did me a favour? If anyone owes anybody anything, then it's you, Finn Gelf.' I rammed my index finger into his chest. 'I made you rich. I made it possible for you to play the bigshot publisher in the book trade. Without me you would be nothing, ZeitSign would have folded long ago and the only contact you would have with books would be selling them in a shop.'

Finn said nothing, he merely stared at me as if I had spoken Chinese.

I pushed my way past him and left the cubicle. Behind me I heard him protest and call me back, but I was no longer listening.

The payphones were located in the lobby, but first I needed a drink. I made my way to the bar in the corner furthest from the entrance. All seats were taken so I stood at the counter and ordered two beers. I drank the first one without taking the glass from my lips. People around me stared and muttered to each other, but I didn't care.

I drank beer number two in a more controlled manner while my anger at Finn continued to simmer. Who the hell did he think he was?

Tanked up with beer and bitterness, I went to the lobby. I took out my notebook and some change and pressed Linda Hvilbjerg's number. She didn't answer and I was asked to leave a message. I hung up, waited a couple of minutes and tried again. Still no reply. After four attempts, I capitulated and recorded a message.

'Hello, Linda? This is Frank, Frank Føns. I'm calling because you're in great danger . . . it's a bit hard to explain, but there is a killer who is persecuting me and committing the murders in my books. And now . . . well, now it's your turn . . . I know it sounds completely insane, but please make sure there is someone near you who can protect you or go somewhere you'll be safe, for my sake.' I paused and looked around. People kept pouring into the lobby and there was chaos at the cloakroom. It seemed an absurd contrast to the message I was leaving.

'Promise me you'll take care. And Linda? . . . Sorry . . .'

27

I called Linda Hvilbjerg a couple more times until I ran out of coins. According to the programme, she had no more appearances at the book fair today, so the chances of her returning in the near future were slim. I felt so tired I had to go back to the hotel. At least she would be able to get hold of me there when she got my message.

Ferdinan was behind the reception counter, but I didn't have the energy to speak to him so I merely waved and headed straight for the lift.

'Mr Føns!' he called out when he saw me and motioned me over. His face was pale and his expression grave, very far from his usual cheerful manner.

I approached the counter like a dog with a guilty conscience.

'It's dreadful,' Ferdinan said, shaking his head. It was clear that he wished he didn't have to tell me.

'What's happened?' I asked.

'Your murder,' Ferdinan said. 'Someone has committed your murder.'

I clutched the counter. It was Saturday afternoon. The

guest in room 102 wasn't due to check out until Monday, I knew that from our previous conversation, but something must have gone wrong. It had to be the smell.

'A man has been murdered in room 102,' Ferdinan continued. 'Just like you described. By the book.'

My eyes widened, but my brain worked overtime to determine the appropriate response. I couldn't betray myself, so I had to feign surprise.

'This isn't funny, Ferdinan,' was all I could think to say.

'No, no,' Ferdinan said quickly. 'A man is dead.' His eyes spotted something over my shoulder.

I turned around. A man in a dark suit was sitting in one of the sofas. He had been reading a paperback, but when he met Ferdinan's eyes, he got up with some effort. He stuffed the book into his jacket pocket, but even at this distance I had already recognized the dark cover of *As You Sow*. He walked with gliding, mechanical movements as if he couldn't swing his arms. He didn't take his eyes off me and his small mouth under a black, slim moustache revealed no more emotions than his gait.

'Frank Føns?' he asked in a surprisingly high-pitched voice. It gave the impression he was a boy dressed in his father's clothes.

'That's me,' I replied.

'Detective Sergeant Kim Vendelev,' the boy said, pulling out a badge from his inside pocket without looking at it. His eyes were still firmly fixed on mine.

I looked at his badge, mainly to avoid his eyes.

'What's this about?'

'Do you know Detective Constable Verner Nielsen?'

I looked at him with what I hoped was surprise. Then I shifted my gaze to Ferdinan.

'Is he the one who . . .'

Ferdinan nodded.

I stared at the floor and shook my head, careful not to do it too quickly.

'It can't be,' I said. 'I saw him here just the other day.'

'That's what we want to talk to you about,' the sergeant said. 'We understand that you had dinner with Verner Nielsen last Wednesday night.'

I nodded.

'We've also been informed that you asked after him at the reception the following day.'

'That's right.'

'I'm going to have to ask you to accompany me to the station,' Sergeant Vendelev said, nodding towards the entrance.

The sergeant ushered me out to a black Opel and drove me to Vesterbro police station. His colleagues stared as he led me through the open-plan office to an interview room on the second floor. Verner had told me he wasn't popular with some of his colleagues. Goody-goodies, he called them, police officers who took their job seriously and weren't on the take. Verner did whatever the hell he liked and made little effort to cover it up. This had sparked several clashes with his colleagues, but he'd just tell them to shut up and mind their own business. They usually played ball, not for Verner's sake, but rather from misplaced loyalty between police officers. Being a whistleblower was worse than being a bent copper.

The sergeant opened the door to the interview room.

He asked me to sit down in one of the two chairs and went to get coffee for us both. In his absence, I studied the room.

In my books I had described interview rooms and interviews several times and my present sparse surroundings matched my descriptions accurately. I believed I had a fair idea of what lay ahead of me. The fact that only one officer had been sent to fetch me and that he hadn't charged me already must mean they didn't think I had killed Verner. Not that I had, obviously, but it would be awkward for me if they were to find out I had been to the crime scene.

The sergeant returned with coffee and placed a small black object on the table between us. It was an electronic recording device as far removed from the cassette recorder or reel-to-reel tape as you could imagine. Somehow it contributed to making me even more relaxed. A large recorder with rotating wheels might have made more of an impression. Seeing every one of my words being recorded would have made me nervous.

Sergeant Vendelev pulled out *As You Sow* from his pocket and tossed it on the table.

'I hate crime fiction,' he said, having sat down. 'It's so unrealistic and riddled with clichés that I usually end up throwing the book away in a fit of anger.'

I frowned. I wasn't expecting such an outburst from the boy opposite me. He must have said it to provoke a reaction, I decided; the first lesson in interrogation technique. I shrugged.

'Each to their own,' I said. 'If it's realism you're looking for it's probably not the right genre. Describing a case as it really happens would make for the world's most boring book. Who wants to read about endless telephone calls, penal code references and entering case files on the computer?'

'But that's how crimes are solved,' the sergeant argued.

'Except that's not what the readers want. They want excitement and they want clichés. Of course they want a certain amount of realism, but they still want their expectations met and there's no point in confusing them.'

'With facts.'

'Yes. You and I both know that when a man is shot, he isn't flung through the air, but countless action movies and crime novels have gunshot victims blown through windows, knocked over balconies or railings. The audience expects it and would react negatively if we didn't deliver.'

Sergeant Vendelev appeared to ponder what I had said.

'The public wants to be deceived,' I summed up.

'Have you ever been tempted to do it for real?' he suddenly asked me.

'Do what?'

'Commit the perfect murder,' he replied. 'I mean . . . you've spent most of your life thinking of ingenious ways to kill people. So . . . have you ever felt like having a go yourself? Prove you're smarter than everybody else?'

I shook my head. 'Never!'

'Not even when you read about a murder in the newspaper where the killer is caught because he overlooked some silly little detail?'

I felt a prickling on my scalp and had to force myself not to scratch my head. Why had he made references to a newspaper? Was he about to confront me with the

Gilleleje murder, reveal that he knew the link between that murder and Verner's?

'Perhaps I find it amusing how slipshod people can be once they have finally decided to go through with it, but I have never wanted to have a go myself.'

'You've never put yourself in the killer's shoes?'

'Only for logistical reasons. I review the crime scene through the killer's eyes to make sure everything slots together. Objects need to be in the right places, items of furniture need to be arranged correctly in relation to one another and entrances and exits must fit the plot.' I paused. 'I'm an author, not a criminal.'

Sergeant Vendelev nodded.

It's coming, I thought. Soon he would show me the newspaper with the Gilleleje headline and next to it he would place pictures from the autopsy of Mona Weis, who would stare at me with her blue eyes. He was about to strike.

But he made a placatory gesture.

'All right, all right, just curious to know how you authors work,' he said. 'A lot of police officers don't understand how you can imagine all those monstrous things in your books without being damaged somehow. How can you sleep at night?'

'Not a problem,' I lied.

I knew I looked like someone who hadn't slept for several weeks and the truth was that I usually slept badly. It wasn't so much my own murders that kept me awake, more the feelings that had inspired them. Alcohol normally helped, but it also gave me restless dreams where I could remember only dark, menacing shadows.

'Anyway, murder isn't what it used to be,' I said. 'It's your age now, the age of forensic science. With DNA, mobile telephones and cameras everywhere there's not much real detective work left. When I started writing thrillers, the killer could cover his tracks simply by burning the body or removing teeth or fingertips. That wouldn't get him anywhere today.'

'You sound disappointed,' Sergeant Vendelev observed.

I shrugged. 'I'm just saying the romance has gone.'

'Romance!' the sergeant exclaimed. 'There's nothing romantic about murder.'

'No, but neither is there much dramatic tension to be had from a DNA test or the fact that all potential victims carry mobiles.'

'Is that why you haven't got one?' Sergeant Vendelev asked.

The question took me by surprise, partly because the sergeant appeared to have checked and partly because he might be right.

'Maybe,' I replied. 'I hadn't thought about it, but I'm getting fed up trying to think of reasons why the victims in my book haven't or why there is no coverage when the killer is chasing them.'

'Perhaps it might create a different kind of tension?' the sergeant suggested. 'Being in contact with someone while it happened?' He smiled.

'I'll think about it,' I said, returning his smile.

Sergeant Vendelev clapped his hands together.

'Right, we'd better get started.' He pressed the black object on the table.

*　　*　　*

253

The interview lasted about an hour and was, in contrast to our opening discussion, very factual. He asked about my relationship with Verner, when I had last seen him and what I had been doing at the time of the murder. I had no alibi for the rest of the evening we had dined together, but it didn't appear to worry the sergeant. He didn't ask me if Verner had any enemies, but I reckoned he was already aware of any. He clearly knew Verner well and I would hazard a guess that Verner would have classified Sergeant Vendelev as one of the goody-goodies. Conversely, Verner was probably a stain on the police force in Vendelev's eyes, and if he was motivated to find the killer, it wasn't because he cared about him, but about the job he represented.

The Gilleleje murder was never mentioned, and I was grateful that police sergeants appeared to have too much taste to read my books.

Overall I thought I handled the interview well. The questions relating to Verner's murder were sufficiently precise for me to answer them honestly, but there were undeniably some unfortunate coincidences. I had been the last person to see Verner alive and then there was the manner of his death, obviously. Sergeant Vendelev approached these circumstances with some hesitation; he merely prodded them only to conclude that they weren't ripe yet and swiftly proceeded to other questions.

When we said goodbye, I had to assure him I wouldn't leave the country – that cliché held true – and I knew I hadn't seen the last of Sergeant Vendelev.

I walked back to the hotel alone.

Ferdinan was at the reception, still with the same

mournful expression. His movements seemed slow compared to his usual bounce. When he saw me, he shook his head again.

'It's just awful,' he said.

I nodded, but said nothing.

'And the police . . . they're all over the hotel,' he carried on, miserably. 'What must my guests be thinking?'

'I'm sure they don't blame you for anything,' I said.

'Perhaps . . . but how can they ever feel safe here again?'

I put my hand on his shoulder and squeezed it. 'They'll catch him. And then you will have another story to tell.'

Ferdinan looked at me with gratitude in his eyes.

'But, imagine, if you had booked that room,' he said. 'It could have been you.'

'I really don't think so,' I declared. 'It seems more like an act of revenge.'

'Like in the book?'

'Just like in the book.'

28

Inner Demons got a rough reception in the press, but the sales figures spoke their own easily measurable language – it was a hit.

Finn Gelf was over the moon. *Outer Demons* had financed ZeitSign's offices in Gammel Mønt and now it looked like *Inner Demons* would ensure the company's financial stability for years to come. There was enough left over for him to buy himself a villa in Spain and replace his old Fiat with a BMW.

For my part I was happy and relieved to know that I had still got it in me to attract readers. I was even grateful I had followed Finn's advice and dropped *Join the Club* in favour of the moneymaker that was *Inner Demons*.

The familiar merry-go-round of interviews, book signings and talk shows started all over again and I was more or less absent from home for three weeks around the time of publication. Line, who was still on maternity leave, looked after the two girls on her own, far too busy to take part in the media circus and so pressed for time that she didn't read the book until two months later.

When she finally read *Inner Demons*, she left me.

The main character and killer in the story, Ralf Sindahl, had been born in traumatic circumstances. His mother, a Red Cross aid worker, fell in love with another aid worker in Africa and became pregnant, but shortly before she was due to give birth she was abducted by an African tribe who raped her before performing an improvised Caesarean section with a machete. The infant boy was sold or stolen from tribe to tribe where he was starved and abused until he was bought by a rich white couple, who couldn't have children of their own. Growing up on the family farm, however, didn't spell an end to the child's troubles. The husband was a sadist, not only towards the staff who worked under slave-like conditions, but also towards his wife and the most recent victim, little Ralf. The boy in turn takes out his frustration on the workers, who are too scared to resist or tell his father, and his attacks become increasingly vicious, the older he gets. At the age of fourteen, he kills his father, who is trying to stop the boy beating up a pregnant black girl. Ralf decides to run away, but before he leaves, he ransacks the house looking for money. He discovers a report that describes his violent entry into the world and contains information about his real parents. He flees to Denmark with the report, where he tracks down his biological father, Claus, who takes him in. Claus, however, soon realizes there is something seriously wrong with the boy and, a few months after their reunion, he is forced to hand him over to the authorities. The boy knows nothing of fear or humility and his brutality puts him on the path to a career as a successful criminal. Soon he has more money than he can spend. However, it isn't money that interests him, but power. He is obsessed by the thought that his strength is the direct result of his brutal birth, and in an attempt to create small monsters in his own image, he kidnaps pregnant women whom he tortures right up until the birth, after which he kills them. He leaves the babies in hospitals or orphanages, convinced he is their psychological father through the shared bond of a traumatic birth. He believes the children will grow up with his powers and rule the world one day. Ralf's fate and downfall comes in the shape of a strong pregnant woman, who outwits him and kills him with a sledgehammer.

But his 'children' are still out there . . .

Not terribly original, I know, but there were still a few people who hadn't read or seen *The Boys from Brazil* and so thought it was quite cool. However, most reviewers agreed that *Inner Demons* was rubbish – a cynical exploitation of people's need to be frightened and outraged.

Once more I was Mr Splatter and *Inner Demons* was condemned by some as a wicked and dangerous book that people should stay away from – which only served to boost sales even further. A number of libraries, acting as moral guardians, refused to let anyone under the age of eighteen borrow the book. The result was that schoolchildren would steal my books from library shelves in order to read the bloodiest extracts in secret, and among teenagers a cult arose around the book and my authorship. At a school in Aalborg, teachers discovered that a group of boys had founded the Deadly Poets Society, whose purpose was to collect and read the most graphic depictions of torture in literature. My two *Demon* books were practically their bibles; they read aloud from them and made drawings of some of the scenes with a precision worthy of a police report. Families were shocked, parent–teacher associations furious and right-wing politicians spoke about bans, censorship and introducing a minimum age requirement for books as is the case with films. Many of my fellow authors queued up to denounce my work. It had nothing to do with literature, they claimed, and hinted that the paper would have been put to better use in a lavatory.

Meanwhile, sales soared.

Around the same time, people started ringing me and making threats. Furious voices called me the worst names and described how I should be put down in ways so vile I wouldn't even have used them in my books. We got an unlisted number, which put an end to the calls, but it didn't stop the letters. As my address was also secret, this so-called fan mail was sent to my publishers and a sackful would be waiting for me each week. To begin with I opened and read every letter, including those that smeared me, but in time I became so practised I wouldn't even need to open the hate mail – I could sense the outrage oozing from the handwriting on the envelope.

However, some readers still supported me and wrote letters of appreciation. In public, few people would admit to having read my books and fewer still to liking them, but the letters painted a different picture. Many wrote of powerful reading experiences, not only from the violence in the book, but also from its characterization. They mentioned scenes and images that had moved them in a way they hadn't been moved for years.

In between these two extremes were letters from a third group, and they were the ones that really worried me. They were fanatical declarations. Initially, these letters resembled fan mail, but they quickly assumed a more disturbing tone. The senders wanted specific information about certain scenes, how I had researched the effect of the murder weapons, or they pointed out mistakes in terms of the body's reaction to certain influences. Some had re-enacted passages from the book and would either praise me for my accuracy and insight or draw my attention to errors, for example, certain bodily positions that were impossible. A few told me how they had used episodes from the book in sex games and thanked me for the experience; one even attached a series of photos as evidence to prove it.

Despite the – for me – enormous attention, I had no problem being out in public. Of course people recognized me, but it was rare for anyone to approach me directly. Perhaps they were scared of me, scared I would turn into one of my notorious killers if they came too close. The few people who did come up to me were friendly and usually only wanted an autograph. One woman told me she couldn't sleep after having read *Inner Demons*, and another, heavily pregnant and sweating, said she simply had to stop reading and would have to finish the book after she'd had her baby.

It seemed as if everyone had an opinion about the book,

whether or not they had read it. But a great many people bought the book and did read it.

Except Line.

After a month, it started to irritate me. Of course she was busy with the children while I ran around doing interviews and attending receptions, but she could have shown a bit more interest, I thought. I nudged her, but it was another month before she picked it up.

To this day, I wish I had never encouraged her.

She started reading it while I was in Germany. Finn was with me; we were meeting with the German translator and settling some contractual issues with the German publisher. When I phoned home from the hotel that evening, Line had just started the book. She remarked that it was rather bloodthirsty, but that was all. We talked about the children and I told her about the German publisher, who had turned out to be a whisky connoisseur and was determined to prove it later that night. The following day she didn't answer the telephone and on the third day, I got the answering machine.

I was surprised, but not worried. She had probably gone to stay with her father as she was on her own with two children, so I didn't regard it as cause for concern.

When I came home, exhausted after three days of talking literature and drinking whisky, the house was empty and *Inner Demons* was lying on the kitchen table.

A note stuck out from it.

> *It's over.*
> *I'm scared to leave you alone with the children now.*
> *Line*

I must have read that note a hundred times, thinking alternately that it was all over or that she would probably come back. The German publisher had presented me with a bottle of 37-year-old Highland Park for special occasions, but it was opened that night and when I woke up next morning only a quarter was left. I hadn't tried to call Line even though I was fairly sure she had gone to stay with her father. Somehow I knew it would be pointless and I needed to think, to come up with a strategy before contacting her, but no useful plan had materialized during the night so, after a cup of pitch-black coffee, I rang my father-in-law.

I had expected rejection, that Line would refuse to talk to me, but after a moment she came to the telephone. She even sounded composed and resolved as she explained that she didn't feel safe with me and would never leave her children in my care again. When I pointed out that they were my children too, she hardened her voice and informed me that she was scared I might hurt them, unless she was around.

The most idiotic thing I could do was lose my temper, so that's what I did. I screamed at her down the telephone and spewed out stupidities I have regretted ever since, but I felt unfairly treated. It was for their sake that I wrote what I did. It was so they could live comfortably in the house in Kartoffelrækkerne and have the holiday cottage in Rågeleje that I had gone the whole hog with the book.

Line said very little during my outburst. She waited until I had finished, then, when my torrent of justifications and accusations had run dry, she informed me that I would be hearing from her solicitor. I couldn't think of anything to say. I was knocked for six, exhausted by my attacks on her, and I realized that everything I had said and done had only served to convince her she had made the right decision. Finally I begged her to at least let me speak to Ironika. She hesitated for a moment, which sparked a slender hope in me, but then she declined and hung up.

In the days that followed I tried various forms of lobbying with Bjarne, Anne and Line's family, but everyone was of the opinion that this time I had gone too far and they neither could nor did they want to help me. A letter arrived from her solicitor. Even up until that point I had been deluding myself I could talk my way out of it, that Line would forgive me and return after some days or weeks, but the formal, legal language and dry presentation of facts hit me head-on like an express train.

Line wanted full custody and banned me from seeing my children. The lawyer pointed out that I had myself supplied the most damning proof by virtue of my two books *Outer Demons* and *Inner Demons*, which clearly demonstrated that I fantasized about torturing and killing my wife and children. To substantiate their claim, they would produce the interview with Linda Hvilbjerg and witness statements in connection with the cut to Ironika's thigh.

I knew the battle was lost. There would be no court hearing or arguments over the children because I had no defence. All I could do was hire a lawyer and let him do what was necessary. I couldn't subject my children to years of court proceedings that I would probably end up losing anyway. It would only make matters worse. In time, I might be allowed to see them, but for now I was beaten.

263

My mental state and lack of self-worth made me considerably more generous than strictly necessary. I gave Line the house in Kartoffelrækkerne, unencumbered, and would of course be paying alimony and child maintenance until the girls grew up. I kept the cottage and initially moved in with Bjarne and Anne in my old Scriptorium room. They were sympathetic, but I couldn't talk to them about the break-up. I suspected they sided with Line and therefore couldn't see the point of bringing up the subject.

Instead I pretended that Line had ceased to exist and threw myself into the life of a bachelor, which nearly proved to be the death of me.

29

Darkness had spread over Frederiksberg. It was cold and I wrapped my jacket around me as I walked from the taxi to the Forum entrance. I showed my invitation and was admitted.

The dinner was taking place in the large restaurant across the entrance foyer. I could see tables had been laid and candles lit, but only a few guests were here already. The authors would probably be among the last to arrive, too snobbish to arrive early and too greedy to stay away. The other guests would be the interviewers, mostly members of the press, and editors from publishing companies, publishers and other helpers from the book fair. I had never attended before, but it was understood that tonight everyone let off steam, tired after two busy days at the book fair and desperate to recharge for the final day, a very long Sunday.

I, however, had only one thing on my mind: finding Linda Hvilbjerg.

When I reached the restaurant, I nodded to the twenty or so people who were there. I didn't know any of them so

I didn't have to chat to anyone and I proceeded straight to the bar. The beer kegs were as yet unmanned so I helped myself to a glass of white wine, set out as a welcome drink. I knocked it back in one go, took another glass and sat down near the bar where I could keep an eye on the entrance.

The guests started to arrive. Some would appear from behind the stands and head for the restaurant, others from the entrance where they crossed through the exhibition hall as if taking part in a parade. Soon so many people arrived that I could no longer make out who was there. I got up for a better look and took the opportunity to fetch another glass of wine at the same time.

Quite a few people I knew had arrived by now and I couldn't get away with nodding, but was forced to have actual conversations. They were people I hadn't seen for several years so we had very little to say. The exchanges were clumsy and only lasted until one of us could think of an excuse to move on.

I tried to keep moving – it was the best way to avoid small talk – so I only heard snippets of conversations around me, all about books and publications even though the speakers had done nothing all day but talk about the same subject.

'Frank?' I suddenly heard behind me. 'What are you doing here?' It was Finn. He stared at me in disbelief. 'You're the last person I expected to see here tonight.'

'Yeah, I know.' I headed for the bar with Finn on my heels. 'Cheers, Finn,' I said, having got hold of another glass of white wine.

'Cheers,' Finn said, sipping his welcome drink. 'And

here was I thinking you were out hunting criminals.' He laughed out loud. 'I tell you, you almost had me there.'

I had given up convincing him so I shrugged. 'Well, you know me.'

Finn laughed again. 'Good to see you, Frank. I think you need to get out more. Mingle with colleagues, network, show your face and all that.'

I nodded and swallowed the rest of my white wine.

Finn couldn't think of anything else to say and pointed over my shoulder.

'We're sitting at one of the tables over there at the end. You're welcome to join us.'

I mumbled a reply that could be taken either way, but Finn appeared satisfied and walked off in the direction he had pointed out.

There was no seating plan so people sat down wherever they wanted to. As a rule, editors would stay with their authors to look after them, but also to prevent other publishers from wooing them. It presented the editors with something of a dilemma because they all wanted to poach new writers as well. I imagine they got very little to eat, busy as they were running around trying to fit in everything they had to do.

In the bar, I finally managed to get a beer. I stayed there and scanned the hall. There had to be more than three hundred people present and I had lost track of things.

The organizer of the book fair, a short balding man with a small moustache and a tight-fitting suit, climbed up on a chair and welcomed us. He gave a speech that was far too long, praised all of us and eulogized literature. I could tell from people's faces that all they cared about was eating and drinking, not listening to the pretentious rubbish he was spouting, but we had to wait like good little boys and girls, including the uniformed waiters with their hands behind their backs.

To my great surprise, I discovered I was hungry. A quick review of the day so far revealed that I hadn't eaten since breakfast, unless I included alcohol, so when the introduction finally ended I was just as keen as everyone else to get to the buffet. I piled up a large plate of food and tried to spot a vacant chair. I wasn't tempted by Finn's offer. I didn't feel like talking to him or anyone else from ZeitSign.

I sat down among a group of young bookshop assistants who let me eat in peace. They were more interested in getting drunk and telling jokes while I concentrated on clearing my plate. My hunger abated, but I felt I needed to eat more to cancel out the amount of alcohol I had consumed.

Back at the buffet, I picked more substantial foods, such as meat and potatoes, and was so preoccupied with my foraging that I didn't notice the scent of sweet perfume slowly enveloping me.

'I hear I might be in your next book?'

It was Linda Hvilbjerg.

30

I spun around and came face to face with Linda Hvilbjerg. She was holding a plate and had a small wry smile on her lips. Her slim body was poured into a long, black dress with thin shoulder straps. Her breasts pressed against the fabric as if they were part of the dress. Her dark hair had been curled since the interview and her lips glistened in a vibrant, traffic-light red. Her pupils revealed that she had recently applied her beauty powder.

I forgot all about what I wanted to tell her and simply stared at her.

'I presume your message refers to your next book?' She fluttered her eyelashes a couple of times and smiled. 'Just between us, shouldn't you try to keep work and reality apart?' She laughed.

I still couldn't think of anything appropriate to say.

Linda Hvilbjerg came up very close to me and made a point of looking around the room.

'But could it be true? Am I really in danger?' She giggled. 'And are you the hero who'll save me from the baddies?'

I decided to play along.

'This ain't no joke, ma'am,' I said with the thickest American detective accent I could manage, possibly inspired by my recent encounter with the police. 'Your life and honour are at stake and I'm the only man who can save them both.'

'Oh,' Linda Hvilbjerg exclaimed. 'Is that really true, Mr . . . ?'

'Pinkerton's the name. Dick Pinkerton, at your service.' I tried to bow, but stopped just in time to prevent my food from sliding off the plate.

'Oh, the great Dick Pinkerton. What an honour.'

'The pleasure is entirely mine, ma'am.'

'And what precisely is your mission?'

'I'm afraid I'll have to keep you under surveillance for the rest of the evening.'

'Close?'

'Very close.'

'It sounds like I'm in very good hands, Mr Pinkerton.'

'These hands will take good care of you, ma'am.'

Linda Hvilbjerg laughed and I laughed with her.

I don't know how I was able to laugh or where the words came from, but I sensed I was on the right track. It seemed utterly impossible to explain the situation to her as we stood there, tipsy, by the buffet, and the next best thing was to make sure I was near her. This wasn't only a gallant motive for protecting her from the killer. I have to admit that when I saw her in the black dress with her red lips, I was horny as hell.

However, it's still beyond me what turned her on that night. I had been drinking heavily for several days and

I think I was still wearing the same clothes as when she interviewed me the day before. All I can think is that she was so high that she overlooked my appearance or perhaps she saw something else, something her body demanded, like a fry-up for a hangover.

We continued our charade for most of the evening and I think we both enjoyed burying the hatchet for a while. We immersed ourselves completely in our little game and flirted with words, looks and light touches so at last it was only a question of where and when we finally lost our inhibitions.

Even though I carried on drinking and she had been out to 'powder her nose' a couple of times, I controlled myself and didn't simply take her down the hall and screw her behind one of the stands while books cascaded around us. I restrained myself because it was my only chance to protect her, but also because I longed for the warmth of a woman.

Heavily intoxicated and exceedingly horny, we took a taxi back to Linda's around midnight. I was enormously pleased with myself. Admittedly, I hadn't told her that she was genuinely in danger, but I was with her and I imagined that in itself would deter the killer. In fact, I regarded myself as something of a saviour and felt so confident that I decided to relax and enjoy myself now that I was there. I deserved it, I convinced myself, and I surrendered to her increasingly intimate groping in the taxi. I noticed the taxi-driver's eyes in the rear-view mirror, but decided to ignore him.

We carried on play-acting. She was the doe-eyed client and I was the hard-boiled detective who was there to protect her and tend to her needs in every way. To this end a thorough physical examination was required, I insisted, to determine what state she was in and also to check for possible wires or other electronic equipment she might be concealing about her person.

Linda giggled at my suggestions and wanted to hear more. Would I be devoting extra attention to certain areas of her anatomy? Did I have special equipment to explore her body? I readily confirmed this and demonstrated how I could examine her mouth most effectively with my tongue. While we kissed, she checked out the rest of my equipment and she was duly impressed at the erection she could feel through my trousers. I, too, was surprised. Despite drinking heavily all day, I still had a hard-on like a teenager.

We were so randy that I almost forgot to pay the driver when we finally reached her house, a two-storey villa in Valby. We spilled out of the taxi and headed for the front door where Linda rummaged through her handbag for the keys. I grabbed her buttocks and kneaded them. They were small and firm, like two balls, and she moaned tenderly and pushed them out towards me.

Finally, she managed to unlock the door and we tumbled into the hall. She didn't switch on the light, but dropped her handbag and turned around to embrace me. We kissed again. In a thick voice, I suggested that she undressed.

Linda Hvilbjerg took one step back. Moonlight shone through a small window above the front door and on to her torso. She wriggled out of her shoes and reached around to her neck. The thin straps fell and with a snakelike movement the black dress slithered over her slim, white body. Her nipples were hard and bobbed up and down towards me like an invitation every time her breasts heaved and fell with her breathing. Her arms were still raised above her head and her back was arched. The skin on her belly was covered with goose pimples and her pubic hair was a close-cropped black rectangle that disappeared between her white thighs.

She asked if I could see anything and I replied that everything looked very, very good, but that I had better carry out a hands-on examination. I stepped towards her and unfairly blocked the moonlight. She let her arms fall around my neck, but I caught them and lifted them back over her head. She giggled, grabbed hold of the coat rack above her and pushed the rest of her body towards me. I kissed her nipples and her laughter was replaced by a small gasp followed by a low moaning. My hands caressed her arms, breasts and stomach. She quivered and the goose pimples rose prouder on her stomach. She sighed loudly and her body trembled as I touched her groin. She was warm and very wet.

I whispered softly that I might have found something and she whispered something affirmative. I took a step back to allow the moonlight to illuminate her body again. She stood with her eyes closed, squirming as if even the light tickled her. I expressed the opinion that it was necessary to use tools and she acquiesced with a sigh. I quickly undressed and left my clothes in a pile on the floor. I was fully erect and the blood was rushing around my body. My hands trembled as they seized her hips and turned her so she stood with her back to me. She pushed her arse towards me and spread her legs. I grabbed her buttocks, bent my knees slightly and entered her in one slow movement.

The word count has reached a critical mass. I wouldn't be able to stop now even if I wanted to, and the sheer magnitude of the manuscript forces me to sleep less and less.

When I finally sleep, I dream about running, not away from something but towards a door or gate that is ajar. It closes just as I reach it, no matter how fast I run, and I wake up on sweaty sheets in the kind of silence that follows a scream. For a long time I lie there, listening, unable to fall asleep again.

It wears me out. I write in a haze. Sometimes I can't even remember having written the sentence I have just concluded with a full stop. And, from time to time, I don't recognize the tone that colours it. I take this as evidence that my project is succeeding, my filter has definitely gone, the words flow without being weighed or measured by my vanity or pride, as if they have been written by someone else – something inside me that urges me on and keeps me going.

I'm ready for the final sprint; this is it, from now on it's going to get very difficult.

Sunday

31

Sometimes when you wake up, you instantly know that something is wrong. When I started writing full-time I would often get this feeling. I would suddenly open my eyes, convinced I was late for work, until I remembered that I was master of my own fate and could turn over and go back to sleep if I wanted to. In the minutes that pass before you realize what sort of day it is and what plans you have for it, the slightest thing sends you into a flat spin because everything just feels wrong.

When I woke up in Linda Hvilbjerg's bed, I knew straightaway that something was up. I had slept heavily, very heavily, but that wasn't surprising. I hadn't slept very much in the last few days and last night's physical exertion had also taken its toll. I was sore all over. We had mated like wild animals. Made love in every single room and in every imaginable position. Even though I had been about to explode from lust, I had been able to last for what felt like hours and it wasn't until we finally ended up in her bed that I surrendered to Linda's ferocity and she rode us both to orgasm. I must have fallen asleep shortly afterwards because I don't remember anything after that.

But it was neither the exhaustion nor the strange surroundings that explained the feeling in my body. It was something else I couldn't put my finger on.

I looked around. The bedroom was done entirely in white and in the grey light cast by the sombre sky outside, it seemed clinical and sad. Linda wasn't there. I sniffed the bed linen. It smelled of sex and sweat like after a pub crawl. From the bed I could look out of the door, out on to the landing from where steps led down to the living room. Images of us fucking our way up the stairs flashed before my eyes.

I shook my head, but stopped when I felt a headache hit it like a hammer. My throat was parched and my stomach complained with a loud rumbling.

Slowly, I sat up in the bed. My legs trembled as I stood up and I had to wait a moment until the dizzy spell passed. I shuffled through the door and across to the stairs. Small lithographs hung on the walls all the way down. I clutched the banister and started my descent. The lithographs appeared to be telling a story, but it wasn't until I reached the foot of the stairs that I recognized it. It was the *Divine Comedy*.

I smiled to myself at this discovery and turned my head.

The sight that met me made me jump back with a cry.

Linda Hvilbjerg was hanging from the balustrade on the landing with a rope around her neck.

Her dead eyes were wide in terror as if they had just witnessed something incomprehensible, something unbelievably terrifying. Dark lines of coagulated blood flowed from her neck down her white, slender body. The lines traversed her breasts and continued down between her legs. Her groin was a bloody pulp and a massive object had been forced up her vagina.

It was a book.

I averted my eyes and stared at the white wall. My whole body was shaking and I had to sit down on the steps in order not to fall. I breathed deeply in an attempt to regain control of myself.

A few minutes later I slowly turned my head.

Linda Hvilbjerg's naked body was still hanging there. A large puddle of blood had gathered on the floor beneath her. It was dark, black almost, and seemed viscous like oil. An overturned chair lay nearby. Footprints had been left on the floor around the body, numerous bloody shoeprints as if someone had outlined the choreography of a complicated dance.

My heart pounded and the nausea spread from my stomach up through my chest and throat. I tumbled forwards, landed on all fours and threw up at the foot of the stairs. Every spasm felt like a blow to the stomach and it carried on long after my stomach was empty. When I could throw up no more, I started to sob. I struggled to breathe and my crying was chopped into intermittent outbursts, like that of a little boy.

I crawled over to the puddle where I knelt down and stared up at Linda's body.

Even without having touched her, I knew she was cold. Her colour and immobility told me that the warm body I had enjoyed in the night had now been reduced to a lump of dead meat. Still I reached up and took hold of her foot, which dangled roughly half a metre above the floor. The coldness caused me to let go, but I made myself grab it again. Her toenails were painted purple, a detail I hadn't noticed before and which was now completely irrelevant.

I released her foot and stood up. I was almost eye-level with her groin and I had to swallow repeatedly not to throw up again. The book that had been forced up her vagina was bent double and soaked in blood, apart from a few pages that glowed eerily white in contrast to the blood and the flesh. Her stomach and breasts were streaked with blood and my eyes followed the lines upwards. The blue nylon rope around her neck dug deep into her flesh. Under the rope, cuts had been made to her throat, some all the way to her veins from where the blood had flowed freely. Scrunched-up pages had been stuffed into her mouth and I knew that they had been ripped out of the same book.

In *Media Whore*, the killer had placed his victim on a chair and raped her with a book after which he had hoisted her up on the chair and tightened the rope around her neck, so she could only avoid strangulation by standing on her toes. Then he had made the first incisions into smaller veins causing her to slowly lose blood. She began to weaken and was finally unable to keep upright. The moment she collapsed, he severed her artery and spun her around so the blood sprayed the walls like a garden sprinkler. The body was emptied of blood and in her death throes, the victim kicked over the chair.

My naked body shook with cold and shock. True, I had described the terrifying scenario in front of me in detail, but I had never imagined the horror of actually experiencing it. The only discrepancy I registered was that the blood hadn't sprayed all the way up the walls as I had imagined in the book, but the scene was macabre enough without this detail. Everything else fitted my description. I wouldn't need to turn Linda Hvilbjerg's body around to see that her hands were tied behind her back with gaffer tape. Even so that's what I did and was proved right. Her body slowly swung back when I let go of it and again I was staring at her groin.

Using my thumb and index finger, I took hold of the book. I tried pulling it out with quick tugs, but it refused to move and only caused the body to swing towards me. I gave up and stepped back, frightened, and wiped my fingers on my chest.

I steeled myself and approached the body again. I steadied her hip with one hand and grabbed the book with the other. Then I yanked downwards until the book came out, but it was too slippery to hold on to and it fell from my hand and landed in the puddle on the floor. A large amount of blood that had been held back by the book followed and splashed over the book and floor and up my legs.

I instantly released the body and knelt down by the book. The cover was smeared with blood and I had to wipe the title with my fingers to be able to read it. It was – as I had known all along – a copy of *Media Whore* and, when I opened the book, I could see that my signature was there too, the signature I had last seen in Hotel BunkInn.

I cursed loudly. If only I had stayed in room 87, or at least taken the book with me, I might have been able to prevent it. If only I had done *something*.

My body was covered in blood and I could barely make it obey me. Yet I managed to crawl over to a white sofa, where I climbed into a corner and curled up. I had had sex with Linda on that sofa a few hours ago – or how long was it really?

I looked around for a clock, but couldn't see one. It was daylight outside, but the murky sky didn't reveal what time of day it was. How long had I been asleep?

There was no avoiding it this time, I knew that. I had to contact the police immediately. Yet I remained on the white sofa, which was now stained with blood, for at least half an hour.

Finally, I pulled myself together and sat up.

A telephone was mounted on the wall near the door to the hall. I summoned all my strength and stood up. I staggered to the door and grabbed the telephone. The line was dead. In despair I yanked the receiver so the cable snapped and I hurled it at my feet. Plastic fragments scattered over the parquet floor.

I went out into the hall. This was where our love-making had started. I expected to find my clothes where I had thrown them in a messy heap on the floor, but instead they lay neatly folded on a chair next to a full-length mirror. My shoes had been placed under the chair.

As I approached, I sensed that something was wrong. My shoes were slightly shiny. When I picked them up, I saw this was because they were coated with blood. I glanced back at the living room where the shoeprints performed their dance. There was also blood on the soles of my shoes. I put them down and picked up my trousers from the chair. When I held them up I realized what had happened.

The killer had dressed in my clothes and shoes for the murder.

Suddenly I was convinced he was still in the house, watching me. I could almost hear him chuckling to himself somewhere, relishing my horror when I realized that the prints on the living-room floor in Linda Hvilbjerg's blood had been made with my own shoes.

A violent rage exploded inside me and I vented it by storming naked around the whole house, snarling like a guard dog, determined to tear my prey to pieces once I caught it. It was a desperate, impulsive action, I was unlikely to be able to do anything if the killer really was here. But I had to know for sure. If only to see his face, yank those sodding sunglasses off him, look him in the face and demand an answer. I had to know who was trying to ruin my life, force an explanation out of him somehow.

But there was no one.

Exhausted, I flopped down on the sofa again. My footprints on the living-room floor now mingled with the killer's shoeprints. It looked chilling. My feet and my shoes, that was how it would look to the police. And it wasn't as if they would be short of evidence. We had left fingerprints and DNA all over the house during the night and for some reason I knew the killer hadn't.

The daylight was fading and I guessed it must be late afternoon. I hadn't shown up for the last interview at the book fair and Finn must have been bombarding the hotel with telephone calls. That meant nothing now.

I knew I had to leave the house. As I couldn't call the

police, I had to drive to the station and report the murder. It didn't occur to me to try the neighbours. The only person I needed to talk to was Sergeant Vendelev. He would undoubtedly arrest me. All the evidence pointed to me, I knew that, and yet it must speak in my favour that I had come of my own free will. Besides, there was my warning on Linda's mobile; they would have to take that into consideration.

Her mobile. I jumped up and ran out into the hall. Linda's handbag hung on a peg under her jacket. I emptied out the contents on the floor. Make-up, receipts, car keys, pills and paper tissues. No mobile.

What did that mean? That the killer had stolen her mobile and cut the connection to her landline? Why? To prevent her calling for help or delay my contacting the police? It was now a matter of urgency that I got hold of Sergeant Vendelev.

My clothes were soaked in blood so I went upstairs and searched her wardrobe. All of Linda's clothes, sorted according to colour, lay in neat piles or were suspended from hangers. The insides of the doors were mirrored. I froze temporarily when I caught sight of my own reflection. My hair was tangled, my eyes red from crying and my body and legs covered in blood. I felt even worse than I looked.

The only suitable item of clothing her wardrobe could offer me was a white shirt. I took it and went out into the bathroom. There I washed the blood off my body as well as I could and put on the shirt. Then I went down to the hall and put on my bloodstained trousers, socks and shoes, and jacket.

I picked up her car keys from the floor where they had landed when I emptied her handbag and took one last look into the living room where Linda's body hung from the landing. Again, I was overcome by nausea.

I pushed down the door handle firmly and opened the front door.

There was a thud at my feet.

An object had been leaning against the door and it fell over when I opened it.

A book.

32

After Line left me, I stayed with Bjarne and Anne. The first few days were almost like the Scriptorium days with whisky and deep conversations until the early morning hours, but Bjarne and Anne both had jobs to go to and soon I felt like a relative who has outstayed their welcome. I checked into the Marieborg Hotel, my first encounter with the hotel that would later feature in *As You Sow*.

Deep down I think Bjarne and Anne were glad to see the back of me. I was their friend, but I knew they believed the break-up was entirely of my own making. It was my fault that Line had left me and I had lost the most precious people in my life through my own carelessness. They never said so directly, but I could see it in their eyes and hear it in the silences that followed whenever I entered the room. There was nothing for it but to move out.

There were still talks to give and receptions to go to and, as I didn't fancy sitting alone falling apart in the cottage, the hotel proved to be the answer. It was cheap and relatively near the city centre.

There was no need for me to be bored. Wealth and fame means it is never hard to find company and company was what I craved. Every time I was on my own, I had a panic attack. It was like sinking into a dark ocean. The shadows of strange creatures swam around me, but only rarely came close enough for me to be able to make them out. Sometimes they were mermaids in the shape of the Line or the girls, other times they were shapeless crossbreeds of marine animals and mammals.

It was highly likely that these visions were the result of the alcohol and drug abuse I was undertaking with the commitment and precision of a participant in a highly amoral research project. I consumed doses in exact quantities and at such intervals that enabled me to party for as long as possible without feeling either too much or too little. I balanced on a knife edge, constantly focusing on my next fix: an upper or a downer, a beer or spirits. Fortunately, I had the money to buy whatever I wanted, and when the money is there, getting booze, drugs or friends is never a problem.

I met a lot of people whom I mistakenly believed to be my friends. They were on the same ride as me, a roller-coaster in permanent motion with our hands raised high above our heads and our eyes staring straight ahead. Every night we met up at Dan Turèll, Konrad, Viktor or whichever bar was the 'in' place that week and prescribed for one another throughout the night until the place closed or some woman dragged me into a taxi. There were plenty of women and there were several days in a row where I didn't sleep in my hotel bed at all. I wouldn't feel remorseful until the next day and even then my contrition only lasted until I had had my first drink. I slept with Linda Hvilbjerg a couple more times – this was before I vented my spleen on her – and a paparazzo managed to snap a photo of us together at a party. This wasn't something that worried either of us. The following week we were photographed with other people and soon Linda in general and me in particular were regular fixtures in the gossip columns. Or so I was told. I didn't read them myself and nor did I care all that much except when the women I tried to chat up in bars turned me down with a snooty comment that they had no wish to be on a tabloid front page. Still, it never deterred me from moving on to the next woman who either hadn't heard about my escapades, wasn't bothered or actively courted publicity and viewed me as a shortcut. There was a surprisingly large number of the latter.

The circle around me grew. Some joined, others dropped off, but eventually I had acquired an entourage. They followed me everywhere, but I usually picked up the tab. At the start it didn't worry me. I had plenty of money. But I slowly realized they had no intention of ever getting their wallets out.

One night I spotted Mortis. He was sitting on the edge of the group, close enough to be part of it, but so far away that he could leave unnoticed.

I didn't confront him immediately. Instead I carried on buying rounds, which he was quick to accept, and I watched him when he wasn't looking.

He was, if possible, even paler than I remembered him, his black hair long and lank. A trench coat hung over his frail body and underneath it was a white shirt that didn't appear to have been washed for a long time. Mortis, along with a couple of other guys, seemed to thrive on the periphery. They had formed their own club within the club and they were laughing at their own jokes, which were out of my earshot. I had a growing suspicion they were laughing at me.

A couple of hours later I could no longer ignore them.

'Bloody hell, isn't that Mortis?'

He was startled and, for a moment, looked like a thief caught red-handed.

'It certainly is,' he said, and tried to smile, revealing a row of yellow teeth.

'Bloody hell . . . how long has it been? Three, four years?'

He shrugged. 'You could be right.'

'So what are you up to?'

'Well, you know . . . a bit of writing,' he replied. He emptied his glass and looked expectantly at me.

I ordered another round. He grabbed the glass with gratitude.

'You're doing all right, eh?' he said, nodding to me. 'You've managed to get your . . . books published?' He spat out the word 'books' with an ill-concealed snarl that caused those sitting closest to snigger.

'I can't complain,' I replied. 'How about you? Have you got your tattoo yet?'

Mortis glared at me and drank his drink before replying. 'Not yet.'

Some people started an animated discussion about tattoos and those who had one showed it to the others in the group. This new game generated excitement and we became the centre of attention. Mortis look away when I took off my jacket and shirt to boast of my ISBN tattoo. He said nothing the rest of the evening; he simply knocked back the drinks that were placed in front of him. I didn't expect to see him again, but he appeared the following evening and watched from the sidelines without joining in.

Late one night I had finally had enough. It wasn't only Mortis. I was surrounded by five or six scroungers who had no intention of contributing and weren't even capable of entertaining me; they merely grinned and nodded every time I said something.

I don't even think they heard what I said because when I told everyone to get lost, they didn't react. When I repeated it and this time added 'parasites', a couple of them laughed, but when I shouted it a third time, the smiles disappeared and the grinning subsided as they exchanged nervous looks. The fourth time it finally sank in and they did as they were told, but not until they had knocked back the drinks I had just paid for. They filed out of the bar, a few muttering insults such as pretentious git, skinflint and drama queen.

Mortis said nothing, but smiled with infuriating superiority and touched an imaginary hat as he left.

Everyone in the bar was staring at me, but I turned my back on them and ordered another bottle. I had had it up to here with all of them. Every single one of them wanted my money, free drinks or a little touch of stardust by touching the hem of my robe. At that time reality TV shows had become big business and I had watched with revulsion how programmes such as *Survivor* and *Big*

Brother attracted the very types who had gathered around me like flies.

I downed a couple of drinks, for once not thinking about the effect. This was about getting drunk on my own. I had no need of deadbeat friends who were there only for a thrill. No more wannabes, thank you very much. No *Survivor* centrefolds looking for the experience of a lifetime. Piss off, amateur singers who expected TV to give them an instant career that required no sacrifices. Go away, brain-dead teenage hopefuls who thought being famous was a job. Get lost all of you who believed there was a shortcut to fame and that it came without a price tag. I had toiled for mine. And I paid the price. A high price. So high I could barely recognize my own life any more.

The outrage grew inside me until I couldn't contain it any longer.

The bottle of booze of which I had drunk nearly half was standing on the counter. I grabbed its neck and smashed it against the edge of the bar. Then I spun around and screamed for anyone looking for a life-changing experience to come and have a go. I would change their lives beyond recognition. They wouldn't need a television or a desert island to feel alive; I could take care of that right here and now, free of charge.

At first there was silence.

I waved the bottle in the air and carried on yelling. Was anyone looking for a new direction? Who wanted to be catapulted out of their humdrum lives, like they all secretly hoped and prayed for? Conversations resumed as if nothing had happened. Raising my voice made no difference. No one dared look at me, for fear of drawing attention to themselves. That didn't stop me. If anyone wanted to change their life, all they had to do was come over and I would take care of it.

I was seized from behind by two bartenders, one for each arm. One of them hammered my wrist into the counter so I dropped the bottle. People in the bar tried to ignore the incident, but they watched out of the corner of their eyes. I was still howling, called the bartenders and everyone present the worst names I could think of. They frogmarched me through the room and out into the street where they pushed me so hard that I landed in the road. I sat up and carried on ranting while they went back inside the bar. One of them stayed behind the door, keeping an eye on me.

I don't know how much time passed, but at some point a police car arrived and took me down to the station. I only remember glimpses from that night. I was led down deserted, neon-lit corridors that reminded me of a World War II asylum. I went berserk again, out of fear this time, and more police officers appeared. The next thing I remember was my belt and my shoes being taken from me. Then the cell, an ice-cold concrete box with a steel toilet and a thin mattress. After they had closed the door, I screamed abuse for a while. How long for, I don't know. At some point I must have fallen asleep. I woke up the next morning stiff and sore all over.

I had lost my voice and the desire to use it. I felt revulsion towards city life and the company of others so when I was released I went straight to the hotel, packed my things and left Copenhagen.

Three months had passed since Line threw me out, three

months where I had constantly been under the influence of alcohol, drugs or both. I couldn't even remember if I had enjoyed myself. All the days merged into one. I had visited the same bars, met the same people and heard the same stories. Even the women I had seduced were foggy memories where, at best, all I could remember was the colour of their hair or the bedroom I had woken up in the next day.

Nor had it been cheap. Three months in a hotel was a huge extravagance and I didn't even dare think of how much money I had spent drinking. I could afford it, no doubt about that, but when I reflect on what I got out of it, it was the worst investment of my life. My reputation was in tatters and the acquaintances I had made were worthless beyond the saloon bar and the fellowship of intoxication.

All I wanted was to be alone and avoid other people as much as I could. The cottage was the answer. Initially I had regarded it as somewhere to store my stuff until I found a place in the city, but now I had the option to disappear, barricade myself in for as long as I wanted. It was early spring, towards the end of March, and the holiday season wouldn't start for a long time so I would be undisturbed, left to wallow in my own misery.

Even the drive up there was liberating. The further away I got from the city, the easier it became to breathe. The darkness I had found myself in slowly faded and grew lighter until it dissolved completely as I drove up the gravel drive to the Tower.

My belongings had been moved up there a couple of months ago and the boxes were still in the middle of the living room where the removal men had left them. The air was damp and stuffy so I opened all the windows and doors and went outside. I hadn't been there for more than six months and the garden was in a sorry state. There were fallen branches everywhere, blown down during the winter, and the grass was yellow after the winter snows.

Though there was just about enough wood to light a fire, I took off my jacket and split ten or fifteen logs myself. It was hard work, the sweat dripped from me and my wrists ached, but at the same time it was incredibly good to feel my body again. Back inside I closed the windows, lit a fire and sat down in front of the flames with a glass and a bottle of whisky.

At that moment, I never wanted to leave the cottage again. Ever.

However, that wish lasted only as long as it took me to drink the house dry. I was forced to go out, though the very thought of other people made me sick. Even the sound of voices made me close windows and doors and lie down on the sofa with a blanket over me. I had unplugged the telephone after it rang twice. It was with great wariness that I made my first foray to the shop. I executed my mission like a soldier from a specialist unit, get in, get out, no hesitation or impulse-buying, and it was a success. Nothing happened. I wasn't attacked and no one tried to talk to me. Slowly, I gained more confidence and eventually I was following a routine that became my life for the next two months. Every morning I would buy fresh bread, six strong beers and a miniature of Gammel Dansk bitters. I would drink the miniature on my way home. It was still early spring, so the warmth from the alcohol was as welcome as a warm coat. I washed down my breakfast with some beers, after which I went out into the garden. There I would chop more firewood, cut the grass or carry out other strenuous tasks.

Pleased with my efforts, I would reward myself with a few more beers, at which point I would discover that I had none left. This always came as a surprise and a second trip to the shop for more soon became a regular feature of my day, something you could set your watch by. The second trip was by bike, an old gentleman's bicycle that had come with the house when we bought it. The chain was rusty and several spokes were missing or bent, so I must have been a pathetic sight, a long-haired, bearded creature on a rattling boneshaker, stamping on the pedals and swaying my upper body from side to side.

As the days passed, people got used to me, and on my late morning trip I always encountered the same two or three men sitting on the stone circle outside the shop. They greeted me faithfully every time, but to begin with I didn't deign to look at them. I didn't need human contact and I certainly wasn't in need of drinking companions. I managed perfectly well on my own, thank you very much.

After the trip to the shop, my day consisted of sitting on the terrace if the weather stayed dry or in the living room in front of the stove if it rained and working my way through the day's catch. Typically this meant ten or fifteen strong beers or a bottle of spirits, sometimes both. I often bought some food, but more often than not I didn't get round to eating it.

The day would end with me falling asleep in front of the stove.

Writing was out of the question. I had lost the urge and the mere sight of books made me want to throw up. Four of the removal boxes in the living room were full of books, but I couldn't bring myself to unpack them. The boxes remained unopened, a constant reminder of the life I had left behind.

One night, I tried to burn some of the books. The flames turned blue as they ate their way through the cover and the laminate bubbled like boils while the illustrations darkened until they were black all over and caught fire. The pages burned badly because they were too dense and I had to break them up with the poker to make them burn properly. It was slow and laborious work and failed to provide me with the satisfaction I had expected, so after three or four books I gave up.

One day, on my way to the shop for that day's rations, I noticed that one of the men on the stone circle was holding a book. Even from a distance, I recognized it as *Outer Demons*. I was on the verge of turning around and probably would have done so had I not been as parched as I was. I ignored the men on my way in, but on my way out I couldn't help glancing at them. There were three of them. Two of them were sitting down, probably to support the weight of their huge stomachs, and the third looked up. He was the one holding the book and I now recognized him as my neighbour. He waved the book and erupted in a broad smile.

'Got you,' he said, grinning.

I think I smiled and shrugged, but I exchanged no words with them and hurried home without looking back.

The weather was growing milder and I could sit outside on the terrace most of the afternoon. That was what I was doing that day, lazing in a deckchair with a wobbly frame and perished fabric that protested every time I shifted position. In order not to have to get up too often, I would get three beers on every trip. I was sitting with one in my lap; the other two were within easy reach, shaded by the garden table until it was their turn. This number meant my urge to urinate corresponded perfectly with my need to fetch fresh supplies.

'Hello, neighbour,' a voice suddenly called out and the man with the book appeared around the corner of the house. He was carrying a plastic bag.

I was about to return his greeting, but discovered I couldn't get a word out. Looking back, I couldn't even remember when I had last used my voice.

'I hope it's OK, me barging in on you,' he continued, as he came closer. He was limping slightly and he held out his hand to me.

I nodded, straightened up as the deckchair groaned and shook his hand. It was dry and warm and I realized I hadn't been in physical contact with another person for several weeks.

'But . . . as we're neighbours and all that' – he pulled the book out of the bag – 'please could I have an autograph?'

I gestured to one of the plastic garden chairs.

'Yes, please,' he said quickly and sat down.

'Would you like a beer?' I asked in a croaky voice, pointing to my stock under the garden table. I was offering not because I wanted to, but because I felt I had to.

'No, thank you. I've already got some.' He rattled the bag and the bottles clinked invitingly.

A huge wave of relief washed over me. I'd been dreading he was yet another scrounger, just like the people I had fled.

'By the way, my name is Bent,' he said, taking out a bottle of Fine Festival beer.

'Frank,' I volunteered, nodding towards the book he had placed on the garden table.

Bent grinned. 'Yeah, mate, I worked that one out.' He produced a bottle opener, polished to perfection by frequent trips in and out of his back pocket. He opened the beer, put the bottle top in the plastic bag and carefully removed any foil left around the bottleneck.

'Cheers, neighbour.' He held out his bottle to me. I held out mine and we toasted. While I drank, I watched how his Adam's apple bobbed as he swallowed nearly half the beer.

'Ah,' he sighed when he finally removed the bottle from his lips.

I got up to fetch a pen and when I came back, Bent was busy opening the next beer.

'I'm not usually much of a reader,' he said. 'But I just loved that shit. Bloody brilliant book!'

'Thank you,' I said, taking the book. It was a paperback, tattered and yellowed by the sun. My photo was on the back and I was struck by how serious I looked. My beard was trimmed with a ruler and my dark hair brushed back, smooth and a tad glossy like a 1930s crooner. However, it was the eyes that surprised me the most. They stared coldly and a little provocatively from the back of the book and I remember how hard it had been to look so aloof. There had been absolutely nothing to be cross about. After all, I had written a book Finn had assured me would be a bestseller, I was married to the loveliest woman in the world and had an angel of a daughter. The photo had been taken only four years ago, but it felt as if it was from a parallel universe, one where I was a successful author and not a bum.

'A really good book,' Bent repeated. 'Gory details. Wicked descriptions of the murders, wicked!'

I flicked through the pages in my mind's eye while he carried on praising the book. Several pages were dog-eared. At the start, they were close together, but later in the book the distance grew and the last quarter had no folded corners at all. I signed my name and handed the book back.

'Thanks a lot, Penpusher,' he said holding it to his heart. 'Viggo and Johnny wanted to borrow it, but I said no, and I won't let them have it now, no way. They can buy their bloody own.' He carefully returned the book to the bag as if it was as fragile as the bottles. 'I've started another one. I can't really remember the name of the guy who wrote it, but it's not a patch on yours.'

Looking back, that first meeting with Bent, the sight of the turned-down corners and especially the frequency of them, was crucial for my return to writing. I told myself I had done a good deed. A heathen had been converted to the true faith. A non-reader had been converted to a reader and, better still, one of *my* readers. I was flattered. This wasn't hollow praise from colleagues or the jet set, but a totally spontaneous gesture, as if I had found a source of pure water in a desert with nothing but poisoned wells.

Not that we were drinking water. We drank the bottles we had and Bent went off for fresh supplies several times. For the first time since my arrival, I opened the book crates. I wanted to introduce him to my favourite readings. Soon the floor was covered with books. He had reignited my voice and I let it talk and talk, words that had built up in the past weeks poured out of my mouth without me censoring what I said. I think I spoke completely over his head, but he showed no sign of being bored – on the contrary. I gave him a copy of *Inner Demons* and told him he could borrow books from me any time he wanted to.

Bent introduced me to the others on the stones in front of the shop and in the weeks that followed I became a member of their circle. I learned about Bent's army career, which later formed the basis for *A Bullet in the Chamber*, and gained insight into Viggo's and Johnny's lives as long-term unemployed in an area otherwise inhabited by wealthy tourists and second-home-owners from the capital.

If meeting Bent inspired me to write again, then Viggo and Johnny gave me the motivation to get started. After only two weeks, they were repeating the same old stories, and I discovered to my horror that I was doing it too. I saw in them what I would become a few years from now if I didn't do something to prevent it, and the thought frightened me.

Overnight I reduced my alcohol intake drastically – in fact, I switched to whisky, a marked contrast to my usual menu of beer and schnapps. It was partly a return to what used to be my favourite tipple while I wrote. The taste of good whisky alone seemed to revive my writing brain cells.

I started planning *A Bullet in the Chamber*. It was the perfect comeback book. I wouldn't even need to leave the cottage to carry out research; all I had to do was wait for Bent to stop by with his bag of Fine Festival beer. He did so every day and the book quickly took shape.

I even ventured to contact Finn to tell him to expect something and his relief was palpable. When I left Copenhagen, he had been forced to turn down a number of interviews and opportunities to promote *Inner Demons*, but my disappearance had in itself been a great story. Sales had benefited from the coverage, admittedly fairly critical and condescending, of the missing author and Finn himself had been interviewed about my sudden exit. He knew very well where I was and probably why I had left, but he stuck to the vanishing act story and didn't shy away from telling everybody about it.

The urge to promote myself or the book didn't return along with the urge to write it. I discovered the optimum working method for me: isolation and a mixture of fixed writing times, physical labour in the garden or the cottage and someone to drink with when I wanted to. My life played out within a fifteen-minute walk that contained the cottage, the shop and the beach where I strolled when I needed fresh air.

I needed nothing more, only my imagination.

A Bullet in the Chamber was a story about soldiers in Iraq. The book wasn't at all political, but the foreign setting, the discipline and the secrecy between interpreters, soldiers and their superiors inspired me to write a Ten Little Indians-style murder mystery about a group of men who are isolated at a guard post at the Iraqi border. The deaths initially look like accidents, but the killings become more and more brutal and eventually the men can no longer ignore the facts. As their numbers diminish, an atmosphere of distrust builds up and accusations fly between the soldiers. The victims begin to be mutilated, suggesting a religious motive. The obvious suspect, the interpreter Maseuf, is lynched by the frenzied group who literally rip him to pieces, but when another murder is committed it becomes a fight for survival among the men who are left. When they are down to two, the real hero of the book, Bent Kløvermark, traps the killer in a minefield where he dies and Bent himself loses a leg.

When the script was finished, I was pleasantly surprised. It was quite a respectable pile of paper, 325 pages, and they proved I could at least still call myself a writer now that I had been stripped of the title of husband and father.

33

Whoever had leaned the book against Linda Hvilbjerg's front door – and it had to be the killer – hadn't bothered wrapping it. No envelope this time and nor did I need to turn it over to know which book it was. I recognized my breakthrough novel, *Outer Demons*, from the back alone.

I took a step back and stared at the book. My heart started to pound. The sense of being under surveillance returned. It was as if someone was watching me from a control room with monitors everywhere to display every reaction of my body and face and microphones to pick up every sound I uttered. Graphs illustrated my pulse, sensors registered my sweat production and body temperature, and an emoticon conveyed the information about my current state of mind.

Right now the emoticon would signal horror. It would look like *The Scream* by Edvard Munch.

But I didn't scream. I was too scared to scream.

Minutes before I opened the door, I had been ready to go to the police and tell them everything. I was prepared to run the risk that they might imprison me, suspect me of murder – not unreasonably – and I had braced myself for long painful interrogations in a dark interview room with bright lights, good cop/bad cop routines and all the other clichés.

The book changed everything.

Even before I opened it, I knew I couldn't go to the police. I knew that whatever I was about to find out would mean I couldn't talk to anyone. When I discovered the book with Linda's photo at Hotel BunkInn, I had believed it would give me a head start, that I could anticipate the killer's next move and would have enough time to do something about it, but now it seemed to me that I had fallen in with the killer's plan. It had always been his intention that I would contact Linda and put myself in a situation where I would be the one to discover her body.

But the game wasn't over yet. That was what the book was telling me. It signalled that I had no will of my own, but would have to keep on playing for as long as the killer was entertained.

Outside birds were chirping. A breeze wafted mild air through the hall, a welcome change to the smell of death in the living room.

I looked up from the book and across the street. There was no one around. The area seemed deserted by all other life forms except birds. Only the trees moved in the wind, scattering autumn leaves on the pavement.

Slowly, I took a step forwards and knelt down. Still looking across the street, I picked up the book and pulled it towards me. I stood up, stepped back, closed the door softly and locked it. The sound of birdsong disappeared.

I went back to the living room and sat down in the chair.

Linda's body was hanging with her back to me as if she had turned away in contempt. I turned the book over with shaking hands and realized I had been right. It was *Outer Demons*, a cheap paperback copy, but apparently unread, like the other greetings the killer had sent me.

I found the photo roughly halfway through the book. My heart stopped.

If I hadn't just seen my daughter, Ironika, at the book fair, I would probably have struggled to recognize her from the picture. She seemed very grown-up, but in that slightly affected way children sometimes have when they mimic their parents. Her eyelids were dark and she wore a little blusher on her cheeks. Her hair was carefully tousled and she had a challenging, almost defiant expression in her blue eyes. A curtain or a rug hung in the background, and the lighting was simple but professional. It looked like a school photo.

I turned the photo over. The name of the photographer, Inger Klausen, the name of her company, K-Foto, and their telephone number were listed on the back. At that moment, I hated Inger Klausen for even having looked at my daughter.

I put the book and the picture of my daughter on the table in front of me and buried my face in my hands. A howling sound started to build up inside me and it travelled up to my chest. It couldn't be suppressed, but rolled out through my throat and mouth. My entire body shook from crying, despair and impotence.

I clenched my hands, stood up and screamed at the ceiling. The sound frightened me, but gave me some relief, so I carried on until I had no more air left in me.

The tears were streaming down my cheeks and a mix of wailing, shouting and snarling erupted from my throat.

I went over to Linda's body, stood in front of her frozen face and howled as loud as I could. A last remnant of self-control prevented me from bashing away at her.

'What do you want?' I yelled. 'What is it you want?'

Linda Hvilbjerg didn't reply. She only stared stubbornly back at me.

It started to get dark outside. The living room turned grey and alien and its designer furniture was reduced to unrecognizable shapes. The stench of death and decay was pronounced. I could no longer ignore it and ultimately I think that was what drove me on.

With the police out of the picture, I didn't need to worry about leaving the house, or the crime scene as it now was, undisturbed. Besides, I owed Linda Hvilbjerg some respect. I took off my jacket and the shirt I'd taken from Linda's wardrobe, and went out into the kitchen to fetch a knife. In the living room I cut Linda down and carried her upstairs. She was heavy, heavier than anything I had ever carried, and when I laid her down on her bed, my naked upper body was covered in sweat and blood. I removed the paper from her mouth, closed her eyes and pulled the duvet over her. At the door to the bedroom I gave her a final glance.

I washed myself again, put the shirt and jacket back on and picked up the novel before I left the house.

Linda owned a Mercedes Smart, one of those cars you can park in a phone booth and costs a small fortune despite its size. I didn't know where to go. The smell of death haunted me and I was aware of the state of my clothes. First I had to find something clean to wear.

The engine started at once and I headed for the city centre. It was early Sunday evening, and there were few people in the streets of this Copenhagen suburb.

Close to the local railway station, I found what I was looking for. A Salvation Army charity shop was located in the basement of an older building facing Vigerslev Allé. The steps leading down to the shop were piled high with black bin bags, donations from well-meaning people who thought that others might find a use for the 1980s bell-bottoms they had now definitively outgrown.

I parked on the pavement, close to the entrance and got out after checking there was no one around. The steps down to the shop were wide and deep and around ten bin bags were lying there. I squatted down on the edge of the top step, grabbed hold of the first bin bag and tore it open. The tear revealed pink colours, white tights, princess dresses and teddy bears. I threw the bin bag aside and took a new one. It was full of suits, but I soon discovered that they were far too small for me.

When I ripped open bin bag number three, I was joined by a tall, thin man in a long coat. His dark hair was wispy and his stubble revealed it was a while since he'd had a shave. I threw him a frightened look, but he merely nodded to me and sat down on the steps where he started on the bin bag I had just discarded. He didn't waste time rummaging through the bag, but tipped out the contents in front of him and studied the clothes through narrow eyes. He held up a jacket, but realized – as I had done – that it was too small and tossed it down the steps.

MIKKEL BIRKEGAARD

I copied his example and emptied the contents of my bin bag on the pavement. It was full of curtains and bed linen. I kicked them aside and started on the next one. The man held up a small pink princess dress. Something made his eyes light up and he stuffed it inside his long coat and smiled with satisfaction. Then he took out a packet of cigarettes and lit one. In the glow from the lighter, I saw that his face was pockmarked and it was dark around one of his eyes. He hummed to himself as he stretched his lean body and grabbed another bin bag.

My next bag contained children's clothing. Small socks, shorts and T-shirts spilled out and buried my feet. I kicked them out of the way. People really did throw away an unbelievable amount of children's clothes. Surely there must be something somewhere I could use. Irritably, I glanced at the man next to me. He had found a pair of corduroy trousers. He turned them over and over while nodding to himself, then he stood up and held the trousers up to his waist. His cigarette dangled from the corner of his mouth and he looked down himself with approval. A little ash fell on the corduroy trousers and he brushed it off carefully.

The anger rose inside me. Those trousers would have suited me. In fact, they were too big in the waist for him and a little too short for his long skinny legs. I was supposed to have found them. I was there first. They belonged to me.

I got up and stepped over to him. At first he didn't notice. He was focused on his trophy and grinned idiotically at his luck. Finally, he looked up. His half-open eyes stared into mine with wonder and he frowned.

Without a word, I grabbed hold of the corduroy trousers and yanked them from him. However, he had a strong grip and I only succeeded in pulling him closer.

'What the hell are you doing?' he grunted.

'Let go,' I said. 'They're mine.'

'No, they're bloody not,' he replied tugging at the trousers. 'I found them, find your own.'

I let go of the trousers, but only to shove the man hard in the chest. He fell backwards and the cigarette slipped out of his mouth. His eyes were no longer half closed, but wide open, and he stared at me in disbelief.

'Give them to me,' I ordered him.

He tried to get back on his feet, but I pushed him and he fell again. His head snapped backwards and he hit it against the pavement with a sickening thud.

'Shit!' I swore and knelt down by his side.

Wailing noises were coming from his mouth and his eyes closed for a moment. When he opened them again and looked at me, there was fear in them. He let go of the trousers and scrambled away from me.

'You're a psycho, man.'

I took a step towards him and held out my hand. 'I'm really—'

'Stay away from me!'

I picked up the trousers and got back to work. The bin bag he'd ripped open lay exposed like a cadaver and I searched through it quickly. There were several pairs of trousers, jumpers and even a pair of shoes. I cradled everything in my arms and walked back to the car. With some effort I managed to open the door to the passenger side and dumped the clothes on the seat.

The man in the long coat had reached the next set of steps where he sat down, hugging himself and glaring at me.

I ignored him, got in the car and drove off.

34

I changed clothes in the car. It wasn't easy. A Mercedes Smart has roughly the same floor space as a shop cubicle, but is only half as tall. Apart from the corduroy trousers, the bin bag had yielded a jumper that fitted me, while the shoes, a pair of blue deck shoes with tassels, were one size too big, but at least they weren't covered in blood.

I dumped my blood-soaked trousers and shoes in a skip in the car park where I had changed. I felt relieved and, as I also abandoned the car, I felt I had put as much distance between me and Linda Hvilbjerg as I could. I couldn't banish the images of her naked body hanging in the living room, but I did my best to keep them at bay. I had to.

Now my daughter was all that mattered.

I had tried to protect Linda, but being with her had made no difference. She had been murdered right before my eyes – all right, so they had been closed and I had been in a deep sleep, but it had happened while I was near. So how would I be able to protect my daughter?

I walked back to the hotel without finding the answer. It was a long walk and I had money for a taxi, but I preferred walking. I think better when I walk and I needed some time out. I reviewed the murders. I tried to imagine the person who was capable of carrying out these killings exactly as I had described them in my books. It was risky. Murder was my home turf, not his, which ought to give me an advantage, or at least a chance to understand him. But what was he hoping to achieve? Did he mean to punish me, challenge me or was it a tribute? I was fairly sure he expected me to make the next move. He had done that with Linda. Like a chess player, he had set a trap and waited for me to make my move, a move by which I would expose myself and thus lose my knight. Now he was going for my queen and it wasn't enough for me to lose her, I also had to *feel* that I had lost her.

Chess had never been my strong point, but murder was. For more than half my life I had planned murders. I had described the psyche of countless murderers to explain why they did what they did, and even though it had become just a business over the years, it was always important to me that it made sense. To me, job satisfaction was the moment everything added up. I was proud when a scene or a detail slotted into the story like a missing cog that makes everything else turn. The sensation never lasted long, but it made it all worthwhile.

I was vain about my plots. I hated it when readers sent me letters pointing out inaccuracies in the killings, things that were physically impossible or errors in the narrative. There was always some tiny piece of information it hadn't been possible for me to check. They were usually trifles with no impact on the story, certainly not given the genre, but it still irritated me.

Take the fish in the Gilleleje murder, for instance. In the book I had described how the fish had nibbled away at the victim's body and swum off with large chunks of her flesh. When Verner told me this hadn't been the case, I had experienced a certain amount of pique. The same pique had hit me when I saw the colour of Verner's hands. In *As You Sow* I had described them as purple and swollen, like a pair of dark leather gloves, but in the hotel room they had the same colour as the rest of his body.

Perhaps I wasn't the expert after all.

I stopped in my tracks.

My heart must have skipped a couple of beats and was now trying to make up the shortfall. I staggered to the nearest bench where I sat down and concentrated on my breathing. I closed my eyes and pressed my palms against my ears to block out sound and make room for thought. I was on to something. I was convinced of it. It felt just like when I was close to solving a problem in a novel. An intoxicating feeling. Better than sex.

I knew what the killer wanted.

He didn't want to punish me or celebrate me.

He wanted to educate me.

It may sound strange, and thinking back it certainly is weird, but at that moment I felt relief. I believed I now understood what the killer wanted from me, and the first step towards stopping him was precisely that. It was the cornerstone in practically all my books.

The killer had shown me there were inaccuracies in the murders I had described. In the Gilleleje murder it was the fish, at the hotel it was the hands, but Linda Hvilbjerg? I recreated the image of her hanging like a lump of meat in the elegant living room. I had received several letters regarding that murder. I hadn't read all of them, but a couple had pointed out that the victim's blood pressure wouldn't be high enough after the blood loss to produce the garden sprinkler effect.

Truth be told, I had suspected that when I wrote the book, but for once I had ignored the facts. I was more concerned with writing a spectacular crime scene and had knowingly allowed this factual error.

Linda's killer had to be an expert. It shook me – physically as well – as I sat there on the bench. All the time I had regarded myself as an authority in the field, but it was clear that I didn't have the necessary practical experience to describe all the details accurately and this was what had enraged the killer. He knew more about the body's reaction than I did. He wanted to educate me, highlight my inadequacy and my errors.

I had met my master.

Impressions from the world around me slowly returned. I noticed the traffic and the sounds from the street. The wind got hold of me and reminded me of the season and my flimsy clothing. I opened my eyes and looked around. I had walked almost in a trance before I sat down and now I saw that I was outside the Zoological Garden in Frederiksberg.

There was still another two kilometres to my hotel, but I covered the distance with brisk, purposeful steps.

I pushed open the door to the lobby with both hands and crossed the room. Fortunately the reception was un-staffed so I picked up my key and went straight to the lift.

It took for ever before the doors started to close and just before they met, they were blocked by a hand. The doors opened again and revealed Sergeant Kim Vendelev, the boy detective from Vesterbro police station.

'Frank Føns,' he said and entered the lift.

I held my breath and waited for the inevitable continuation. He would arrest me and take me down to the station. He briefly looked me up and down, but his facial expression didn't change even though I was wearing my spoils from the charity shop: blue shoes, brown corduroy trousers, a red pullover and my own black jacket, which by now was rather crumpled. I was still holding the book and I sneaked my hands behind my back to hide both the book and their shaking.

'Glad I caught you,' he continued. 'There's something I want to ask you.'

The doors closed and the lift started pulling us up inside the building.

'I was just about to go home,' he said. 'We've taken forensic samples all day, but we've almost finished now.' He exhaled heavily.

As did I, mentally. If he wanted to arrest me, he would have done it by now.

'Have you found anything?' I asked, although I didn't want to know.

'There's plenty of evidence,' he said. 'Too much, almost, but this is a hotel. A lot of people pass through so there's a mountain of paperwork to process – you know, the kind that solves crimes.'

'You'll get there in the end,' I said. It was hard to keep calm. Two people in a lift take up a lot of space and it wasn't easy to hide my nerves. I was sweating and I couldn't help tapping my foot.

'But while we were working, I heard some of my colleagues say something about the deceased.'

'Yes?'

'They said that Verner Nielsen had shown an interest in a murder on the north coast, more specifically in Gilleleje. That's near where you live, isn't it?'

I started to feel faint. My body was swaying slightly and I had to fix my eyes on the doors in order not to fall.

'Are you OK?' Sergeant Vendelev said, placing his hand on my shoulder.

At that moment the doors opened and I fell on my knees out into the corridor. I dropped the book when I instinctively tried to cushion the fall with my hands and it landed a short distance from me. I started wheezing.

'Do you want me to call a doctor?' Sergeant Vendelev asked anxiously.

I shook my head.

'It's OK,' I panted. 'I just don't like lifts.'

'Perhaps you should have taken the stairs?' Vendelev suggested and picked up the book with one hand while helping me to my feet with the other.

I staggered towards my room.

'I think I had better make sure you get to bed in one piece,' the sergeant said.

Vendelev supported me to my door where I struggled to insert the key with my still trembling hands. He led me to the nearest chair into which I collapsed and placed the book on the coffee table. The top of the photo stuck out so you could see my daughter's eyes. The sergeant went to the bathroom to fetch a glass of water. I accepted it gratefully and gulped half of it down.

'I didn't know you were claustrophobic,' Vendelev said, sitting down opposite me. 'But then again, I don't suppose there are many lifts in Rågeleje?'

I shook my head and drank the rest of the water.

'Because that's where you live, isn't it?' He didn't wait for a reply. 'It's a remarkable coincidence that Verner shows an interest in a murder near where you live, after which he's murdered at a hotel where you're staying, don't you think?'

I agreed that it looked like more than a coincidence, but suggested that this was what separated reality from fiction; in fiction nothing was coincidental. He appeared to reflect on this and nodded to himself with his eyes fixed on *Outer Demons*, which lay between us. He reached for the book.

'Yes, it's very strange that—'

'Thanks for helping,' I interrupted him and took the book before he could pick it up. 'But I think I had better get to bed.' I nodded in the direction of the bedroom.

'You're sure you're feeling better?' he asked and got up.

I nodded.

He kept looking at me. 'The power of phobias is extraordinary,' he said. 'I've seen grown men break down in aeroplanes and police officers run away from a domestic spider . . . By the way, haven't you written a novel based on phobias?'

I tried to swallow the last drops of water from the glass.

'Yes,' I replied. '*In the Red Zone*.'

'*In the Red Zone*,' he repeated. 'I'll make a note of that. Phobias are fascinating, perhaps I ought to read it.'

My breathing had almost returned to normal, but my heart was still pounding like a marathon runner's.

'I think you should,' I said and managed a smile.

'Right,' Vendelev exclaimed. 'I'll leave you in peace so you can recover. We can always discuss Verner's pet project some other time.'

I nodded and smiled, even though I knew that if I ever saw Sergeant Vendelev again, it would be in handcuffs.

35

The first thing I did when Sergeant Vendelev had left me alone in my hotel room was to take off my clothes and have a shower. My body smelled of sex and death and Linda Hvilbjerg's blood was still smeared across my legs. I showered for more than half an hour before I felt clean again.

I put on a fresh set of clothes and sat down on the sofa with *Outer Demons*. My strongest feelings of horror had subsided and been replaced by a sense of purpose, prompted by my discovery. I had found out what motivated the killer: factual errors in my books. Now I had to think of a way to stop him.

Outer Demons was my third book and I hadn't put much effort into researching it. Verner had helped me with minor aspects, but the book had practically written itself and I didn't want to wreck it by making it technical or didactic. Consequently, I might be looking for several factual errors; it was only a question of which ones had offended the killer the most.

After its publication I had received quite a few letters,

but I couldn't remember anyone complaining about specific details. Many felt it was a disgusting book they could barely bring themselves to read to the end, but this was because of the graphic violence, not because it was unrealistic.

I stared at the photo of my daughter. I was gripped with panic and it spread through my body. I placed the picture on the coffee table face down and concentrated on the book. I started flicking through it page by page. There were no notes, no marks or clues to guide me. When I had finished, I closed the book and pressed it to my forehead as if I could extract its secret through the power of my mind.

Outer Demons is a book about a monster, Henrik Booring, a rich man who has inherited the family fortune and need never lift a finger for the rest of his life. He can buy anything he wants – houses, cars and women – and he does so with no regard for the cost. Slowly, his tastes become more and more perverted and other people become his playthings. When he tires of straight sex, he pushes his limits with sadomasochism, sex with men and domination, but nothing really turns him on. After all, it's only a game, an arrangement between consenting adults, and what he wants is the real thing, real pain, unadulterated horror. Booring's first project is his neighbour's daughter, a busty 15-year-old he has been spying on while she sunbathes. He tortures her in his newly built dungeon but, due to his inexperience, she dies far too quickly. Disappointed and dissatisfied, he starts to practise. He abducts several teenage girls and takes detailed notes during their torture to refine his methods. By closing up wounds quickly, transfusing blood, administering different types of medicine and even a defibrillator, he can keep his victims alive for longer, and he feels ready to attempt to crown his achievements: the Princess. He has become attracted to a 13-year-old beauty, the daughter of one of his domestic staff, and he knows instantly that he must possess her . . . fully.

In the meantime, the Flying Squad has started investigating the case. Inspector Kenneth Vagn is its public face, a thankless job as the media quickly lose patience and demand that the case is solved. Booring takes pleasure in the police's frustration and taunts Inspector Vagn. Through a complex network of intermediaries and a series of riddles, a line of communication is established so that the two opponents can write to each other. Booring hints that soon he will be ready for the Princess, the object of all his efforts and the last girl he intends to abduct. He has perfected his methods of torture and thinks he can keep her alive for as long as he wants to. Inspector Vagn senses that time is running out and works on the case day and night. He is a walking zombie existing on coffee and pills. The Princess is abducted and Booring sends Vagn detailed descriptions of what he is doing to her, observed with the precision of a forensic examiner and a thriller writer's talent for generating horrifying images. The inspector wears himself out following up every lead, no matter how vague or insignificant it appears, and in the end his persistence leads to the breakthrough. A builder who helped construct the dungeon in Booring's house noticed several unusual features, including extensive soundproofing, air filters and a complex locking and alarm system. When the recent victim can be linked to Booring through her father who works for him, Inspector Vagn strikes. On his own, he pays a visit to Booring, and it ends with a showdown in the dark corridors of the dungeon where the inspector finally kills the murderer with a fatal shock from the defibrillator.

The Princess is still alive, but will never have a life.

Torture scenes and detailed descriptions of how the victims die made my career, but I was failing to make a breakthrough now and see where I had gone wrong.

The photo had been inserted on page 209, roughly halfway through the book. I leafed back and forth a couple of pages, searching through my own words to find the hidden meaning.

This section didn't, unlike the other passages the killer had selected, concentrate on the actual killing or the torture of the victim. It took some time before that particular penny dropped. This was significant, but how? Frantically, I flicked back and reread the whole section. My frustration grew. I stood up, went back to the start and read the text aloud to myself while I gestured with my free hand.

No matter how many times I read the passage, I couldn't understand what I was looking for.

It was a description of the police tailing one of the go-betweens for the correspondence between Inspector Vagn and the killer, an operation that turned out to be a dead end as the courier knew nothing about anything. The physical handover took place via a PO box – a rather antiquated means of communication today, but the internet wasn't particularly widespread when I wrote the book and an anonymous email address wouldn't have provided the same possibilities for suspense.

I tossed the book aside.

Had I been mistaken? Was the place where the photo had been inserted irrelevant or had I just failed to find the clue? I sank into the armchair beside the coffee table, leaned my head back and closed my eyes.

The post office where the PO box was located was in Østerbro. It was a majestic-looking building with broad steps and columns either side of the oak front door. I tried to replay the scene in my head. Plainclothes police officers were watching the post office, a relatively straightforward task as the building faced Fælledparken. In front of the entrance was a large gravel square with several benches where the observers could sit down. The courier, a young man with horn-rimmed glasses and a ponytail, cycled down Østerbrogade and turned into the post office.

I opened my eyes. Something didn't add up.

I leapt up and went to pick up the book, which had landed on the floor by the window. The title page had been bent after its flight. With shaking hands I found page 209. The description of the courier was correct and he did indeed cycle down Østerbrogade.

However, in real life the post office was located on the corner of Blegdamsvej and Øster Allé, not Østerbrogade as in the book.

I frowned. It was an almost unforgivable mistake. The geography of my novels is always thoroughly checked so it was beyond me how this howler had slipped through proofreading and several editions. It was one thing that I had made a mistake, that was embarrassing in itself, but that no one had spotted it was unbelievable.

I went over to the console table where the telephone stood. In one of the drawers I found the telephone directory and opened it at the front, where there was a map of Copenhagen and the area of Østerbro. Ten seconds. That's how long it took me to verify the location of the post office.

The description in *Outer Demons* was wrong.

36

My comeback novel, *A Bullet in the Chamber*, was fairly successful, but it would have had more of an impact if I had been willing to promote it. I stayed in the cottage and let my editor talk to the press. Finn was unhappy. He preferred his authors to flog the goods. Let the punters see the rabbit.

He was, however, delighted with the book.

'Great craftsmanship,' he said several times and that was precisely how I saw it. I had no deeper feelings towards *A Bullet in the Chamber* than a builder towards a floor he has laid or a carpenter for a shed he has put up. Yet the publication marked a turning point in my career as a writer. If I had once kidded myself that I was destined to write world-class literature, *A Bullet in the Chamber* was my epiphany. I now knew that I would never write the great Danish contemporary novel, but I could easily see myself as the kind of bread-and-butter writer we had always despised back in the Scriptorium days. In a way, I was relieved.

My neighbour was downright chuffed. Bent threw

himself into his own promotional tour around the holiday resort. In the months that followed publication, he always carried spare copies in his old Fjällräven rucksack. He was never modest when it came to explaining his role in the creation of the book, and many people must have got the impression that he was really my ghostwriter or that I had simply taken dictation from him. Not that I cared. Bent was due some of the credit that the book had been written at all, so he deserved a pat on the shoulder. I had certainly no need for attention.

Whether it was Bent's enthusiasm or Finn's marketing that did it, I don't know, but the novel sold well, although without ever reaching the heights of *Outer Demons*. It received a fair amount of press coverage. Some interpreted it as a critical response to Denmark's participation in the first Iraqi war – completely unintentional from my side – but the association stuck and has haunted the book ever since. Because of this I received numerous letters from soldiers who had been posted to Iraq, and again later when Denmark joined in for the second half. Many of them told of physical and psychological trauma. They were surprisingly frank about excess drinking, family problems and the difficulty of readjusting after returning home.

A few letters contained direct threats against my life, either because I, in the sender's opinion, had given a completely distorted picture of serving in Iraq, or because the sender felt that outsiders shouldn't be allowed to write about it when they had never been there and seen comrades killed by IEDs or had snipers take pot shots at them.

I kept all these letters in a box like old family photos

you haven't got the heart to throw out. I sensed a kinship with those lost souls who now lived alone with only the bottle for company and the memory of a family who no longer wanted to know.

But at least I had something to do, something that could occupy my thoughts for several hours every day and provide me with a living. Writing became my fixed point and I adhered to my working routine with military precision.

I quickly discovered that being a writer is the world's best excuse for being alone and I often used it as justification for getting rid of guests. Sometimes I would use it to stop people from visiting in the first place. If I pretended I would be writing all day, people respected it and didn't disturb me.

Apart from giving me something to do, writing also became an outlet for the anger I discovered inside me. My divorce from Line took place through lawyers and it was a bitter experience to see my former life disappear like that.

As a result, I wrote *Nuclear Families*, a story about a group of housewives who are taken hostage by a robber in a supermarket. They overpower the robber, who dies when he is impaled on an umbrella stand, and the women discover they have something in common. Apart from being resourceful, they share a passion for morbidity and are all trapped in unhappy marriages. They start to meet in secret and strike a deal to murder the husbands while each wife has a rock-solid alibi. It quickly turns into a sport, one murder becomes more spectacular than the next, and the more the husband suffers the better. A police officer,

329

a male chauvinist and a bragging caricature of Philip Marlowe, suspects a link between the murders. He has his own marital problems and it isn't until he finally uncovers the group that he realizes the conspiracy is greater than he first presumed. His own wife has arranged for his female boss to kill him while she herself is at bingo. The police officer dies in a shooting accident on the last page of the book, just as his wife wins a full house.

Nuclear Families was a furious attack on all women and their sisterhood. It was my antidote to the injustice I felt when Line took my children from me. It wasn't a very good book, nor was it terribly popular with my readers, but it did its job. The critics slated it, but I was used to that by now and it didn't upset me. A sole critic enjoyed the stereotypical gender depiction and was of the view that it was a big fat ironic response to the wave of girl power that had started to spread. But there was no truth in that. It was simply a bad book.

Financially, *Nuclear Families* wasn't a success, either. It paid for itself as far as ZeitSign was concerned, but once I had paid alimony and child maintenance, there was nothing left for me. Fortunately I still got royalties from the other books and public lending rights, but I had to cut my consumption down considerably, something that turned out to be easier than I had expected. There wasn't much to spend money on in a holiday area, at least not during the winter, and as I didn't mix with people, there was a limit to how much money I could spend on petrol and clothes. The biggest item in my household budget was alcohol, but I could always switch to a cheaper label.

At this point, it didn't really matter how many years my whisky was aged.

Some months after the publication of *Nuclear Families* I had a visit from Line.

It was a late afternoon in May, warm enough for me to sit outside, but still a little too chilly for shorts. I sat in the garden with my Scotch, a Macallan, and studied the lawn.

'Frank?'

I heard her voice as if in a dream. It was a very long time since I had last heard it and now it didn't sound like her at all or else I had forgotten how she spoke. That possibility frightened me. I had imagined her voice countless times, imagined what she might say in this or that situation, and sensed her approval or scepticism from her intonation when I asked her advice about something or other. Now her voice was alien to me.

'Frank. Are you there?'

It was her, no doubt about it, and I panicked. I looked at myself. My clothes were a mess. A white T-shirt under an old fraying cardigan which – would you believe it – used to be her father's. Then a pair of jeans with no belt, holes in the knees and on my feet I wore a pair of slippers that had been in the house when we bought it. I thought about hiding, but it sounded as if she was just around the corner and my car was in the drive, so I couldn't see how I could avoid her.

I put the whisky bottle behind my chair and buttoned up the cardigan. It was missing a button midway.

'Ah, there you are,' Line said, coming into view.

'Hello, Line,' I said, as casually as I could. My throat felt dry and parched, but I suppressed the urge to grab my glass and swallow the rest of my whisky. 'I didn't hear you.'

But then I saw her and it was like a punch to the stomach. She had put up her hair so her neck was bared. A black top, a pair of tight jeans and white trainers made her look young and fresh. And then she smiled. I had fallen for that smile once and at that moment I did so again. There was no need for her to say anything, all she had to do was state her demands and I would have signed instantly in my own blood and agreed to whatever she wanted.

I got up, a little too quickly, and accidentally pushed the chair back and knocked over the bottle behind it. It didn't smash, but the noise was unmistakable. Line's gaze flickered and I needed no speech bubble to tell me what she was thinking. I chose to ignore the sound and walked towards her. Having wiped my hand on my trousers, I offered it to her. She took it and squeezed it.

'Good to see you,' she lied.

'You too,' I replied and meant it.

'I apologize for turning up unannounced,' she said and let go of my hand. 'But you weren't answering the telephone, so I started to worry.'

'Telephone?' I said, looking at the cottage. I remembered ripping out the cable in a drunken rage. It was several months ago. 'Oh, right, it's broken.'

Line nodded towards the garden chairs. 'May I sit down?'

'Of course,' I replied quickly and dusted one of them down. 'Do you want a drink?'

'I'm driving,' she said. 'But a glass of water would be great.'

I rushed inside the cottage and into the kitchen. It was overflowing with several days' worth of washing-up and there were no clean glasses. I quickly rinsed one and wiped it with a piece of kitchen towel. While I waited for the water to turn cold, I opened the fridge and drank a mouthful of vermouth straight from the bottle. The taste made me grimace.

When I returned to the garden, Line was standing with her back to me at the far edge of the terrace, as if she was balancing. It was impossible to tell that her body had given birth to two girls. She was slim, narrow around the hips and had the same elegant posture she had always had and which I had always admired.

'The lawn needs cutting,' Line remarked, yanking me back to reality.

I shrugged. 'I might be going for a natural look.'

Line laughed and took the glass I was offering her. I could kick myself for not having waited until the glass cooled down. She had definitely noticed that it was still warm after I had washed it and guessed why. I sipped my whisky while she drank her water. We sat down in our garden chairs.

'I'm worried about you, Frank.'

I brushed it aside with a wave of my hand. 'Nah, no need for that. Like I said, the telephone is out of order.'

'No, that's not it,' Line said, looking earnestly into my eyes. 'I've read the book.'

I looked away and swallowed a mouthful of whisky. 'And?'

'I couldn't recognize you at all, Frank.' She shook her head. 'All that rage scares me.'

'Relax,' I said. 'It's only a book.'

'It's never been "only a book" with you.'

I was aware of irritation growing inside me. My enchantment had been transformed into distrust. What was she doing here? Why was she confronting me in this way? How was it any of her business what I wrote and whether or not I cut the grass?

'Perhaps I've grown wiser.'

'Have you?'

It was always the same with her, simple questions that were so hard to answer, but it wasn't the question that had upset me. I felt ambushed. Partly because she had turned up without warning so I had to receive her unshaven, unwashed and with a house that hadn't been cleaned for several months. Partly because she confronted me with my own cowardice in writing *Nuclear Families* without her being able to defend herself. All I wanted was for her to leave as quickly as possible.

'I suppose we all grow wiser every day,' I replied and tried to smile.

Line looked away. 'You're avoiding the question.'

'What do you want me to say?'

She leaned forward, stretched out her slender hand across the table and placed it on top of mine. 'I want you to say that you forgive me and that you forgive yourself. I want you to say you'll take better care of yourself and start to go out a bit more.' She fixed my gaze and I could tell from her eyes that she really meant what she had just said.

I cleared my throat. 'I forgive you. I forgive myself and I'll take better care of myself and I'll start to go out a bit more,' I said, trying to match her tone of voice as accurately as I could.

Line withdrew her hand and shook her head. 'I don't know why I came,' she said, laughing bitterly. 'Perhaps I thought you would listen this time, that you needed me, needed some help.' She sighed. 'There are still people who care about you, Frank. You don't need to hate yourself and the whole world.'

She stood up and pressed her arms to her sides.

'I'll drive back now,' she said. 'But there's something I want to tell you before you hear it from other people.' She paused. 'I . . . I've met someone. His name is Bjørn . . . he's moving in with us next week . . . the girls are crazy about . . .'

I heard what she said, saw her struggle to express the words and serve them up like tiny hand grenades wrapped in cotton wool. I noticed the little ripple of a smile that formed when she spoke his name and noted her frustration when her reassuring words ended up sounding like gloating.

A fire ignited within me, bombs and stars exploded in my body and I felt like throwing up until my guts were spread out in front of me. But I focused all my strength on staying calm. I transformed my face into a cast of Frank Føns, a death mask that reproduced his final emotions before the execution.

'Did you hear what I said?' Line asked.

I responded by raising my whisky glass towards her.

'Congratulations,' I said and drained the glass.

She shook her head. 'Goodbye, Frank,' she said. Her voice broke and she clasped her hand over her mouth as she hurried away from me, around the corner of the house, out of my field of vision. Soon afterwards I heard the sound of a car starting and driving off.

I stared at my glass and then across the garden.

Suddenly I felt like cutting the grass and maybe chopping down a couple of trees.

Media Whore followed soon after *Nuclear Families*. I finished it in record time, expelled it from my body with the rage and impotence I felt at losing Line and my girls. Someone had to pay and ultimately it was all Linda's fault, wasn't it? Of course it wasn't, but at the time that wasn't how I saw it. After Line's visit I could no longer hate her so I had to find someone else to vent my fury on. Linda had made me betray my family and, in my opinion, that was the beginning of the end.

Media Whore proved to be moderately successful. Even though I had written it for myself, some critics felt that it captured the spirit of the age and its obsession with celebrities, and it received considerably more coverage than it deserved. Linda Hvilbjerg herself never referred to it once.

My next victim was Bjørn, Line's new husband and my daughters' stepfather.

You Don't Have To Call Me Dad is about a paedophile who lives several double lives with different women, all of whom are ignorant of each other's existence. It's the kind of story you hear about from time to time without ever understanding how it can be possible, but I took it one step further. My main character and killer, Bjørn

Vibe or Bjørn Jensen or Bjørn Christoffersen, as he also calls himself, selects single mothers with daughters, as many as possible. He charms his way into the family so effectively that the mother ends up accepting his marriage proposal – what else would she do? Bjørn is great with the kids, good-looking and has a well-paid job as a travelling sales manager. After the wedding, Bjørn's personality changes. He batters both the mother and her children and it escalates to actual slavery where he abuses everyone in the family. His alleged job enables him to travel from one family to the next, always without warning, so they never know when he will be back or when he will leave. At some point in the relationship, he kills one of the children to assert his power, usually pretending that the mother has transgressed in some minor way. She is forced to cover everything up or her other children will suffer. Bjørn is finally punished for his attacks when one of his wives discovers the existence of one of the others. They track down the remaining wives in his harem, set a trap and torture him over a weekend. All the wives are involved and participate in the final execution where they stab him until he is one bloody pulp. At the end, the women decide to join forces, seek out men with similar tendencies and subject them to the same treatment.

It was inexcusable to portray Bjørn in this way and I hope my daughters never read that book. In fact, I hope they never read *any* of my books. Even though writing is my job and I wrote in order to provide for them, I don't like the thought that they might one day read what I have written. I would dearly love them to be proud of me, but I blew that chance long ago.

If they were to read anything of mine, I hope it will be these pages. Perhaps it will help them understand me better, but I seriously doubt they will ever have an opportunity to read this.

Linda Hvilbjerg was right. My literary output is one long string of attacks on everyone around me and my next book, *As You Sow*, was no different. Now it was Verner's turn. I camouflaged it as a vigilante story where the murdered characters somehow deserved to die, but I was really out to get Verner. In my eyes, he had it coming. The incident at Line's party alone justified it, but it was just as much because I had hurt Line by having anything to do with him. Maybe things would have been different if I had distanced myself from Verner from the beginning. This was my thinking, and that was why he had to be wiped off the surface of the earth in the book.

Line never visited me again and my behaviour ensured that I was denied access to my children. My books were used as evidence when the court order was reviewed. The frequent violence and the obvious link between the plots of my books and the girls' family circumstances made it easy for the judge, and the court order was extended. The wording of the court's decision came as close to calling me unbalanced as is possible without actually stating it.

Not being able to see my girls was the worst. I had thought it would get easier in time, but it didn't. Every day I wondered how they were, what they were doing and if they thought about their dad. This probably happens to every parent when their children leave home, but I had been separated from them so early that I couldn't imagine how they could be prepared for life's trials and tribulations without me. I believed I had hard-earned experience to pass on to them and dreamed several times that they stayed with me in the cottage in the holidays so they could get to know me.

The years in the cottage in Rågeleje seemed to me one long writing retreat. I wrote more than seven books in the Tower and every single day centred on producing my 2,500 words.

Astonishingly, I rarely felt lonely. I had become addicted to the silence in the holiday resort. Here it could be quiet like nowhere else. Another person in the house would have disturbed the cocoon of calm I surrounded myself with. The sea would often break the silence, but that wasn't irritating, it merely emphasized the absence of other sounds.

Silence became important for my work. Previously I had been able to write anywhere, in any situation, while all sorts of things were happening around me – even children playing – but no more. I had to be alone and free from intrusive noise. Music was out of the question. Even the racket of chainsaws or lawnmowers sometimes destroyed my rhythm.

I felt best when I rose at the same time, ate the same breakfast, wrote roughly the same amount of text during the day and finally rewarded myself with a whisky in the afternoon with Bent.

I'm sure that a totally predictable life would have made me want to scream in the Scriptorium days. Back then we wrote in response to experiences and unique events, not in routine and repetition. If anyone had told me then that I would spend ten years writing in a holiday cottage, I would have laughed at them. I had wanted to travel, see the world, and I never wanted to write the same story twice.

The reality turned out to be something else. Reality was a day with fixed working hours, weeks all the same and months distinguished from each other only by the changing weather and the nature of gardening tasks.

My days were filled with thoughts of when to rake up leaves while I typed my way through quotas of words and sentences with the regularity of a train timetable.

This rhythm was only rarely disturbed – until the telephone rang one morning.

Monday

37

From the moment I discovered *Outer Demons* on Linda Hvilbjerg's doorstep, I felt the next move was up to me. The killer had held off murdering Linda until I had taken my place on the stage and everything suggested the ball was now in my court. I knew the victim – my own daughter – and it was impossible to do nothing.

The more I thought about it, the clearer it became what I had to do. Pointing out the error regarding the Østerbro post office must be an invitation. Just like the killer in *Outer Demons*, he was offering a way we could communicate, a chance for me to contact him rather than wait for his messages.

In the book, the killer sent his letters straight to the detective, Kenneth Vagn, who replied via the PO box. This was my opening: I would write to him and he could reply directly to me.

Monday morning I checked out of the hotel.

Ferdinan apologized profoundly and gave me a substantial discount. He placed the entire blame on his own drooping shoulders and, when I left him in reception, he didn't look like a man who wanted to stay in the hotel business. But then I probably didn't look like someone who wanted to stay in the book business.

My time in Copenhagen was far from over, but I couldn't bear to stay at the hotel any longer. I had to get away from the strained atmosphere and Ferdinan's wounded eyes.

When I finally sat in my car, my body filled with relief. I felt in control, not just of the car, but also what would happen next.

It was time for me to play my part.

My first stop was Nordhavn station. There I bought a newspaper, some magazines, sweets and crisps. I made sure to get the right change for the photo booth. Then I drove to the post office where I bought a large envelope in which I placed my message and delivered it to the PO box mentioned in *Outer Demons*. I didn't doubt for a moment that the killer had taken the same box as was mentioned in the book. When I posted the envelope, I had the feeling the act forged a bond between us, that a connection was established like a conversation through a switchboard.

Now all I had to do was wait.

That was why I had bought something to read. But newspapers and magazines weren't a substitute for whisky. I parked by the post office and walked across Trianglen and down Nordre Frihavnsgade. Vinbørsen appeared like an oasis. I bought two bottles of Oban single malt, an 18-year-old, and a set of rustic whisky glasses in a gift box. Back in the car, I ripped off the wrapping paper and poured myself half a glass. The first mouthful made me shudder, but I forced down the rest of the contents and placed the glass by the handbrake.

I had no illusion of catching the killer on his way in or out of the post office, so I turned the key in the ignition and drove off. It was mid-morning, the traffic was tolerable and there were plenty of parking spaces in the otherwise busy Østerbro area.

I wasn't going far. Kartoffelrækkerne lay around a kilometre from the post office. After less than five minutes I turned into the street where I lived ten years ago. Property prices had more than quadrupled since then and it was clear that the rise in values had given the area a facelift. Several of the more than 100-year-old, two-storey terraced houses had been fitted with new windows and roofs and the small front gardens were well tended and practically all of them displayed teak garden furniture and Weber barbecues.

I parked a short distance from the house where Line now lived with another man. The man my daughters regarded as their father. No one appeared to be in. Line must be at work and the girls at school. Their front garden gave the neighbours a run for their money. The area was landscaped with tiles, flowerbeds and a few areas of freshly mown grass. This had to be Bjørn's doing. Line had never been one for gardening, though she was otherwise very practical. I smiled to myself at the memory of Line who with graceful movements offered to help out in the garden, but quickly had enough and invented an excuse to leave. 'Why don't I make us a cup of coffee?' she would say and disappear into the kitchen. Half an hour later she would appear with the world's best cappuccino with an intricate pattern painted in the froth.

I sank into my seat so I could just about see over the

dashboard and poured myself another whisky. The warmth from the alcohol and the memories spread through my body. Once upon a time I had lived here, worked here and been happy. I had everything I could ever want. A house, a wife, children, and the job that made it possible to provide everything they needed.

I have always despised people in interviews who claim they have no regrets or that they wouldn't have done anything different in their lives. Everyone has hurt someone or acted selfishly and others have suffered as a result, but very few are prepared to admit it. The worst offenders are those who acknowledge they have upset other people, but almost celebrate it under the mantra: 'It made me who I am today'. Who the hell do they think they are? What's so special about them that it's OK for them to hurt others? And if they hadn't done it in the first place, wouldn't they have been better people? If they don't wish to change anything about their lives, aren't they lacking in self-awareness or, at least, imagination?

I had imagination in spades.

A few drops of rain started falling on the windscreen and hit the roof like little water spears. The sound of drops hitting the metal was loud and steady and it increased slowly. The drops diminished in size but grew in number and at last generated almost constant noise as they hammered down on the car. In a few minutes, the temperature inside had plummeted. I shivered and pulled my jacket tighter, sinking further into the seat.

It was impossible to make out contours outside; everything was distorted by the veil of water cascading down the windscreen. Every now and then I could make out people darting through the rain, enigmatic figures with distorted limbs moving behind the water curtain.

I thought about switching on the wipers, but dismissed the idea. I had no idea how long I would be sitting there and didn't want to draw attention to myself. If communicating through the PO box really did work, it might not be necessary for me to stay so close to my former family, but if the killer wanted to carry out his plan regardless, then this was the only place I should be.

The sense that I had done what I could, the only thing I could do, helped me relax. I flicked through the newspapers, ate some sweets and slowly drank my way through the bottle. Outside the rain slackened off. It didn't stop altogether, but persisted stubbornly in its gentler form as it grew darker. People returned to their homes and lights came on behind the windows.

Suddenly, the light was switched on in the house I had been watching. I hadn't seen anyone return home, but it could easily have happened while I read the newspaper. From my position, I couldn't see directly into the living room, all I could see was that the lamp on the windowsill had been turned on. I had no way of knowing whether it was Bjørn, Line or the girls who had returned home.

I had no intention of contacting them, but as I sat there in the emerging darkness with the chill creeping through every layer of my clothing, I wished I was on the other side of that window, inside the warm living room with the cosy lighting where the sound of the rain couldn't be heard over children's voices and dinner preparations in the kitchen.

I closed my eyes and could almost smell the food cooking.

Tuesday

38

Someone tapped on the window.

The sound was loud and insistent. Slowly, I opened my eyes. It was morning. I squinted in the light and looked around to identify the source of the tapping. I was cradling the whisky bottle like a baby I was shielding from the cold. The glass was on the dashboard. There was still a drop left, but a feeling of nausea made me look away.

Someone knocked again. Close to me.

I turned to face the side pane and wiped away the condensation. Line was standing outside. She was leaning forwards, staring at me with a mix of incredulity and anger.

'Frank?'

I think I mustered a smile, but it might have been a snarl because I had yet to surface completely. Slowly I found the handle for the side window and rolled it down. During this process the whisky bottle slipped from my lap and hit one of the pedals with an audible clonk.

'What are you doing here?' Line asked, before I had managed to roll down the window in full. She leaned forward even further, but flinched when the smell from the car hit her nostrils. She frowned slightly.

'Hi, Line.' My voice croaked and I cleared my throat. I was still drowsy from sleep and had no idea what to say. All I registered was a powerful urge to hug my ex-wife. 'Any chance of breakfast?'

Line shot me a look of resignation. Her eyes scanned the car, the empty sweet wrappers, the newspaper and the whisky glass.

'Have you been sitting here all night?'

'Just a cup of coffee,' I continued. 'That would be nice.'

'That's not a good idea, Frank.'

'I promise to behave . . . I . . . I'm not drunk.'

Line kept looking at me. Then she straightened up and glanced up and down the street.

'There's something I have to tell you,' I said. 'It's important.'

She took a deep breath, still looking down the street as if to make sure we hadn't been seen.

'One cup of coffee,' she said. 'That's all. I'm going to work in an hour.'

I nodded eagerly and started wriggling out of my seat. My limbs were stiff after sitting so long in the same position and I groaned silently as I got out of the car. Line had walked on ahead of me. She was wheeling her bicycle. The rear light was still on.

'I've just taken Mathilde to school,' she said, unlocking the front door. 'I think she's embarrassed I still take her.'

'They've grown so big,' I said. I cursed myself inwardly at the banality of my response.

Line sighed. 'If only you knew,' she said. As soon as she

said it, she gave me a frightened look. She looked away again. 'Sorry.'

I shrugged. 'It's OK . . . my parents keep me updated.' That was a lie, but I hadn't come to embarrass Line. In fact, I still didn't know why I was here.

Much had changed since I lived in the house. Everything had been renovated and redecorated in pale colours. The furniture had been replaced and photos and bric-a-brac told stories of the inhabitants' shared lives. I would like to have studied the photographs more closely, but Line carried on walking. The kitchen had been rebuilt and expanded to include a dining area and this was where we sat down. I was still wearing my jacket. Line hadn't suggested that I take it off and I didn't want to impose. The warmth in the house was welcome and I clutched the mug of coffee with both hands to drive the cold from my fingers.

'What were you doing out there?' Line asked after a moment's silence.

'Ironika visited me at the book fair,' I said. 'I barely recognized her.'

Line nodded.

'She doesn't want us to call her Ironika any more,' she said. 'She raised it herself at a family meeting some months ago. It took us completely by surprise. She just stood up and said she didn't like being called Ironika and she wanted us to use her real name from now on.' Line smiled to herself. 'I was sad and proud at the same time.'

'She has inherited her mother's strong-mindedness,' I said trying to ignore that Line had used the words 'family meeting'.

'The book fair was her idea, too,' Line continued without acknowledging the compliment. 'She didn't tell me until afterwards.'

'Yes, I was a bit surprised.' I heaved a sigh at the memory of our conversation in the little cubicle. 'I think she caught me at a bad time.'

'She mentioned that you behaved a little strangely.'

I nodded. 'These are strange times.'

'Is that why you're here?'

I shifted my gaze to the coffee mug in front of me. It was good coffee. Strong and warm, brewed from organic beans in a cafetière. Line took milk or cream, but I always took my coffee black and she had remembered that.

'I'm here because I'm worried about you,' I said at last.

Line was about to say something, but I held up a hand to indicate that I would explain.

'I've got a . . . fan,' I began. 'A very pedantic fan who has taken offence at some mistakes in my books. He sees it as his mission to educate me about my shortcomings, show me my errors, prove how it's really done.'

Line threw up her hands. 'There will always be people like that,' she said. 'I remember some of the letters you used to get—'

'This is different,' I interrupted her. 'This guy wants to show me how it should have been done. Do you understand? He wants to *show* me.'

Line frowned. 'Are you saying . . .'

'He has killed people,' I said.

Some seconds passed where neither of us spoke. Line scrutinized me as if she expected me to burst into either laughter or tears.

'He acts out scenes from my books, right down to the smallest detail, to show me I got my facts wrong. It's like a teacher marking my essay, except the red lines aren't drawn in ink.'

Line shook her head. 'Frank, are you sure . . .'

'Verner is dead,' I said.

Line's eyes took on a confused expression as if she had to retrieve the name from a drawer she had closed a long time ago.

'He was murdered at the Marieborg Hotel, just like I described it in *As You Sow*.'

'I never read that,' Line said quietly.

'It doesn't matter, but I can assure you that it's not a very pleasant way to die and someone went to a lot of trouble to reconstruct the entire scene.'

'Why . . .'

I shrugged. 'To mock me, to educate me, punish me, who knows?'

'What do the police think?'

'They think his murder was an act of revenge.'

'But you haven't told them about your "fan"?'

I shook my head. 'I can't. Linda Hvilbjerg is dead, too. She was murdered, while I was asleep upstairs . . .' I clammed up when I saw the reaction in Line's eyes. A trace of resignation had crept into them.

'You need help, Frank.'

'I can't go to the police,' I said.

'No, that's not what I mean,' Line replied. 'I mean, you need to see a psychologist.'

I clasped one of her hands with both of mine. 'What I need is for you to believe me,' I pleaded.

355

'Why? What can I do?'

She tried to withdraw her hand, but I refused to release it.

'You can protect our daughter.'

Line shot up from the table so forcefully that I was forced to let go of her hand. 'What?'

'I think I've got it under control, but . . .'

'What's this about Veronika?'

'She might be next.'

'But, Frank, you're sick!' Line shouted and took one step away from me. I held up my hands.

'No, wait . . .'

'If she needs protecting from anyone, then it's you!' She shook her head. 'It's always been you. You've never been able to distinguish between fantasy and reality, have you? Everything that happens in real life is a story to you, isn't it? Something you can exploit, something you can write about. And everything you write becomes real.'

I shook my head. 'You don't understand,' I tried. 'It may have looked like that, but now—'

'You need help, Frank.'

I got up and started walking around the table towards Line.

'No. Stay away from me! Stay away from me and from my family, do you hear me?' She took another step backwards and put her hand on the handle of the door that led to the small back garden.

'Line, please let me—'

'Get out, Frank!'

I was desperate. Why wouldn't she believe me? If it hadn't been for her eyes, I would have grabbed her and held tight her until she listened and understood, but her eyes exuded rage and, worse than that, fear.

'Like I said,' I began, forcing my voice to be calm. 'I think I've taken care of it, so it won't come to that.'

Line simply stared at me.

'I'll go,' I said. 'Only . . .' I felt my throat constrict. 'Please take care of our children, OK?' I begged her in a thick voice. At that moment I knew I would never see Line or my daughters again. 'Tell them . . . tell them I'm sorry about everything. I know I'm asking a lot of you, but please tell them I love them more than anything.'

Line had raised her hands to her face and covered her mouth. Tears welled up. I started walking backwards, away from the kitchen table and out into the hall.

'I love you too, Line. I always have. Remember that.'

I turned round and left the house

39

Line's reaction upset me.

I had expected her to need convincing, but not that she would reject me out of hand. Maybe the news about Verner hadn't reached the papers yet, but when it did, she might believe me. Or she might become even more scared. Of me.

At best, there would no headlines because I had imagined it all, like Line had suggested. Perhaps the murders of Mona Weis, Verner and Linda Hvilbjerg and the yellow envelopes and the photos were a delusion, a construct of my own mind. After years of inventing stories my brain could no longer distinguish between fantasy and reality, exactly Line's point.

As I left the house that had once been my home, I wished more than ever that this was so. I genuinely hoped that I had lost my mind and the rest of the world was as it should be. I hoped that men were checking out Mona Weis as she walked down Gilleleje High Street, I wished that Verner was pestering the prostitutes in Vesterbro and that Linda Hvilbjerg was busy dashing the dreams of yet another budding writer.

I would have given anything for Line to be right.

Reality returned with a vengeance when I got back in the car. It was cold and clammy and stank of whisky. The windows were foggy, which made it was difficult to see out. The whisky glass was still on the dashboard, the bottle on the floor, only a quarter full.

Everything was just as I had left it.

Except for the envelope on the passenger seat. It was the same one I had sent to the PO box yesterday.

I stared at it.

My slender hope that my brain had been playing tricks on me died, but I wasn't surprised. When I picked up the envelope, I could see it had been opened with a knife or some other sharp instrument.

I took out the sheet of paper. It was the message I had written the day before with the addition 'OK' in blue pen at the bottom. It had been printed in capital letters and revealed nothing about the sender; no graphologist would get anything from those two characters. Everything else was still in the envelope.

I took a deep breath. My plan appeared to be working. I had managed to communicate with the killer and he had accepted my challenge. I was tempted to go back to Line to tell her that she could stop being scared, that I had taken care of it, but at that moment a police car came down the street and I changed my mind. The police were the last thing I needed.

I started the engine and drove off as quickly as I dared. In my rear-view mirror I saw the police car park outside Line's house. I didn't blame her. She had done what she needed to do to protect her family and the police might even do the job I was incapable of. However, what did worry me was that I had mentioned Linda Hvilbjerg. She was unlikely to have been found yet, but if Line repeated what I had said, the police might follow it up and find the body sooner than they would otherwise have done.

Not that this made any difference to my plans.

I drove north, towards Hillerød, and stopped once at a petrol station. I filled up the car and bought newspapers, which I skimmed before I drove on. There was nothing about Verner or Linda Hvilbjerg. In Hillerød I went to the bank and emptied out my bank accounts. They added up to 150,000 kroner. The cashier studied me closely and demanded that I answer a series of security questions before handing over the money. It felt strange to hold so many notes in my hand. I couldn't resist the temptation to sniff them before stuffing them in my inside pocket.

Then I drove on to Helsinge and onwards to Rågeleje. As I drove down Store Orebjergvej, I slowed to a crawl. Nearly all the leaves had fallen from the trees. The wind knocked them about on the roadside and shook the naked branches of the bushes. I could see from a distance if I had visitors. I hadn't. The drive was empty and the Tower was deserted, just as I had left it. The trip from Østerbro to North Sjælland had taken roughly two hours, but the police didn't appear to have discovered Linda yet. Still, it was only a matter of time before they did, so I mustn't waver now.

I parked the car, got out, went straight to my front door and let myself in. Once inside, I locked the door behind me. The heating had been off during the five days I had been away; the autumn chill had accepted the invitation and seeped through the walls. The air was cold and damp.

I scrunched newspapers into balls and chucked them into the stove with some kindling. The fire was reluctant to accept the cold paper and wood, but after a couple of minutes the flames took hold and could look after themselves. I went upstairs and opened the trapdoor to the attic. It wasn't very big; there was only room for three or four removal boxes. I grabbed one and eased it through the narrow opening and down to my study. I opened it to make sure it was the one I wanted. It was.

Back downstairs, I opened the box again. It was full of letters from my readers, letters I had received during my almost twenty years as a writer. Many of them had never been opened.

I took a handful and stared at them. They contained praise and criticism, admiration and abuse, flattery and disgust. I threw them on the fire, which seized the paper immediately, opening letters I had never opened and consuming the contents I myself hadn't read.

Handful after handful of letters was thrown on the fire, which repaid me with a radiant blast of heat in the cold living room.

But I didn't burn the letters to get warm.

Nor was it out of concern for the real victims, the people who had so generously shared their fear and horror with me. Burning the letters was part of the deal. I might not have promised to do so in the message I sent to the PO box, but it was implied that I would.

If the killer had written to me previously to mock me

or to point out my mistakes, his letter might be in the box and there was a danger of someone finding it. As I didn't know which sender to look for, they all had to go. Wasting time burning them was risky, but it was necessary in order to fulfil our agreement.

The fire transformed the paper into thin flakes of ash that took up more and more room in the stove. They fluttered at the slightest gust of wind and some whirled into the living room where they settled on the floor, on me or on the furniture around me. My clothes were soon sprinkled with ash and I stood up to dust myself down.

At that moment I heard someone try to open the front door.

I froze in mid-movement, just as I was brushing ash off my sleeve, and held my breath.

There was a knock on the door.

'FF?'

It was Bent.

'Are you OK, neighbour?'

Even though he couldn't see into the living room from that side of the house, I still tiptoed to a corner that couldn't be seen from any of the windows.

'I saw your car,' Bent called out on the other side of the door. 'How was Copenhagen?'

I heard his steps move away from the front door and around the house. He was talking to himself. The decking on the terrace creaked. Soon I heard him tap on the window.

'Frank? Is everything all right?'

He couldn't see me in the corner, but I could see his shadow fall through the French windows. He was leaning towards the glass, cupping his hands either side of his head to peer inside.

'Come on, Frank,' he said, sounding mildly annoyed. 'I can see that you've lit a fire.'

I clenched my teeth. Why couldn't he just go away?

Bent knocked harder on the window.

'Bloody hell, Frank.'

His shadow moved away.

'Frank!' Bent shouted. 'Are you upstairs?'

I could hear that he had been drinking. The slurring in his speech would indicate five or six beers, which would be about right, given that it was one o'clock in the afternoon.

'Fraaaank!'

I had a strong urge to open the door and tell him to piss off, but he persisted.

'Frank, for Christ's sake.'

I heard him shuffle across the terrace.

'I know you're in there!' he called out from the garden. 'Come on, Frank . . . I'm not going to go away, you know.' He laughed briefly.

Ten or fifteen seconds passed when I could only hear mumbling. Then his tone changed.

'Bloody writer,' he sneered. 'Bloody writer!' he said again, now sounding like a petulant child. 'You've always been so stuck up. You think you're too good for the rest of us, eh. But let me tell you something.'

He fell silent for a few seconds as if he was plucking up the courage or waiting for a reaction.

'You're no better than the rest of us. Not one bit. Or you wouldn't be rotting away up here like us, would you? No! But you think you're so bloody clever and that we're all so bloody lucky that you choose to hang out with us.'

Shouting appeared to sober him up. At any rate, he had stopped slurring.

'But you're no better than the rest of us,' he scoffed again. 'You're worse. Good neighbours give and take. But not you. You've only ever taken and always when it suited you. You let us come over when you felt like it, the rest of the time you would just ignore us.'

Shouting had made him breathless and he paused.

'Do you know something, Frank?' He waited a couple of seconds for a reply. 'Screw you! You're on your own from now on, you stuck-up wanker!'

I heard him march through the garden back to his own house. A few minutes later, I moved out of the corner and went back to the stove. Bent's words hadn't upset me. I was almost relieved that he had ended our neighbourly relationship. One less thing to worry about.

The fire was dying down from lack of nourishment and I chucked in the rest of the letters in one big pile. The flames flared up with gratitude. I made sure they were burning properly before I ran back upstairs. In my bedroom I packed a suitcase of clothes that I left downstairs by the front door. Then I returned to my study and started unplugging computer cables. I carried the monitor downstairs, then the computer itself and the keyboard. Finally I brought down the printer as well as bag of essential cables and a ream of paper.

The letters in the fireplace had burned away. Only a few yellow envelope corners remained in the ashes. A gust of wind found its way down the chimney and wafted black flakes of burned paper out on the floor.

I opened the door a little and peered outside. Bent was nowhere to be seen. I grabbed the suitcase and sneaked out to the car. Carefully, I opened the boot and slid my suitcase over the parcel shelf and down on the back seat. Then I went back for the computer and the rest of my equipment.

I didn't waste time locking up the cottage, but I stood for a moment staring at the place that had been my home for many years.

Then I got into the car and drove off.

40

I followed the coast past Vejby, Tisvildeleje and on towards the west. In Hundested I caught the ferry across the fjord to Rørvig. The crossing only took twenty minutes, but I felt I was leaving behind an entire continent.

I found a holiday homes letting agency near Rørvig Harbour. The agent was delighted to have a customer this late in the season, but surprised that I needed a place immediately and that I paid cash, both the deposit and eight weeks' rental. I chose a house with a sea view and relatively isolated from its nearest neighbours. Even outside the tourist season it was expensive, but the location was crucial.

I gave my name as Karsten Venstrøm, the name of the murdering psychologist from *In the Red Zone*. The agent wanted to chat, but I ignored him and completed the paperwork as quickly as I could. Twenty minutes later I got into my car with the keys to the house in my pocket.

I shopped in a supermarket in Nykøbing and quickly filled a shopping trolley with enough groceries for a couple of weeks if I rationed my supplies carefully.

Then I drove to the house, which lay further out on Odden.

It was a large house, far bigger than I needed, with a Jacuzzi, a sauna and a huge conservatory with a wood burner. It slept twelve, but I chose the smallest bedroom, where I unpacked my clothes and made my bed. I closed the doors to the other rooms and switched on the heating in the rooms I intended to use. I put the computer and printer at the end of an enormous dining table that seated at least ten. I checked my computer would start and that I could print. Everything worked.

Apart from the conservatory, there was a dining room, a living room and a television room with a wooden floor, black leather furniture and a fireplace. The television was a large flat-screen model. I turned it on and checked the text TV news. There was nothing about Verner or Linda. I left the television on while I went back to the car. I was able to remove the registration plates with my hands and I threw them both into the boot. Then I drove the Corolla further into the grounds so it couldn't be seen from the road.

Afterwards I walked around the area. Most of it was covered by heather or trees. The nearest house was over two hundred metres away and there were conifers in between to block the view across. The garden consisted of a lawn, decking and a shed containing garden furniture, a round barbecue, a lawnmower and other gardening tools.

Back in the house the heating from the electric radiators had kicked in, but I lit a fire in the television room all the same. I switched the television to the news channel and fetched a bottle of whisky I had bought in the supermarket. I reclined in the soft leather armchair, a glass of whisky in my hand and the bottle within reach, and spent the next couple of hours following the 24-hour news. The murders weren't mentioned; they only covered trivialities such as the Danish government's budget negotiations and silly contributions to the immigration debate.

I proposed several toasts. I drank to my health and erupted in laughter every time. I felt confident. Step one of my plan had succeeded and I had a sense of being in control, or at any rate no longer mystified. That night I allowed myself to relax – a day of rest before the great exertions in the weeks ahead.

I didn't need my bed that night. I fell asleep in the armchair in front of the television and I awoke to images of suicide bombers in the Middle East. Dusty streets filled the screen with people running around, crying and screaming about injustice and revenge. In Denmark they were still discussing the budget.

I switched off the television and didn't turn it on again.

After a modest breakfast of a heated roll and coffee, I sat down in front of the computer. It started up with a slow humming. The envelope with my handwriting lay on the table. I opened it and took out the photograph. It was one of five pictures I had taken in the photo booth at Nordhavn station. My hair was a tad messy, my beard a little denser and stragglier than usual, but it was the eyes that attracted attention. They were empty and seemed to look into a dark place.

I leaned the picture against the screen.

*   *   *

The computer had finished starting up. The desktop was an old photo of the cottage taken one summer's day. It was almost like sitting in my study in the Tower and looking out at the garden.

I opened the word-processing program and created a new document. This was always a special occasion, a little bit like a painter starting a new painting on a brand-new canvas, but this time I didn't relish it. I missed the feeling of freedom that normally inspires me at the sight of a blank page. This time I knew precisely what I would be writing and it terrified me.

I took my letter from the envelope and placed it next to the keyboard.

It was a brief synopsis, written with trembling hands. The desperation and the terror seeped out from the jagged handwriting.

I copied the title from the letter to page 1 of the document:

Death Sentence

by

Frank Føns

I saved the document with practised keystrokes, an acknowledgement that there was no way back.

I took a deep breath and began . . .

'Until recently I had only killed people on paper.'

Today

Final Chapter

I didn't sleep last night.

Eight days have passed since I sent this script to the box at Østerbro post office and two days since I received a reply. It was a postcard of the Little Mermaid. All the card had on it was today's date. The postmark was Nykøbing, the largest town in the area, approximately fifteen kilometres away. I don't know what to deduce from that. Is he staying locally? Am I under surveillance or was it some smokescreen? Ultimately, doesn't matter.

I can feel that the time has come.

My body is in a heightened state of alert and nothing escapes my attention. I hear every sound, see every colour and feel the slightest gust of wind against my skin. It's as if my entire being wants to absorb every single impression while it still can. My hands refuse to relax. They constantly seek surfaces and objects to touch and I register details of the tabletop and the windowsill that I hadn't noticed before. The veins in the wood feel like mountain ranges and I detect unevenness in the polished marble surface. My taste buds deny me whisky, the taste is too sharp, and

I discover nuances in the flavour of tap water I had never noticed before. I drink a lot of water. It tastes heavenly and my throat feels constantly dry.

Outside I watch the birds pecking at the breadcrumbs I have scattered. It's almost as if I can hear their beaks split open the seeds in the bread. When they spread their wings and take off, I see them in slow motion and I tell myself I could catch them quite easily. I would be able to anticipate their every move and there is a suppleness in my muscles that convinces me I'm faster, better controlled than they are. A sudden urge makes me run around the garden. I feel the wind against my face and the grass under my bare feet. The exertion doesn't affect me. My breathing is under control. I can hear the air pass in and out of my lungs and airways in a steady rhythm, like mechanical bellows.

When I go back inside, the stuffy air in the house nearly suffocates me. The air feels viscous and slows down my movements. I open all the windows and doors for fifteen minutes before the air is tolerable again. A faint scent of pine from the trees outside remains after the windows have been closed. I empty the bin, which smells of the fry-up I had yesterday. The fridge is empty, but that's all right. Even though I'm hungry, I know that my taste buds won't allow themselves to be touched by any old food and there is no prospect of a major gourmet experience in this area. Besides, I can't leave the house.

I'm expecting guests.

The items we will need are laid out on the dining table. I pick up the scalpel and test the blade, even though I did so earlier this morning. It's incredibly sharp and makes a small cut in my thumb. The blood seeps out in an ever-growing drop. I swear briefly, replace the scalpel and stick my thumb in my mouth as I head to the bathroom. I get the first-aid kit from the cabinet above the sink and find a plaster. Before I attach it, I run cold water over my thumb until it feels almost numb. When the plaster is in place, I study it closely to see if the blood is still running, until the absurdity of the situation dawns on me.

I start to laugh. I can't stop. My laughter grows louder and louder and I have to leave the bathroom to find enough room for the sound of my merriment. The whole house resounds and dust is lifted by my outburst. I start to gasp for air and have just about managed to control myself when I happen to glance at my thumb and start laughing all over again.

At last I stagger, still laughing, back to the dining table to make myself stop. The sight of the objects has the required effect and my laughter fades. I wipe the tears from my eyes and blow my nose in a piece of kitchen towel. My throat feels raw again and I drink more water.

My gaze lingers on each item on the table. I have collected them from all over the house, the kitchen, the bathroom and a locked shed outside, which I broke into with the poker from the cast-iron stand next to the wood burner. Ordinary things and tools you would find in most holiday homes. This is what I do, this is my strength: turning everyday objects into something that can wipe the smile off anyone's face.

The light outside is fading. The days are short in December. It occurs to me that it's nearly Christmas. The television hasn't been on since my first night here, but now I turn it on and I see that the whole world is excited about the holidays. They're showing the old Christmas movies, and advertising breaks are packed with colourful promotions for must-have plastic toys waiting to gather dust in children's bedrooms. My eyes spurn the flat television image. I switch it off.

During the short time I have watched television, the last of the daylight has died away. I'm annoyed at having missed it and turn on the lights in the house. The final light I switch on is the outdoor lamp, which signals I'm ready. Then I chuck more logs on the wood burner. A large stack of logs from the shed outside is piled up next to it. More than enough.

It's nearly time.

I listen out, but all I can hear is the roaring in the wood burner and the wind in the trees outside.

The knock on the door startles me. It's a loud, insistent knocking on the glass window in the front door. My heart races and I think I can hear the blood rush around my veins as I go to answer it. My hand grips the cold metal handle, I push it down and open the door. A cold wind slips past the figure standing outside.

You're wearing an overcoat and in one hand you're holding a white plastic bag with the items I was unable to get hold of and the script. Your other hand is buried in your coat pocket. It may be holding a pistol, but you have no intention of letting me know. The hand I can see is covered by a tight-fitting black leather glove.

This time you're not wearing sunglasses. There is no need for disguises or guesswork any more. All masks are off. Only the writer and the reader are left, ready for the final act.

You look down at my hand and the thumb with the plaster. A smile forms around your lips and you might have quipped something like 'Have you started without me?', but I have decided there will be no dialogue.

What is there to say?

I step back so you can enter. You close and lock the door behind you, then you follow me. Your eyes scan the living room as we proceed through the house. I'm four or five steps ahead of you until we reach the dining room. My legs are trembling slightly, but I try to conceal it and sit down on the chair at the end of the dining table. It's a solid wood chair with armrests and I place my arms on them and look at you apprehensively. You take a roll of gaffer tape from your bag and toss it to me.

I find the end and tear off a long section, which I use to tie my ankle to the leg of the chair. Then I tie my other ankle to the other chair leg. In the meantime, you're standing some distance from me, watching my efforts closely. I tie my right arm to the armrest with difficulty. When I have done that, I place the tape on the table. You nod and feel safe enough to leave me while you check the other rooms in the house. You find nothing and return to the dining room.

From your bag, you pull out the bottle. It's a 21-year-old Spring Bank whisky, drawn directly from the cask and almost impossible to get hold of.

With my free hand, I push the two glasses that I have set out earlier towards you. You fill my glass generously, pour a more moderate amount for yourself and sit down on the chair opposite me. We take our glasses, raise them and study the golden liquid before we drink. My taste buds welcome the whisky. I close my eyes and savour the taste. It's round and mild and the aftertaste lasts for several minutes.

When I open them again, our eyes meet. You nod with approval before you take another sip. I follow your example and before long we have both emptied our glasses.

You get up abruptly, take my free hand and press my wrist against the armrest. You hold it in place with your knee while you tie my lower arm to the chair. Then you check the other bindings by pulling the tape, but find that you're satisfied with my work.

You seem to relax more now that I'm tied up and you put your coat on one of the other chairs. You take out the script from the plastic bag, put it on a chair a bit further away and open it somewhere near the ending. Page 378 is my guess. Then you go to the dining table and inspect the tools. I have arranged them in the order in which they will be used, the scissors first. You pick them up and start cutting away my right sleeve. It's drenched in sweat and that makes it difficult for the scissors to cut through, but after some minutes my upper arm is exposed.

The tattoo has become a little blurred in time, like ink on poor-quality paper, but the ISBN number is still legible.

You toss the scissors aside and take the scalpel from the dining table. Kneeling on my lower arm and with a hand on my shoulder, you hold me down while you sink the blade into my flesh, just above the tattoo.

The pain is like an electric shock that shoots through

my whole body. I grit my teeth and clench my fists until the pain starts to subside. You take a step back without removing the scalpel and observe how it sits quivering at an angle of 90° from my upper arm. Surprisingly little blood is running from the cut, but then it's only half a centimetre wide, so far.

You step forward again, place your knee as before and take hold of the scalpel. With a slow sawing movement, you extend the cut round my arm above the tattoo. It hurts, it hurts like hell, but it's no longer a surprise, so I endure the agony without screaming.

When the cut reaches all the way round, I look down. The blood is running from the long incision and covers the tattoo and most of my arm down to my elbow. You take a cloth from the table and clean away the blood, but it keeps dripping so your efforts are futile.

The scalpel is sticky with blood and you wipe it on kitchen towel before proceeding to cut number two. The blade sinks in below the tattoo this time and you perform a parallel incision all the way round my arm. You use the cloth to mop up enough blood so you can check that both cuts are unbroken. They form a ribbon around my upper arm.

With an almost casual movement, you cut across the band and let the blade curve under one end which now dangles like a piece of tape. You throw the scalpel on the table and pick up the pincers lying ready.

I close my eyes while the jaws of the pincers grip the skin flap. I feel your hand on my shoulder and how you push your foot against the seat of the chair between my legs.

Then you pull.

Though I have closed my eyes, I'm blinded by a sudden explosion of light and my body arches. I can't suppress the scream and I howl out into the living room, a prolonged primal scream that carries on until I run out of air. Then I gasp for breath, greedily sucking in the air around me, and the scream is replaced by moaning.

A moment later, I open my eyes. They are full of tears and sting with sweat dripping from my forehead, but I see you standing in front of me, studying the skin flap hanging from the jaws of the pincers. Blood is dripping from it and you drop the flap on the tiled floor, where it lands with a squelch.

My eyes can't resist returning to the cut on my upper arm. A two-centimetre-wide piece of skin has been torn off, including the subcutaneous layer, so I can make out the contours of the muscles through the blood. To my horror, I see that less than half the ribbon has gone. Again, I gasp for air and avert my eyes. You come back and force me to lean forward as far as I can, so you can reach the last piece.

I hold my breath when I feel the pincers grip and wait for the explosion. It follows soon and I fling myself back. The chair would have fallen over if you hadn't been standing there. Again, I scream the place down. My head and torso slump forwards and I shake all over. My breathing has become a hissing and saliva has gathered at the corners of my mouth.

I'm aware of you walking past me and stopping in front of me again. The wound burns as if a red-hot iron ring is gripping my arm, but it's a constant pain and I can cope with it. You drop the pincers with the remaining skin flap on the floor between my feet.

I see that the whole tattoo has now gone and experience a kind of relief. Not only because no more yanking will be required, another kind of relief emerges. By losing the proof of my inauguration, I have been freed of the burden of being a writer. *In the Dead Angle* has been undone.

The ring around my arm is still smarting, but I try to keep calm. I hold my fingers in a cramped, crooked position and they look like gnarled twigs. The smallest movement tugs at the arm and makes the pain soar.

You pour another glass of whisky. I hear you take a sip and express your appreciation. Then you fling the remains at the open wound. My body stretches as far as the tape will allow and I yell at the ceiling. When I'm sitting down again, wheezing and panting, you show me the lighter. It's a cheap yellow disposable lighter that I found in a kitchen drawer, but it works, and you demonstrate this a couple of times in front of my half-open eyes.

The whisky ignites reluctantly. The flames are small and move drowsily across the wound and down my arm. It takes a moment before I feel the heat. It begins as an almost pleasant sensation, but quickly grows hotter until it becomes unbearable. My body reacts instinctively by trying to get away from the fire. I struggle under the tape, throwing myself from side to side in the chair, but I can't get out. The smell of burned hair and flesh reaches my nostrils and I cry out in despair.

You beat out the last flames with the cloth. My arm still feels as if it's ablaze and I have to look to check the fire really has been put out. The hairs have been singed off and my lower arm is red. The wound is covered by a black crust, which has cracked in a few places where the blood has seeped through. But the bleeding has practically stopped.

My face is drenched in sweat. Snot hangs from my nose and tears fill my eyes. I want to spit all the time and rising nausea makes me take quick, deep breaths. My fingers have started to tingle and I feel woozy. My head lolls from side to side. I try to get my breathing under control. I breathe through my nose and spray snot on to my chest, which heaves and lowers at a manic pace.

The dizziness subsides and my fingers stop tingling. I hear you pick up something from the dining table and go over to the wall, where you insert a plug into a power point and flick a switch. You put the iron on the floor near the chair. I can see the red light that indicates it isn't hot enough yet.

My heart starts to beat faster. Not because of the iron, but because of what will precede it.

I shake my head and cry. A dry sobbing fills my chest and leaves my mouth in spasms that make my whole body convulse.

You're standing by the chair with the script, flicking a couple of pages ahead as you nod with satisfaction. Everything is going according to plan.

The red light on the iron goes out.

I try to push the chair backwards, but you place a foot on the seat between my legs to prevent it from moving. You have picked up the garden shears from the table without me noticing and you grab hold of my right hand. I clench it as hard as I can and thrash around in the chair. You let go of my hand and take a step back. I relax and glare at you with hate through my tear-stained eyes. You wait with your hands on your hips. Your eyes radiate disgust. There is no pity. And why should there be? I have asked for this, I have written this.

It's no use. There is no way out.

I nod and spread my fingers. When you approach, I turn my head away and close my eyes. Again you place your foot on the chair and grip my wrist. My hand is shaking, but still I keep my fingers extended, straining as if I'm trying to catch a ball. You force the jaws of the shears around the inner joint of my index finger. The metal feels cold against my skin. You tighten your hold of my wrist and press down hard against the armrest. I grit my teeth and hold my breath.

The sound is no different from when I cut branches in the garden at the cottage. A quick snip. Something falls on the floor with a thud. It could be an apple core or a carrot, but in this case it's six centimetres off my right index finger.

My hand contracts as if it has been electrocuted. The pain shoots up my arm, hurtles through my shoulder and drills into my spine, which straightens up with a jerk that sends the excess energy like a whiplash out through my mouth in the form of a long, high-pitched wail. My brain seems to expand and press against the inside of my skull. The howling dies out when I have no more air left in my lungs. My teeth are clattering as if from cold, but the rest of my body is on fire.

Slowly, I turn my head back and force myself to open my eyes. I straighten out my fingers. They're twitching and beads of sweat sit in the tiny hairs on every one of them. When I see the stump of my index finger, I scream again, not from pain, but from terror. There is one centimetre left below the knuckle, and the cut is unnaturally clean. The blood drips on the floor at a steady pace. In the puddle, I can see the severed finger. It looks unreal, as if it had been transformed into a papier mâché copy as soon as it was liberated from my body.

You seize the chance to grip my open hand and twist the stump upwards. With your other hand, you take the iron and, without hesitation, you press it against the stump. It hisses and a little puff of grey smoke rises from under the sole plate. My hand contracts, but you have a firm hold and you press the iron firmly against the cut. The red light comes on and you return the iron to the floor.

The smell of burned flesh finds my nose and I can no longer suppress my nausea. I fling myself forwards and throw up on the floor between my feet. You step back a little while my stomach forces its contents up through my throat in powerful spasms. I nearly choke. It feels as if there isn't enough room for my lungs to expand and that's the reason I can't breathe. You slap my face and the shock makes me gasp. I cough and splutter and my breathing is jolted back into action like an old tractor.

My finger is no longer bleeding. A black crust covers the cut and the heat has formed blisters on the rest of the stump so it looks as if my finger has melted from the end right down to the knuckle. I try to throw up again, but only produce a sensation of choking and eerie noises in my throat.

I didn't notice where you put the shears while you

cauterized the wound, but suddenly you're standing there holding them again. The jaws open and shut in front of my eyes.

You have to use both hands to sever my thumb. I can't help clenching my hand, but you force the shears around the thumb so I can do nothing to prevent the blades from sinking into the flesh and crushing their way through the bone until it gives in. I don't hear the stump falling – I'm too busy screaming.

You've got fed up with the noise, perhaps you're also concerned that someone might hear me, so you tear off a piece of gaffer tape and press it across my mouth. Breathing through my nose is difficult for me so you make a cut in the tape to enable me to breathe, but not scream very loudly.

When you have finished, I look at my hand. I must have pulled my hand back hard while you cut. A couple of centimetres of skin have been scraped off and the cut is at the outer joint. The exposed bone stump glows white against the blood. The tip of my thumb is lying on the floor, still displaying the plaster I stuck on it some hours before. I'm reminded of my earlier fit of laughter and I grin hysterically before the pain makes me clench my jaw.

The uneven cut makes it hard to seal the wound with the iron and the stench envelopes us both. Halfway through you take a couple of steps back and cough, but I'm not afforded the same luxury and am overwhelmed by nausea. The tape turns my coughing into an intermittent mumbling and the exertion makes my temples throb.

When the wound has finally been sealed, you get to work on the rest of my fingers.

At some point, I pass out. I don't know how long for,

but my first impression when I resurface is of the sound of Christmas carols. When I open my eyes, you're sitting in front of the television with a whisky. For a moment I don't know where I am, but when I remember I panic and thrash around while I try to scream through the tape.

Reluctantly, you take your eyes off the television and study me as if you're deciding whether or not I intend to stay conscious.

Then you get up, put down your glass and sever the rest of my fingers to the sound of Christmas carols sung by a girls' choir in a village church.

The soleplate of the iron is black with burned flesh and blood. I have grown used to the pain, but when all ten stumps are lying at my feet, I still scream. Perhaps from the recognition that I have permanently lost my tools and, consequently, my identity. I'm no longer a writer. It's physically impossible for me to type on a keyboard and communicate my fantasies to paper. The instruments I used to hurt the ones I love are no longer part of my body. My hands have been turned into shapeless lumps of meat and bone – burned, bloody and swollen beyond recognition. The critics would have a field day. This must be what they think I deserve – Frank Føns reduced to a whining freak incapable of ever writing another word. The victim of my own abominable sentences. The world will be a better place without my scribbling to taint literature.

My worst critic waits until I have stopped screaming into the tape before ripping it off in one quick pull. I don't feel pain, but I'm aware that skin from my lips comes off with it and the taste of blood fills my mouth. I swallow all the air I can in one deep breath, cough and spit blood.

Suddenly you appear with the two wedges I have spent the last couple of days making. I got the wood from one of the shelves in the kitchen cupboard, sawed them into triangles and sanded them down. The angle had to be just right, as wide as possible, but small enough to reach all the way in.

I swallow a couple of times before I open my mouth. You press one wedge into the left side of my mouth with such force that my jaw is nearly dislocated. I groan to the extent that I can with my mouth wide open. You insert the second wedge into the right-hand side and tap it into place with the side of your hand. My lips are fully stretched and it feels as if they could snap like elastic at any time.

You bend down and pick up the pincers. They are covered in blood and vomit and slip out between your gloved fingers. You pick them up again and wipe them and your gloves with a cloth. My mouth fills with saliva. I can't swallow so I lower my head to allow it to dribble out of my mouth and down my chin. You place one hand on my forehead and force my head back. You hold the pincers with the other and tap them tentatively against my front teeth. The sound of metal against enamel clatters in my head. I close my eyes.

Your thumb finds my eyesocket while you place your fingers across my forehead. I feel the pincers grip a front tooth and you put your foot on the seat between my thighs. The tooth creaks as you tighten the pincers and when you pull I hear a terrifying grating sound as the roots of my tooth are torn from my jaw. My head snaps back and there is a stabbing pain in my neck. I groan and lift my head again. The pain from my hands drowns out everything else so I have to feel with my tongue to check if the tooth has been ripped out. My gum feels ragged and blood flows into my mouth.

Before I have time to empty my mouth, you get hold of me again, push my head back and clamp the next tooth with the pincers. The blood is running down my throat and I try to cough. Drops of blood spray across my cheeks. You pull again and my head snaps back for the second time.

I slump forwards and the blood runs out of my mouth and drips on to my trousers. The holes where my teeth used to be feel like craters.

You go over to the wood burner while I carry on bleeding. Saliva and blood form a sticky paste that flows out of my mouth like slime. My whole head aches and my jaw muscles are sore from being stretched for such a long time.

It takes five to ten minutes before the poker is hot enough and with some difficulty you hold my head by my hair and press the iron tip against the wound in my upper jaw. It sizzles and when the poker hits my upper lip, I can feel it split. The heat makes me jerk my head so violently that you are left holding a clump of my hair. Irritably you shake it off your fingers like a piece of stubborn Sellotape.

My head dangles back and forth and from side to side. I find it hard to stay focused and I'm not really aware of what is going on around me. It's like I'm sedated, possibly because my body has short-circuited my overloaded nervous system. I don't know how, but through the fog I'm aware that you carry on with the other teeth. When my upper mouth has been cleared, you start work on my lower jaw. This time you don't pull them out, but fetch a hammer and bash them into my mouth with one blow. It sounds like my jaw breaks and a dart of pain penetrates the fog and lights up like a flashlight. I spit out blood and teeth and am almost grateful when you close the wound with the red-hot poker.

There is no mirror, thank God, but I imagine that my mouth is one gaping big hole of blood, flesh and rubble. My tongue sits in the middle, red and untouched like a stigma in a flower.

My woozy state displeases you. From the table you fetch a green plastic bottle which you hold under my nose. The ammonia attacks my nostrils and I straighten up and open my eyes. I see you pick up the pincers and the poultry shears. With an almost dispassionate movement, I try to turn my head, but you push the pincers into my mouth and clamp my tongue. Pulling directly up to the ceiling, you force my head back. The missing teeth provide you with easy access and you cut off my tongue with a V-incision as far back as you can reach. The blood spurts out of my mouth, but all I notice is my severed tongue, which you place carefully on the seat between my thighs. The blood makes it unrecognizable.

My head lolls forwards to drain the blood from my mouth. My jumper is soaked and the floor is red around the chair. It's hard to say how much blood I have lost, but it looks serious and I feel distinctly dizzy every time I raise my head.

You cauterize the wound in my mouth with forceful pressure from the poker. It cools rapidly and you have to go back and forth between the wood burner and the chair a couple of times until you're satisfied, then you yank out the wedges. I can barely close my mouth. My jaw muscles temporarily feel slack, overstretched, so they can no longer function.

My head slumps forward and my chin rests against my chest.

Perhaps I could have stopped it? After all, I wrote the script, but it could have been a trap. What would have prevented me from hiding in the bushes outside and whacking you at the back of your head with a shovel while you waited for me to open the door? I would have tied up your ankles and wrists with the gaffer tape you had brought, dragged you into the living room and drunk the single malt whisky you had brought. It would have tasted fantastic. It would be a victory toast, like a black-and-white photo of a great game hunter with his trophy. When you woke up, I could have forced a confession out of you, tortured you with the same instruments you have used on me until you admitted to killing Mona Weis, Verner Nielsen and Linda Hvilbjerg. I would make sure to record your confession on a dictaphone or on a video camera. Then I would call the police and I would be cleared of every suspicion and proclaimed a hero. I would be on the front page of every newspaper in the country. My books would sell again and this script would be published and turned into a film. Everyone would be dying to hear what had really happened in the holiday home near Nykøbing in my own words. You, too, would become a celebrity. Newspapers and TV companies would offer you lots of money for an interview with you in your cell. You might even write your own version of events and we would meet in talk shows, you handcuffed to two police officers and me in a new suit with manicured nails. Line and the girls would be in the audience and afterwards the four of us would go out for dinner. I would tell them that I had quit drinking and would never write another book again. And I would have kept my word for a very long time . . . or for several months.

Oh, yes, I might have been able to save my life, but I wouldn't have been able to save myself.

The ammonia stings my nose and my body jerks. I cough. Slime and blood are forced from my mouth and stain your clothes. You ignore it. Instead you grab my head and force open an eyelid with your thumb. I try to focus, but it isn't easy and my eyelid glides shut as soon as you let go.

I'm freezing. My clothes are soaked with blood and sweat and my entire body is shaking from a combination of cold and shock.

I feel you pinching my eyelid again, this time with your thumb and index finger, pulling the skin out from the eyeball. The scalpel gleams in the light from the lamp above the table and I see you stare directly into my eye with deep concentration as you slice off my eyelid. I try instinctively to close my eye, but nothing happens and I can no longer keep visual impressions at bay. Blood runs into my eye and dyes the room pink. I shake my head and try to move it as far away from you as possible, but you get hold of my hair and force my head back. I squeeze my eyes shut, but I can still see the scalpel approach the other eye in the red mist. You cannot pinch my other eye-lid and hold my head still at the same time, so instead you sink the scalpel into my skin just below the eyebrow. With a sawing motion, you cut along the brow bone until you reach the root of my nose. You toss the scalpel aside, get hold of the skin flap and pull it off like a plaster that's no longer needed.

When you release my hair, my head drops to the side and comes to rest on my shoulder. The blood makes it almost impossible to see anything but shadows, but I'm aware of you going to the wood burner to fetch the poker. Shortly afterwards you get hold of my hair again, force my head back and seal the wound above the eye with the poker. When you repeat this with my other eye, my body goes into spasms so the metal hits my eyeball, which sizzles. I scream.

The red veil before my eyes is suddenly lifted and I see you standing with a glass in your hand. The water drips from my face and it causes pain to shoot through my tongue stump when I tried to direct some of it into my mouth. My throat feels dry and swollen and I try to ask for water, but the only sound to come out of my crater of a mouth is a dry hiss. Nevertheless, you understand the hint and go out into the kitchen where you calmly refill the glass and return. I lean back my head and open my mouth so you can pour in the liquid. It's like eating ice cubes and firecrackers the same time. The pain makes me cough, but my craving for the water forces me to swallow what I can.

There is a big cotton wool cloud to the right in my field of vision which refuses to go away.

You go over to the dining table. It's starting to resemble a workbench in a slaughterhouse. The scalpel, the garden shears, the pincers and the poultry shears are lying in a pool of blood, and small chunks of flesh and fragments of teeth are strewn between the tools. The neat layout I prepared earlier has been spoiled.

The line of instruments has almost reached the end, only two remain.

I take a deep breath when you pick up the matches. You hold the box up to your ear and shake it. It rattles. It's almost full. Satisfied, you slip it into your back pocket and pick up the petrol can. It's a small chubby container of black plastic. It contains at most five litres, but that will suffice. I found it in the shed, but had to top it up with petrol from my own car. The blend of lawnmower and car petrol probably wouldn't do either of them any good, but it burns all right.

You squat in front of me and open the container. The detachable spout is clipped between the handle and the container, and it appears to be stuck because you almost topple over when you finally yank it loose. I can smell petrol. Even though I try to breathe calmly, I start to hyperventilate. The sweat pours from my forehead and runs from my armpits. No more ammonia is required. My senses are working overtime, every one of your movements is registered with rising terror.

Slowly, you screw the spout to the plastic container's thread and tighten it.

I try to plead for my life, but the only noise coming from my chapped lips is a mix of vowels and sobbing. The tears flow from my exposed eyeballs and I tilt my head.

You look at me, clearly repulsed by the sight, which only seems to motivate you further. You get up and hold the petrol container over me. I squirm in the chair as the liquid cascades over my body. My injuries wake up and pump SOS signals through my nervous system. I writhe, but you carry on pouring. A squirt hits my face and my eyes seem to melt. Colours explode in front of my eyes and the muscles around them instinctively try to close even though there is nothing left to close with. I cough and splutter as the petrol finds its way to my mouth.

The splashing stops and you toss aside the container. It lands with a hollow thud, jumps a couple of times before landing on its side. The smell is unbearable. Fumes force their way into my lungs and cause me to retch, but nothing comes up.

The petrol has dissolved most of the blood on what used to be my hands. They seem to boil in the fluid and my finger stumps wriggle comically in agony.

I hear a rattling noise and I look up. You're holding the matchbox with a wry smile. The pain disappears temporarily and is replaced by terror. I rock the chair back and forth, but it hardly moves.

The first match doesn't catch. I hear sulphur rub against sulphur, but the familiar crackling of a flame fails to follow. You shrug, change your grip of the match and the box and strike the sulphur against the side with a quick movement. Sparks fly and a flame flares up. You hold the match at an angle so the fire can take.

Our eyes meet.

Your eyes radiate a combination of anticipation and respect. I take a breath and hold it.

We have reached the end of the road.

The match spins towards me as if in slow motion. The flame grows small and blue as it goes through the air, but it carries on burning and is heading for my groin. Before it lands, the fumes ignite with a whoosh. The fire is blue, red and yellow. It spreads up across my body in an instant.

The first few seconds I feel nothing at all. I can see the flames, taste them almost, but I don't feel anything. My jumper starts to melt and there is a smell of burned plastic. It starts to get hot from my neck and upwards. My hair is burning and the temperature rises. My hands are starting to hurt. The stumps resemble torches and they twitch, but there is nothing I can do. My body arches and tries to break the chair. It throws itself around in an attempt to avoid the flames. The pain is unbearable. It fills my entire body with a blinding white explosion, an explosion that never ends, but carries on growing without limit or centre. My skin is melting. My screams are muffled into a gurgling sound as if someone had poured liquid lead down my throat. My hair falls off in burning clumps and lands in the blood under the chair with a hiss. The tape comes apart on my left wrist and my arm jumps up towards the ceiling in an attempt to escape my burning body. It looks like a runaway version of the arm of the Statue of Liberty and flails around the air with its newfound freedom. I don't control it, but it soon realizes that it can't tear itself loose and returns to my body. What was once my palm slams into my face and covers my mouth.

The pain has disappeared or has grown so strong that I can no longer contain it. My senses implode. They melt and leave me in darkness and silence. Sounds can no longer reach me, nor can impressions or smells, only darkness. It's nice here. Time seems to have stopped, the moment will last for ever, but I know there is very little time left.

That's OK.

I have got what I wanted.

Hopefully I have atoned for some of my mistakes, made amends to all the people I let down and hurt, paid for the insults and malice I spread about me. It's all far too late, of course. It won't make much of a difference now, but at least the world can carry on without the poison that is Frank Føns.

The foggy spot to the right in my field of vision slowly changes shape, it condenses in some places and fades in others. It turns into a photo. A light-coloured picture, mainly in pale shades. Three figures on a bench. They're all dressed in white and bathed in sunshine. A woman and two girls in summer dresses. The woman is sitting in the middle. She and the older of the girls look knowingly into the camera, while the younger girl is busy with her mother's hair. In the woman's hair is a garland of flowers, tied together a little clumsily and with an uneven distribution of white and yellow colours. The little girl is grinning broadly while the others smile at the lens with more restraint. The older girl's smile is a little ironic, as if she has noticed something about the photographer's face which shouldn't be there, a secret she can share with the others and laugh at. The woman is smiling, too. There are tiny laughter lines around her eyes, which are half closed from her smile and the sunshine. Her mouth is slightly open and you can see the bottom two of her front teeth. On one side of her cheek, you can make out a dimple and, in an extension of that, a small wrinkle.

I think she smiles often.

Note

This manuscript, consisting of 396 loose A4 sheets, was found at the crime scene near the body and has been impounded with the investigation as evidential material, item #09234.07.

The events described in the script, the murders of Mona Weis, Verner Nielsen and Linda Hvilbjerg, match the dates for the discoveries of the bodies. It has not yet been possible to contact Merethe Andersen, also known as Little Marie, a prostitute from Vesterbro.

The final torture, as described in the script, is generally accurate as far as the state of the deceased is concerned. However, there are minor discrepancies that should be taken into account. The whisky was Johnnie Walker Red Label, the body contained traces of Ibuprofen (see the Forensic Examiner's Report No. 6357) and evidence from the crime scene suggests that the severing of the fingers could have taken place later than described in the script.

We await the outcome of further investigations to determine how this affects the sequence of events.

A pair of black gloves (#09234.22) was discovered not far from the crime scene and they match the description in the script. DNA material from two people has been extracted from them, one identified as belonging to the deceased, the other cannot be identified until further analysis has been carried out.

Detective Sergeant Kim Vendelev

The Library of Shadows
Mikkel Birkegaard

Imagine that some people have the power to affect your thoughts and feelings through books. They can seduce you with amazing stories, conjure up vividly imagined worlds, but also manipulate you into thinking exactly what they want you to.

WHEN LUCA CAMPELLI dies a sudden and violent death, his son Jon inherits his second-hand bookshop, Libri di Luca, in Copenhagen. Jon has not seen his father for twenty years since the mysterious death of his mother. When Luca's death is followed by an arson attempt on the shop, Jon is forced to explore his family's past.

Unbeknown to Jon, the bookshop has for years been hiding a remarkable secret. It is the meeting place of a society of booklovers and readers, who have maintained a tradition of immense power passed down from the days of the great library of ancient Alexandria. Now someone is trying to destroy them, and Jon finds he is in a fight to save his new friends.

9780552775021